NEBULA WINNERS FIFTEEN

'Keep in mind that these stories and articles are among the best available today in the judgement of professional writers. The best and most dangerous honours come from contemporaries in your own field. It's nice to have the admiration of fans, yes. That means you've been entertaining and the effort was profitable. When it comes to your fellow writers, though, they are doing what you do; and if they like your work, that's a rarified form of praise. It can be very heady stuff.'

Frank Herbert

Nebula Winners Fifteen

Edited by Frank Herbert

Star

A STAR BOOK

published by

the Paperback Division of
W. H. ALLEN & Co. Ltd

A Star Book

Published in 1983
by the Paperback Division of
W. H. Allen & Co. Ltd
A Howard and Wyndham Company
44 Hill Street, London W1X 8LB

First published in the United States of America by
Harper & Row, Publishers, Inc. 1981
First published in Great Britain by
W. H. Allen & Co. Ltd, 1981

Printed in Great Britain by
Cox & Wyman Ltd, Reading

ISBN 0 352 31227 0

NEBULA WINNERS FIFTEEN

Contents

Introduction

You probably don't know the first damned thing about my prejudices. Do you care? Without that knowledge, anything I write in this introduction to the Science Fiction Writers of America Nebula anthology is virtually useless. Do you know how this book came to be?

Most of the hard work was done by Peter Pautz, SFWA's executive secretary. Like the anchor man on the six o'clock news, I was called in when the material was all assembled. I have read it and now I'm supposed to give you the "definitive critique." That may improve sales but it can be lousy communications.

You want to know what kind of mental safari you are about to take in this book?

A well-known literary critic once asked me if I believed science fiction—he called it sci-fi, a fact I reveal for its value in character analysis—anyway, this character asked me if I believed "science fiction *really* could aspire to the status of Art?"

The capital *A* was audible.

I asked him why he thought any writer should bother his head with such an asinine question. This is especially poignant because I have yet to meet a literary critic who knows contemporary art or Art from a four-letter word which includes the same letters. And yes, I pass the same terrible judgment on myself-as-critic. I think the only reliable critic is time, and I don't mean the magazine.

Does it endure?

Contemporary critics are useful mainly as they reflect your prejudices. They help you avoid things you would consider to be dreck. The Critic as screening system. It's not a perfect system and requires periodic reassessment, but where do you find perfection?

You begin to see my critical approach: Will future teachers inflict it on our descendants? Will our descendants enjoy it and keep it alive?

Even then . . . well, I ask you: Is "The Masque of the Red Death" *really* Art? It's entertaining. It's instructive as a comment on its times. It's required reading in schools. But is it Art?

What's Art? As far as I'm concerned, it's my dentist, Art Krout. You see, if critics don't know, how can you expect a writer to know?

This is not to say that writers and readers should be uncritical. Readers have to protect their eyesight and their valuable time. As a writer, if you're not self-critical, you're not trying hard enough. Your work could become sufficiently sloppy that it would bore even the most ardent fan.

Boredom! There's one of the enemies! Shoot the bugger down!

Look back on the Artists and Critics whose work has endured. They did not bore their contemporaries and they do not bore enough of us today that they are secure for at least another generation. Continue looking back but this time only at the works of enduring Artists. What did they have in common?

They tested limits, their own *and* yours.

They produced something new.

They entertained you. (Remember, stuff that endures does not bore.)

They often addressed very large questions, sometimes in miniature.

They touched a chord which we still call *truth*. (It rings true when you hit it.)

They took you beyond yourself to something you recognized as better. They reminded you of the best in your own humanity.

Ah, there's something: Art is humanizing.

What's that mean, that word there—*human?* You know a human when you see one and so do I. Two-word definition of human: "like me." At bottom, that's the litmus paper we all use.

If it debases you, if it makes you feel diminished, damaged and irrevocably pained, *and that's all it does*, it's not Art. It's something else.

No cheap shots. (My God! That eliminates most movies!)

You ask: "Will the stories in this volume enter those rarefied and enduring currents?"

Patience.

There appears to be some evidence, including this anthology, that sci-fi (we say "skiffy," not "sy-fy") is coming out of a formative phase into something which may endure. Check back with me in a few hundred years and we'll review this question on the basis of better evidence.

Then how did Peter and the rest of us come by these particular anthology selections?

We voted.

Was it an honest vote?

More honest than most.

There was a time when some writers and their friends lobbied hard for inclusion in this prized selection. It got so bad that a number of us considered dropping out of SFWA.

"Stop trying to buy my vote," I said. "It is a poor thing but mine own."

Reasons for the lobbying are obvious. You must know that inclusion in SFWA's anthology rings the cash register. And then there's all that "fame." Good sense appears to be winning, however. Attempts at vote trading and other lobbying efforts have died off because they produced unwanted negative results.

Each of us voted, then, on the basis of our personal assumptions, that set of prejudgments which we identify as private internal reactions. The results are exposed here in this book for you to judge. Now, like birds that have been kicked out of the nest, these stories face an uncertain future.

Keep in mind that these stories and articles are among the best available today in the judgment of professional writers. The best and the most dangerous honors come from contemporaries in your own field. It's nice to have the admiration of fans, yes. That means you've been entertaining and the effort was profitable. This is important because money means the writer has more time to write. When it comes to your fellow writers, though, they are doing what you do; and if they like your work, that's a rarefied form of praise. It can be very heady stuff.

Why dangerous, then? The danger comes in the movement toward the Academy and the reactions of Academe. It can be poisonous when Academics convince a sensitive writer that Academe knows best.

"We know what's Art," they say.

"Yeah! Tell me more!" the writer says.

Listen, they may know what *was* Art, but there's something like hubris in the claim to absolute contemporary good judgment. I'll let you in on a secret. They're guessing. Some of them may make lucky guesses, but don't count on it. The poison comes when praise for the wrong reasons fogs over the self-critical awareness of someone who might have become a great (read *long-enduring*) Artist. What wrong reasons? Only the Artist and time know.

It appears clear to me that these Nebula Awards anthologies may be one of the first steps toward an Academy. Now, that's not necessarily all bad. In the first place, an Academy is something like a double-edged sword with no handle. You can only pick it up by grabbing a sharp place. If you grab it too hard you'll be the first one taken out of the action. How many choices of past Academies have survived into our times? Not many.*

There's another safety valve in the recent reminder by a friend that we don't have an academy tradition in this country. We have schools, lots of them. Grant them good intentions, but we know what kind of a road is paved with good intentions. Some of those schools could be paving roads for lemmings. As for the waves and the movements and the other schools . . . well, all of the votes aren't in yet.

Whatever you do, don't underestimate the strength of science fiction. It flowered in this country for good reasons. We Yanks have a well-earned reputation for winging it, and that's exactly what

---

*If you would like to keep score on current survival rates from "Best of . . ." choices, get a copy of Franson and DeVore's *A History of the Hugo, Nebula and International Fantasy Awards.* It's available at science-fiction conventions and by mail from 4705 Weddel Street, Dearborn, Michigan 48125.

science fiction does best. We rejected a lot of that European stuff a long time ago—unwarranted searches, monarchs, confiscation of arms, self-satisfied academics, funny food . . . I mean, they eat *snails!*

When it comes to European-style Academe, a lot of us crowd into Missouri. We are suspicious. Just what are they trying to sell us? We *know* that European Academe is Fat. This knowledge comes out of the same mythos which prompted a superb writer to tell me once that the best writing is done by people who are either lonely or hungry. Hunger has a long-standing association with Art —garrets, tuberculosis and all of that. Incipient tragedy drives us to greater heights.

Academe in this country has developed a different tradition, more homespun and strongly influenced by the Great Depression, when a thing we had suspected for a long time was demonstrated right before our very eyes: teaching was a safe and secure job even in hard times. They get tenure, you know.

This attraction of security accounts partly for a fact revealed by the results of World War II draft-deferment tests of United States college and university students—most of the then education majors were in the lowest 10 percent of the IQ scale. Maybe our existing intelligence tests are not all that accurate in screening for the best teachers, but they are a screen. And they obviously screen for people who seek some kind of sinecure. We don't know what effects might have come from having at least two generations of students taught mostly by people screened that way. And what of their influence on school administration?

The paradox of security, that grail which supposedly lured so many immigrants to these shores. Hell, the Indians didn't have security and we didn't import it.

To a free-associating science-fiction writer, security is a dirty word. Security has a well-known history of attracting the unimaginative, the noncreative, the people who prefer any yesterday to any tomorrow. We live in a society dominated by a bureaucracy top-heavy with people selected that way—security seekers. Those are the people who gave us Social Security—the biggest chain letter, the most monstrous Pyramid Club, the most outrageous con game in the history of government. You want one mea-

surement of the con? Our bureaucracy has its own private retire-
ment system, as does the Congress. They remain completely independent of the dissolving pyramid which they administer. They
don't want any part of this thing when their own *security* is at
stake.

Yes, this is pertinent to Academe, Academies, to this anthology
and to science fiction in general. I remind you that science fiction
is mostly about tomorrow. Is that a secure tomorrow? Hell, no! Do
our fictional governments perpetrate outrageous con games and
other injustices on their fictional societies? Indeed they do. Do we
offer security with one technological fist while yanking it away
with another hand? Oh my, yes. Is there any reflection of current
realities in all of this? You be the judge. Don't leave that to an
Academy or to Academe.

Which brings me back to the current love affair between Academe and science fiction. We are witnessing a complex phenomenon here. You can identify several dominant movements and mix-
tures of same in the muddy waters.

There are the Academics who praise science fiction as a lever
with which to improve reading skills among the young.

There are those who see it as *what's happening*. It appeals to an
urge for contemporary understanding, to a drive to be part of
history.

Then there are the academics who came in through fandom.
These bring a real interest in the exploration of outré ideas.

All of them analyze, and when they read this, I hope they appreciate taking their turn under the lens of the microscope. I say to
them sadly that analysis does not always lead to understanding. It
is possible to analyze the life out of a subject. You can make it
boring. This has led many a fan to cry out in anguish: "Keep
science fiction in the gutter where it belongs!"

To these fans I say: We don't gain a thing by fleeing in terror
from the current academic enthusiasm. I agree that it is dangerous, but it also is unavoidable and may be beneficial in the long
term. The thing to resist is those forces which push us toward a
hidebound European-style Academy—forces found not only in
Academe but even in fandom and, God forbid, among writers
themselves.

In Europe, Academies not only were used to honor selected practitioners of the Art, they also were designed to control what *could* happen in a chosen artistic field. They were a source of funding and still are. As you might expect, they experience(d) a certain amount of lobbying and other kinds of politicking. Sound familiar?

Enter politics, exit Art.

Politics easily becomes the ultimate boredom. Witness how few people actually vote in the United States, a condition politicians say they would like to correct but which they are very careful not to correct. People recognize that when there is an elitist force at the helm, the single vote doesn't carry much weight. And that's the way it is in a politicized Academy.

Let's suppose that we have something Artistic happening in science fiction—new ways of looking at our universe, poking fun at dearly beloved assumptions while gathering greater and greater economic clout, more and more attention from a swelling population of fans.

That can be dangerous.

Art has always been viewed as at least potentially dangerous in this country, anyway, an attitude attached to our homespun traditions but rooted in far deeper things. Involved with the NEW as it is, Art produces its fair share of surprises. If you break through the limits everyone else believes contain that which is safe and secure, you *may* encounter something which flips existing power structures into new alignments.

Can't allow that! It's bad for business.

The truth is, it's good for business and always has been. However, it has been known to put some people out of business. Thus, political/economic power structures always want to keep firm control of Art. Thus Academies and all the rest of it. Do I have to be the one to tell these people that Art and Firm Control are mutually exclusive, that Firm Control is actually bad for business?

Now you have an idea of where I come from, and I can comment on the selections in this anthology with less fear of being misunderstood. I obviously believe there are some standards by which to judge contemporary work. This anthology contains good work— some of it may even be great. I enjoyed every bit of it, but I don't want that to dominate your judgment. Let me point out something, though, which could be overlooked. Publications of this type can be of extraordinary value to new writers. This is what's being accepted. This is foundation stuff judged by contemporary writers themselves. Don't think of us as an Academy but just as writers. If you write or want to write, go out and do something better. I truly want that.

Think of this volume as an example of where we are today. We writers liked this enough that a majority of us voted to include these works in our most prestigious publication. We do not, however, intend to stand on these laurels. What we write tomorrow may be much better. We will let time be the judge.

—FRANK HERBERT

NEBULA WINNERS FIFTEEN

JACK DANN

Camps

Jack Dann, who began publishing science fiction in 1970 with two stories written with George Zebrowski for *Worlds of If,* has been a Nebula finalist four times—for "Junction" (1973), "The Dybbuk Dolls" (1975), "A Quiet Revolution for Death" (1978) and for the gem in this volume, "Camps," which also was a finalist for the British Science Fiction Association Award. He is well known in science fiction as editor or coeditor of five powerful anthologies—*Wandering Stars, Faster Than Light, Future Power, Immortal* and *Aliens!* and as managing editor of the SFWA Bulletin from 1970 to 1975. His novel *Starhiker* was published in 1977, and another work is now in preparation, *The Man Who Melted.* A collection of his short stories, *Timetipping,* was brought out in early 1980, and the publisher has commissioned him to edit an anthology sequel, *More Wandering Stars.* His novel *Junction* is listed for 1981 publication.

As Stephen lies in bed, he can think only of pain.

He imagines it as sharp and blue. After receiving an injection of Demerol, he enters pain's cold regions as an explorer, an objective visitor. It is a country of ice and glass, monochromatic plains and valleys filled with wash-blue shards of ice, crystal pyramids and pinnacles, squares, oblongs, and all manner of polyhedrons—block upon block of painted blue pain.

Although it is midafternoon, Stephen pretends it is dark. His eyes are tightly closed, but the daylight pouring into the room from two large windows intrudes as a dull red field extending infinitely behind his eyelids.

"Josie," he asks through cotton mouth, "aren't I due for another shot?" Josie is crisp and fresh and large in her starched white uniform. Her peaked nurse's cap is pinned to her mouse-brown hair.

"I've just given you an injection; it will take effect soon." Josie strokes his hand, and he dreams of ice.

"Bring me some ice," he whispers.

"If I bring you a bowl of ice, you'll only spill it again."

"Bring me some ice. . . . " By touching the ice cubes, by turning them in his hand like a gambler favoring his dice, he can transport himself into the beautiful blue country. Later, the ice will melt, and he will spill the bowl. The shock of cold and pain will awaken him.

Stephen believes that he is dying, and he has resolved to die properly. Each visit to the cold country brings him closer to death; and death, he has learned, is only a slow walk through icefields. He has come to appreciate the complete lack of warmth and the beautifully etched face of his magical country.

But he is connected to the bright flat world of the hospital by plastic tubes—one breathes cold oxygen into his left nostril; another passes into his right nostril and down his throat to his stomach; one feeds him intravenously, another draws his urine.

"Here's your ice," Josie says. "But mind you, don't spill it." She places the small bowl on his tray table and wheels the table close to him. She has a musky odor of perspiration and perfume; Stephen is reminded of old women and college girls.

"Sleep now, sweet boy."

Without opening his eyes, Stephen reaches out and places his hand on the ice.

"Come now, Stephen, wake up. Dr. Volk is here to see you."

Stephen feels the cool touch of Josie's hand, and he opens his eyes to see the doctor standing beside him. The doctor has a gaunt long face and thinning brown hair; he is dressed in a wrinkled green suit.

"Now we'll check the dressing, Stephen," he says as he tears away a gauze bandage on Stephen's abdomen.

Stephen feels the pain, but he is removed from it. His only wish is to return to the blue dreamlands. He watches the doctor peel off the neat crosshatchings of gauze. A terrible stink fills the room.

Josie stands well away.

"Now we'll check your drains." The doctor pulls a long drainage tube out of Stephen's abdomen, irrigates and disinfects the wound, inserts a new drain, and repeats the process by pulling out another tube just below the rib cage.

Stephen imagines that he is swimming out of the room. He tries to cross the hazy border into cooler regions, but it is difficult to concentrate. He has only a half-hour at most before the Demerol will wear off. Already, the pain is coming closer, and he will not be due for another injection until the nightnurse comes on duty. But the nightnurse will not give him an injection without an argument. She will tell him to fight the pain.

But he cannot fight without a shot.

"Tomorrow we'll take that oxygen tube out of your nose," the doctor says, but his voice seems far away, and Stephen wonders what he is talking about.

He reaches for the bowl of ice, but cannot find it.

"Josie, you've taken my ice."

"I took the ice away when the doctor came. Why don't you try to watch a bit of television with me; Soupy Sales is on."

"Just bring me some ice," Stephen says. "I want to rest a bit." He can feel the sharp edges of pain breaking through the gauzy wraps of Demerol.

"I love you, Josie," he says sleepily as she places a fresh bowl of ice on his tray.

As Stephen wanders through his ice-blue dreamworld, he sees a rectangle of blinding white light. It looks like a doorway into an adjoining world of brightness. He has glimpsed it before on previous Demerol highs. A coal-dark doorway stands beside the bright one.

He walks toward the portals, passes through white-blue cone-fields.

Time is growing short. The drug cannot stretch it much longer. Stephen knows that he has to choose either the bright doorway or the dark, one or the other. He does not even consider turning around, for he has dreamed that the ice and glass and cold blue gemstones have melted behind him.

It makes no difference to Stephen which doorway he chooses. On impulse he steps into blazing, searing whiteness.

Suddenly he is in a cramped world of people and sound.

The boxcar's doors were flung open. Stephen was being pushed out of the cramped boxcar that stank of sweat, feces, and urine. Several people had died in the car, and added their stink of death to the already fetid air.

"Carla, stay close to me," shouted a man beside Stephen. He had been separated from his wife by a young woman who pushed between them, as she tried to return to the dark safety of the boxcar.

SS men in black, dirty uniforms were everywhere. They kicked and pummeled everyone within reach. Alsatian guard dogs snapped and barked. Stephen was bitten by one of the snarling dogs. A woman beside him was being kicked by soldiers. And they were all being methodically herded past a high barbed-wire fence. Beside the fence was a wall.

Stephen looked around for an escape route, but he was surrounded by other prisoners, who were pressing against him. Soldiers were shooting indiscriminately into the crowd, shooting women and children alike.

The man who had shouted to his wife was shot.

"Sholom, help me, help me," screamed a scrawny young woman whose skin was as yellow and pimpled as chicken flesh.

And Stephen understood that *he* was Sholom. He was a Jew in this burning, stinking world, and this woman, somehow, meant something to him. He felt the yellow star sewn on the breast of his filthy jacket. He grimaced uncontrollably. The strangest thoughts were passing through his mind, remembrances of another childhood: morning prayers with his father and rich uncle, large breakfasts on Saturdays, the sounds of his mother and father quietly making love in the next room, *yortzeit* candles burning in the living room, his brother reciting the 'four questions' at the Passover table.

He touched the star again and remembered the Nazi's facetious euphemism for it: *Pour le Semite*.

He wanted to strike out, to kill the Nazis, to fight and die. But he found himself marching with the others, as if he had no will of his own. He felt that he was cut in half. He had two selves now; one watched the other. One self wanted to fight. The other was numbed; it cared only for itself. It was determined to survive.

Stephen looked around for the woman who had called out to him. She was nowhere to be seen.

Behind him were railroad tracks, electrified wire, and the conical tower and main gate of the camp. Ahead was a pitted road littered with corpses and their belongings. Rifles were being fired and a heavy, sickly sweet odor was everywhere. Stephen gagged, others vomited. It was the overwhelming stench of death, of rotting and burning flesh. Black clouds hung above the camp, and flames spurted from the tall chimneys of ugly buildings, as if from infernal machines.

Stephen walked onward; he was numb, unable to fight or even

talk. Everything that happened around him was impossible, the stuff of dreams.

The prisoners were ordered to halt, and the soldiers began to separate those who would be burned from those who would be worked to death. Old men and women and young children were pulled out of the crowd. Some were beaten and killed immediately while the others looked on in disbelief. Stephen looked on, as if it was of no concern to him. Everything was unreal, dreamlike. He did not belong here.

The new prisoners looked like *Musselmänner*, the walking dead. Those who became ill, or were beaten or starved before they could "wake up" to the reality of the camps, became *Musselmänner*. *Musselmänner* could not think or feel. They shuffled around, already dead in spirit, until a guard or disease or cold or starvation killed them.

"Keep marching," shouted a guard, as Stephen stopped before an emaciated old man crawling on the ground. "You'll look like him soon enough."

Suddenly, as if waking from one dream and finding himself in another, Stephen remembered that the chicken-skinned girl was his wife. He remembered their life together, their children and crowded flat. He remembered the birthmark on her leg, her scent, her hungry love-making. He had once fought another boy over her.

His glands opened up with fear and shame; he had ignored her screams for help.

He stopped and turned, faced the other group. "Fruma," he shouted, then started to run.

A guard struck him in the chest with the butt of his rifle, and Stephen fell into darkness.

He spills the icewater again and awakens with a scream.

"It's my fault," Josie says, as she peels back the sheets. "I should have taken the bowl away from you. But you fight me."

Stephen lives with the pain again. He imagines that a tiny fire is burning in his abdomen, slowly consuming him. He stares at the television high on the wall and watches Soupy Sales.

As Josie changes the plastic sac containing his intravenous saline solution, an orderly pushes a cart into the room and asks Stephen if he wants a print for his wall.

"Would you like me to choose something for you?" Josie asks.

Stephen shakes his head and asks the orderly to show him all the prints. Most of them are familiar still-lifes and pastorals, but one catches his attention. It is a painting of a wheat field. Although the sky looks ominously dark, the wheat is brightly rendered in great broad strokes. A path cuts through the field and crows fly overhead.

"That one," Stephen says. "Put that one up."

After the orderly hangs the print and leaves, Josie asks Stephen why he chose that particular painting.

"I like Van Gogh," he says dreamily, as he tries to detect a rhythm in the surges of abdominal pain. But he is not nauseated, just gaseous.

"Any particular reason why you like Van Gogh?" asks Josie. "He's my favorite artist, too."

"I didn't say he was my favorite," Stephen says, and Josie pouts, an expression which does not fit her prematurely lined face. Stephen closes his eyes, glimpses the cold country, and says, "I like the painting because it's so bright that it's almost frightening. And the road going through the field"—he opens his eyes—"doesn't go anywhere. It just ends in the field. And the crows are flying around like vultures."

"Most people see it as just a pretty picture," Josie says.

"What's it called?"

"Wheatfield with Blackbirds."

"Sensible. My stomach hurts, Josie. Help me turn over on my side." Josie helps him onto his left side, plumps up his pillows, and inserts a short tube into his rectum to relieve the gas. "I also like the painting with the large stars that all look out of focus," Stephen says. "What's it called?"

"Starry Night."

"That's scary, too," Stephen says. Josie takes his blood pressure, makes a notation on his chart, then sits down beside him and holds his hand. "I remember something," he says. "Something just—" He jumps as he remembers, and pain shoots through his distended stomach. Josie shushes him, checks the intravenous needle, and asks him what he remembers.

But the memory of the dream recedes as the pain grows

sharper. "I hurt all the fucking time, Josie," he says, changing position. Josie removes the rectal tube before he is on his back.

"Don't use such language, I don't like to hear it. I know you have a lot of pain," she says, her voice softening.

"Time for a shot."

"No, honey, not for some time. You'll just have to bear with it."

Stephen remembers his dream again. He is afraid of it. His breath is short and his heart feels as if it is beating in his throat, but he recounts the entire dream to Josie.

He does not notice that her face has lost its color.

"It's only a dream, Stephen. Probably something you studied in history."

"But it was so real, not like a dream at all."

"That's enough!" Josie says.

"I'm sorry I upset you. Don't be angry."

"I'm *not* angry."

"I'm sorry," he says, fighting the pain, squeezing Josie's hand tightly. "Didn't you tell me that you were in the Second World War?"

Josie is composed once again. "Yes, I did, but I'm surprised you remembered. You were very sick. I was a nurse overseas, spent most of the war in England. But I was one of the first service women to go into any of the concentration camps."

Stephen drifts with the pain; he appears to be asleep.

"You must have studied very hard," Josie whispers to him. Her hand is shaking just a bit.

It is twelve o'clock and his room is death-quiet. The sharp shadows seem to be the hardest objects in the room. The fluorescents burn steadily in the hall outside.

Stephen looks out into the hallway, but he can see only the far white wall. He waits for his nightnurse to appear: it is time for his injection. A young nurse passes by his doorway. Stephen imagines that she is a cardboard ship sailing through the corridors.

He presses the buzzer, which is attached by a clip to his pillow. The nightnurse will take her time, he tells himself. He remembers arguing with her. Angrily, he presses the buzzer again.

Across the hall, a man begins to scream, and there is a shuffle

of nurses into his room. The screaming turns into begging and
whining. Although Stephen has never seen the man in the opposite room, he has come to hate him. Like Stephen, he has
something wrong with his stomach, but he cannot suffer well.
He can only beg and cry, try to make deals with the nurses,
doctors, God, and angels. Stephen cannot muster any pity for
this man.

The nightnurse finally comes into the room, says, "You have to
try to get along without this," and gives him an injection of Demerol.

"Why does the man across the hall scream so?" Stephen asks, but
the nurse is already edging out of the room.

"Because he's in pain."

"So am I," Stephen says in a loud voice. "But I can keep it to
myself."

"Then stop buzzing me constantly for an injection. That man
across the hall has had half of his stomach removed. He's got
something to scream about."

So have I, Stephen thinks; but the nurse disappears before he
can tell her. He tries to imagine what the man across the hall looks
like. He thinks of him as being bald and small, an ancient baby.
Stephen tries to feel sorry for the man, but his incessant whining
disgusts him.

The drug takes effect; the screams recede as he hurtles through
the dark corridors of a dream. The cold country is dark, for Stephen cannot persuade his nightnurse to bring him some ice. Once
again, he sees two entrances. As the world melts behind him, he
steps into the coal-black doorway.

In the darkness he hears an alarm, a bone-jarring clangor.

He could smell the combined stink of men pressed closely together. They were all lying upon two badly constructed wooden
shelves. The floor was dirt; the smell of urine never left the barrack.

"Wake up," said a man Stephen knew as Viktor. "If the guard
finds you in bed, you'll be beaten again."

Stephen moaned, still wrapped in dreams. "Wake up, wake up,"
he mumbled to himself. He would have a few more minutes before the guard arrived with the dogs. At the very thought of dogs,

Stephen felt revulsion. He had once been bitten in the face by a large dog.

He opened his eyes, yet he was still half-asleep, exhausted. You are in a death camp, he said to himself. You must wake up. You must fight by waking up. Or you will die in your sleep. Shaking uncontrollably, he said, "Do you want to end up in the oven; perhaps you will be lucky today and live."

As he lowered his legs to the floor, he felt the sores open on the soles of his feet. He wondered who would die today and shrugged. It was his third week in the camp. Impossibly, against all odds, he had survived. Most of those he had known in the train had either died or become *Musselmänner*. If it was not for Viktor, he, too, would have become a *Musselmänner*. He had a breakdown and wanted to die. He babbled in English. But Viktor talked him out of death, shared his portion of food with him, and taught him the new rules of life.

"Like everyone else who survives, I count myself first, second, and third—then I try to do what I can for someone else," Viktor had said.

"I will survive," Stephen repeated to himself, as the guards opened the door, stepped into the room, and began to shout. Their dogs growled and snapped but heeled beside them. The guards looked sleepy; one did not wear a cap, and his red hair was tousled.

Perhaps he spent the night with one of the whores, Stephen thought. Perhaps today would not be so bad. . . .

And so begins the morning ritual: Josie enters Stephen's room at quarter to eight, fusses with the chart attached to the footboard of his bed, pads about aimlessly, and finally goes to the bathroom. She returns, her stiff uniform making swishing sounds. Stephen can feel her standing over the bed and staring at him. But he does not open his eyes. He waits a beat.

She turns away, then drops the bedpan. Yesterday it was the metal ashtray; day before that, she bumped into the bedstand.

"Good morning, darling, it's a beautiful day," she says, then walks across the room to the windows. She parts the faded orange drapes and opens the blinds.

"How do you feel today?"

"Okay, I guess."

Josie takes his pulse and asks, "Did Mr. Gregory stop in to say hello last night?"

"Yes," Stephen says. "He's teaching me how to play gin rummy. What's wrong with him?"

"He's very sick."

"I can see that; has he got cancer?"

"I don't know," says Josie, as she tidies up his night table.

"You're lying again," Stephen says, but she ignores him. After a time, he says, "His girlfriend was in to see me last night. I bet his wife will be in today."

"Shut your mouth about that," Josie says. "Let's get you out of that bed so I can change the sheets."

Stephen sits in the chair all morning. He is getting well but is still very weak. Just before lunchtime, the orderly wheels his cart into the room and asks Stephen if he would like to replace the print hanging on the wall.

"I've seen them all," Stephen says. "I'll keep the one I have." Stephen does not grow tired of the Van Gogh painting; sometimes, the crows seem to have changed position.

"Maybe you'll like this one," the orderly says as he pulls out a cardboard print of Van Gogh's *Starry Night*. It is a study of a village nestled in the hills, dressed in shadows. But everything seems to be boiling and writhing as in a fever dream. A cypress tree in the foreground looks like a black flame, and the vertiginous sky is filled with great blurry stars. It is a drunkard's dream. The orderly smiles.

"So you did have it," Stephen says.

"No, I traded some other pictures for it. They had a copy in the West Wing."

Stephen watches him hang it, thanks him, and waits for him to leave. Then he gets up and examines the painting carefully. He touches the raised facsimile brushstrokes and turns toward Josie, feeling an odd sensation in his groin. He looks at her, as if seeing her for the first time. She has an overly full mouth which curves downward at the corners when she smiles. She is not a pretty woman—too fat, he thinks.

"Dance with me," he says, as he waves his arms and takes a step forward, conscious of the pain in his stomach.

"You're too sick to be dancing just yet," but she laughs at him and bends her knees in a mock plié.

She has small breasts for such a large woman, Stephen thinks. Feeling suddenly dizzy, he takes a step toward the bed. He feels himself slip to the floor, feels Josie's hair brushing against his face, dreams that he's all wet from her tongue, feels her arms around him, squeezing, then feels the weight of her body pressing down on him, crushing him. . . .

He wakes up in bed, catheterized. He has an intravenous needle in his left wrist, and it is difficult to swallow, for he has a tube down his throat.

He groans, tries to move.

"Quiet, Stephen," Josie says, stroking his hand.

"What happened?" he mumbles. He can only remember being dizzy.

"You've had a slight setback, so just rest. The doctor had to collapse your lung; you must lie very still.

"Josie, I love you," he whispers, but he is too far away to be heard. He wonders how many hours or days have passed. He looks toward the window. It is dark, and there is no one in the room.

He presses the buzzer attached to his pillow and remembers a dream. . . .

"You must fight," Viktor said.

It was dark, all the other men were asleep, and the barrack was filled with snoring and snorting. Stephen wished they could all die, choke on their own breath. It would be an act of mercy.

"Why fight?" Stephen asked, and he pointed toward the greasy window, beyond which were the ovens that smoked day and night. He made a fluttering gesture with his hand—smoke rising.

"You must fight, you must live, living is everything. It is the only thing that makes sense here."

"We're all going to die, anyway," Stephen whispered. "Just like your sister . . . and my wife."

"No, Sholom, we're going to live. The others may die, but we're going to live. You must believe that."

Stephen understood that Viktor was desperately trying to convince himself to live. He felt sorry for Viktor; there could be no sensible rationale for living in a place like this.

Stephen grinned, tasted blood from the corner of his mouth, and said, "So we'll live through the night, maybe."

And maybe tomorrow, he thought. He would play the game of survival a little longer.

He wondered if Viktor would be alive tomorrow. He smiled and thought: If Viktor dies, then I will have to take his place and convince others to live. For an instant, he hoped Viktor would die so that he could take his place.

The alarm sounded. It was three o'clock in the morning, time to begin the day.

This morning Stephen was on his feet before the guards could unlock the door.

"Wake up," Josie says, gently tapping his arm. "Come on, wake up."

Stephen hears her voice as an echo. He imagines that he has been flung into a long tunnel; he hears air whistling in his ears but cannot see anything.

"Whassimatter?" he asks. His mouth feels as if it is stuffed with cotton; his lips are dry and cracked. He is suddenly angry at Josie and the plastic tubes that hold him in his bed as if he were a latter-day Gulliver. He wants to pull out the tubes, smash the bags filled with saline, tear away his bandages.

"You were speaking German," Josie says. "Did you know that?"

"Can I have some ice?"

"No," Josie says impatiently. "You spilled again, you're all wet."

". . . for my mouth, dry . . ."

"Do you remember speaking German, honey. I have to know."

"Don't remember, bring ice, I'll try to think about it."

As Josie leaves to get him some ice, he tries to remember his dream.

"Here, now, just suck on the ice." She gives him a little hill of crushed ice on the end of a spoon.

"Why did you wake me up, Josie?" The layers of dream are beginning to slough off. As the Demerol works out of his system, he has to concentrate on fighting the burning ache in his stomach.

"You were speaking German. Where did you learn to speak like that?"

Stephen tries to remember what he said. He cannot speak any German, only a bit of classroom French. He looks down at his legs (he has thrown off the sheet) and notices, for the first time, that his legs are as thin as his arms. "My God, Josie, how could I have lost so much weight?"

"You lost about forty pounds, but don't worry, you'll gain it all back. You're on the road to recovery now. Please, try to remember your dream."

"I can't, Josie! I just can't seem to get ahold of it."

"Try."

"Why is it so important to you?"

"You weren't speaking college German, darling. You were speaking slang. You spoke in a patois that I haven't heard since the forties."

Stephen feels a chill slowly creep up his spine. "What did I say?"

Josie waits a beat, then says, "You talked about dying."

"Josie?"

"Yes," she says, pulling at her fingernail.

"When is the pain going to stop?"

"It will be over soon." She gives him another spoonful of ice. "You kept repeating the name Viktor in your sleep. Can you remember anything about him?"

Viktor, Viktor, deep-set blue eyes, balding head and broken nose, called himself a Galitzianer. Saved my life. "I remember," Stephen says. "His name is Viktor Shmone. He is in all my dreams now."

Josie exhales sharply.

"Does that mean anything to you?" Stephen asks anxiously.

"I once knew a man from one of the camps." She speaks very slowly and precisely. "His name was Viktor Shmone. I took care of him. He was one of the few people left alive in the camp after the Germans fled." She reaches for her purse, which she keeps on Stephen's night table, and fumbles an old, torn photograph out of a plastic slipcase.

As Stephen examines the photograph, he begins to sob. A thinner and much younger Josie is standing beside Viktor and two other emaciated-looking men. "Then I'm not dreaming," he says, "and I'm going to die. That's what it means." He begins to shake, just as he did in his dream, and, without thinking, he makes the gesture of rising smoke to Josie. He begins to laugh.

"Stop that," Josie says, raising her hand to slap him. Then she embraces him and says, "Don't cry, darling, it's only a dream. Somehow, you're dreaming the past."

"Why?" Stephen asks, still shaking.

"Maybe you're dreaming because of me, because we're so close. In some ways, I think you know me better than anyone else, better than any man, no doubt. You might be dreaming for a reason; maybe I can help you."

"I'm afraid, Josie."

She comforts him and says, "Now tell me everything you can remember about the dreams."

He is exhausted. As he recounts his dreams to her, he sees the bright doorway again. He feels himself being sucked into it. "Josie," he says, "I must stay awake, don't want to sleep, dream. . . ."

Josie's face is pulled tight as a mask; she is crying.

Stephen reaches out to her, slips into the bright doorway, into another dream.

It was a cold cloudless morning. Hundreds of prisoners were working in the quarries; each work gang came from a different barrack. Most of the gangs were made up of *Musselmänner*, the faceless majority of the camp. They moved like automatons, lifting and carrying the great stones to the numbered carts, which would have to be pushed down the tracks.

Stephen was drenched with sweat. He had a fever and was afraid that he had contracted typhus. An epidemic had broken out in the camp last week. Every morning several doctors arrived with the guards. Those who were too sick to stand up were taken away to be gassed or experimented upon in the hospital.

Although Stephen could barely stand, he forced himself to keep moving. He tried to focus all his attention on what he was doing. He made a ritual of bending over, choosing a stone of certain size, lifting it, carrying it to the nearest cart, and then taking the same number of steps back to his dig.

A *Musselmänn* fell to the ground, but Stephen made no effort to help him. When he could help someone in a little way, he would, but he would not stick his neck out for a *Musselmänn.* Yet something niggled at Stephen. He remembered a photograph in which Viktor and this *Musselmänn* were standing with a man and a woman he did not recognize. But Stephen could not remember where he had ever seen such a photograph.

"Hey, you," shouted a guard. "Take the one on the ground to the cart."

Stephen nodded to the guard and began to drag the *Musselmänn* away.

"Who's the new patient down the hall?" Stephen asks as he eats a bit of cereal from the breakfast tray Josie has placed before him. He is feeling much better now; his fever is down, and the tubes, catheter, and intravenous needle have been removed. He can even walk around a bit.

"How did you find out about that?" Josie asks.

"You were talking to Mr. Gregory's nurse. Do you think I'm dead already? I can still hear."

Josie laughs and takes a sip of Stephen's tea. "You're far from dead! In fact, today is a red-letter day; you're going to take your first shower. What do you think about that?"

"I'm not well enough yet," he says, worried that he will have to leave the hospital before he is ready.

"Well, Dr. Volk thinks differently, and his word is law."

"Tell me about the new patient."

"They brought in a man last night who drank two quarts of motor oil; he's on the dialysis machine."

"Will he make it?"

"No, I don't think so; there's too much poison in his system."

We should all die, Stephen thinks. It would be an act of mercy. He glimpses the camp.

"Stephen!"

He jumps, then awakens.

"You've had a good night's sleep; you don't need to nap. Let's get you into that shower and have it done with." Josie pushes the tray table away from the bed. "Come on, I have your bathrobe right here."

Stephen puts on his bathrobe, and they walk down the hall to the showers. There are three empty shower stalls, a bench, and a whirlpool bath. As Stephen takes off his bathrobe, Josie adjusts the water pressure and temperature in the corner stall.

"What's the matter?" Stephen asks, after stepping into the shower. Josie stands in front of the shower stall and holds his towel, but she will not look at him. "Come on," he says, "you've seen me naked before."

"That was different."

"How?" He touches a hard, ugly scab that has formed over one of the wounds on his abdomen.

"When you were very sick, I washed you in bed, as if you were a baby. Now it's different." She looks down at the wet tile floor, as if she is lost in thought.

"Well, I think it's silly," he says. "Come on, it's hard to talk to someone who's looking the other way. I could break my neck in here and you'd be staring down at the fucking floor."

"I've asked you not to use that word," she says in a very low voice.

"Do my eyes still look yellowish?"

She looks directly at his face and says, "No, they look fine."

Stephen suddenly feels faint, then nauseated; he has been standing too long. As he leans against the cold shower wall, he remembers his last dream. He is back in the quarry. He can smell the perspiration of the men around him, feel the sun baking him, draining his strength. It is so bright. . . .

He finds himself sitting on the bench and staring at the light on the opposite wall. I've got typhus, he thinks, then realizes that he is in the hospital. Josie is beside him.

"I'm sorry," he says.

"I shouldn't have let you stand so long; it was my fault."

"I remembered another dream." He begins to shake, and Josie puts her arms around him.

"It's all right now, tell Josie about your dream."

She's an old, fat woman, Stephen thinks. As he describes the dream, his shaking subsides.

"Do you know the man's name?" Josie asks. "The one the guard ordered you to drag away."

"No," Stephen says. "He was a *Musselmänn*, yet I thought there was something familiar about him. In my dream I remembered the photograph you showed me. He was in it."

"What will happen to him?"

"The guards will give him to the doctors for experimentation. If they don't want him, he'll be gassed."

"You must not let that happen," Josie says, holding him tightly.

"Why?" asks Stephen, afraid that he will fall into the dreams again.

"If he was one of the men you saw in the photograph, you must not let him die. Your dreams must fit the past."

"I'm afraid."

"It will be all right, baby," Josie says, clinging to him. She is shaking and breathing heavily.

Stephen feels himself getting an erection. He calms her, presses his face against hers, and touches her breasts. She tells him to stop, but does not push him away.

"I love you," he says as he slips his hand under her starched skirt. He feels awkward and foolish and warm.

"This is wrong," she whispers.

As Stephen kisses her and feels her thick tongue in his mouth, he begins to dream. . . .

Stephen stopped to rest for a few seconds. The *Musselmänn* was dead weight. I cannot go on, Stephen thought; but he bent down, grabbed the *Musselmänn* by his coat, and dragged him toward the cart. He glimpsed the cart, which was filled with the sick and dead and exhausted; it looked no different than a carload of corpses marked for a mass grave.

A long, grey cloud covered the sun, then passed, drawing shadows across gutted hills.

On impulse, Stephen dragged the *Musselmänn* into a gully behind several chalky rocks. Why am I doing this? he asked himself. If I'm caught, I'll be ash in the ovens, too. He remembered what Viktor had told him: "You must think of yourself all the time, or you'll be no help to anyone else."

The *Musselmänn* groaned, then raised his arm. His face was grey with dust and his eyes were glazed.

"You must lie still," Stephen whispered. "Do not make a sound. I've hidden you from the guards, but if they hear you, we'll all be punished. One sound from you and you're dead. You must fight to live, you're in a death camp, you must fight so you can tell of this later."

"I have no family, they're all—"

Stephen clapped his hand over the man's mouth and whispered, "Fight, don't talk. Wake up, you cannot survive the death by sleeping."

The man nodded, and Stephen climbed out of the gully. He helped two men carry a large stone to a nearby cart.

"What are you doing?" shouted a guard.

"I left my place to help these men with this stone; now I'll go back where I was."

"What the hell are you trying to do?" Viktor asked.

Stephen felt as if he was burning up with fever. He wiped the sweat from his eyes, but everything was still blurry.

"You're sick, too. You'll be lucky if you last the day."

"I'll last," Stephen said, "but I want you to help me get him back to the camp."

"I won't risk it, not for a *Musselmänn*. He's already dead, leave him."

"Like you left me?"

Before the guards could take notice, they began to work. Although Viktor was older than Stephen, he was stronger. He worked hard every day and never caught the diseases that daily reduced the barrack's numbers. Stephen had a touch of death, as Viktor called it, and was often sick.

They worked until dusk, when the sun's oblique rays caught the dust from the quarries and turned it into veils and scrims. Even the guards sensed that this was a quiet time, for they would congregate together and talk in hushed voices.

"Come, now, help me," Stephen whispered to Viktor. "I've been doing that all day," Viktor said. "I'll have enough trouble getting you back to the camp, much less carry this *Musselmänn*."

"We can't leave him."

"Why are you so preoccupied with this *Musselmänn?* Even if we can get him back to the camp, his chances are nothing. I know, I've seen enough, I know who has a chance to survive."

"You're wrong this time," Stephen said. He was dizzy and it was difficult to stand. The odds are I won't last the night, and Viktor knows it, he told himself. "I had a dream that if this man dies, I'll die, too. I just feel it."

"Here we learn to trust our dreams," Viktor said. "They make as much sense as this. . . ." He made the gesture of rising smoke and gazed toward the ovens, which were spewing fire and black ash.

The western portion of the sky was yellow, but over the ovens it was red and purple and dark blue. Although it horrified Stephen to consider it, there was a macabre beauty here. If he survived, he would never forget these sense impressions, which were stronger than anything he had ever experienced before. Being so close to death, he was, perhaps for the first time, really living. In the camp, one did not even consider suicide. One grasped for every moment, sucked at life like an infant, lived as if there was no future.

The guards shouted at the prisoners to form a column; it was time to march back to the barracks.

While the others milled about, Stephen and Viktor lifted the *Musselmänn* out of the gully. Everyone nearby tried to distract the guards. When the march began, Stephen and Viktor held the *Musselmänn* between them, for he could barely stand.

"Come on, dead one, carry your weight," Viktor said. "Are you so dead that you cannot hear me? Are you as dead as the rest of your family?" The *Musselmänn* groaned and dragged his legs. Viktor kicked him. "You'll walk or we'll leave you here for the guards to find."

"Let him be," Stephen said.

"Are you dead or do you have a name?" Viktor continued.

"Berek," croaked the *Musselmänn*. "I am not dead."

"Then we have a fine bunk for you," Viktor said. "You can smell the stink of the sick for another night before the guards make a selection." Viktor made the gesture of smoke rising.

Stephen stared at the barracks ahead. They seemed to waver as the heat rose from the ground. He counted every step. He would drop soon, he could not go on, could not carry the *Musselmänn*. He began to mumble in English.

"So you're speaking American again," Viktor said.

Stephen shook himself awake, placed one foot before the other.

"Dreaming of an American lover?"

"I don't know English and I have no American lover."

"Then who is this Josie you keep talking about in your sleep . . . ?"

"Why were you screaming?" Josie asks, as she washes his face with a cold washcloth.

"I don't remember screaming," Stephen says. He discovers a fever blister on his lip. Expecting to find an intravenous needle in his wrist, he raises his arm.

"You don't need an I.V.," Josie says. "You just have a bit of a fever. Dr. Volk has prescribed some new medication for it."

"What time is it?" Stephen stares at the whorls in the ceiling.

"Almost three P.M. I'll be going off soon."

"Then I've slept most of the day away," Stephen says, feeling something crawling inside him. He worries that his dreams still have a hold on him. "Am I having another relapse?"

"You'll do fine," Josie says.

"I should be fine now. I don't want to dream anymore."

"Did you dream again, do you remember anything?"

"I dreamed that I saved the *Musselmänn*," Stephen says.

"What was his name?" asks Josie.

"Berek, I think. Is that the man you knew?"

Josie nods and Stephen smiles at her. "Maybe that's the end of the dreams," he says, but she does not respond. He asks to see the photograph again.

"Not just now," Josie says.

"But I have to see it. I want to see if I can recognize myself. . . ."

Stephen dreamed he was dead, but it was only the fever. Viktor sat beside him on the floor and watched the others. The sick were moaning and crying; they slept on the cramped platform, as if proximity to one another could insure a few more hours of life. Wan moonlight seemed to fill the barrack.

Stephen awakened, feverish. "I'm burning up," he whispered to Viktor.

"Well," Viktor said, "you've got your *Musselmänn*. If he lives, you live. That's what you said, isn't it?"

"I don't remember, I just knew that I couldn't let him die."

"You'd better go back to sleep, you'll need your strength. Or we may have to carry *you*, tomorrow."

Stephen tried to sleep, but the fever was making lights and spots before his eyes. When he finally fell asleep, he dreamed of a dark country filled with gemstones and great quarries of ice and glass.

"What?" Stephen asked, as he sat up suddenly, awakened from dampblack dreams. He looked around and saw that everyone was watching Berek, who was sitting under the window at the far end of the room.

Berek was singing the *Kol Nidre* very softly. It was the Yom Kippur prayer, which was sung on the most holy of days. He repeated the prayer three times, and then once again in a louder voice. The others responded, intoned the prayer as a recitative. Viktor was crying quietly, and Stephen imagined that the holy spirit animated Berek. Surely, he told himself, that face and those pale unseeing eyes were those of a dead man. He remembered the story of the golem, shuddered, found himself singing and pulsing with fever.

When the prayer was over, Berek fell back into his fever trance. The others became silent, then slept. But there was something new in the barrack with them tonight, a palpable exultation. Stephen looked around at the sleepers and thought: We're surviving, more dead than alive, but surviving. . . .

"You were right about that *Musselmänn*," Viktor whispered. "It's good that we saved him."

"Perhaps we should sit with him," Stephen said. "He's alone." But Viktor was already asleep; and Stephen was suddenly afraid that if he sat beside Berek, he would be consumed by his holy fire.

As Stephen fell through sleep and dreams, his face burned with fever.

Again he wakes up screaming.

"Josie," he says, "I can remember the dream, but there's something else, something I can't see, something terrible. . . . "

"Not to worry," Josie says, "it's the fever." But she looks worried, and Stephen is sure that she knows something he does not.

"Tell me what happened to Viktor and Berek," Stephen says. He presses his hands together to stop them from shaking.

"They lived, just as you are going to live and have a good life." Stephen calms down and tells her his dream.

"So you see," she says, "you're even dreaming about surviving."

"I'm burning up."

"Dr. Volk says you're doing very well." Josie sits beside him, and he watches the fever patterns shift behind his closed eyelids.

"Tell me what happens next, Josie."

"You're going to get well."

"There's something else. . . . "

"Shush, now, there's nothing else." She pauses, then says, "Mr. Gregory is supposed to visit you tonight. He's getting around a bit; he's been back and forth all day in his wheelchair. He tells me that you two have made some sort of a deal about dividing up all the nurses."

Stephen smiles, opens his eyes, and says, "It was Gregory's idea. Tell me what's wrong with him."

"All right, he has cancer, but he doesn't know it, and you must keep it a secret. They cut the nerve in his leg because the pain was so bad. He's quite comfortable now, but remember, you can't repeat what I've told you."

"Is he going to live?" Stephen asks. "He's told me about all the new projects he's planning. So I guess he's expecting to get out of here."

"He's not going to live very long, and the doctor didn't want to break his spirit."

"I think he should be told."

"That's not your decision to make, nor mine."

"Am I going to die, Josie?"

"No!" she says, touching his arm to reassure him.

"How do I know that's the truth?"

"Because I say so, and I couldn't look you straight in the eye and tell you if it wasn't true. I should have known it would be a mistake to tell you about Mr. Gregory."

"You did right," Stephen says. "I won't mention it again. Now that I know, I feel better." He feels drowsy again.

"Do you think you're up to seeing him tonight?"

Stephen nods, although he is bone tired. As he falls asleep, the fever patterns begin to dissolve, leaving a bright field. With a start, he opens his eyes: he has touched the edge of another dream.

"What happened to the man across the hall, the one who was always screaming?"

"He's left the ward," Josie says. "Mr. Gregory had better hurry, if he wants to play cards with you before dinner. They're going to bring the trays up soon."

"You mean he died, don't you."

"Yes, if you must know, he died. But *you're* going to live."

There is a crashing noise in the hallway. Someone shouts, and Josie runs to the door.

Stephen tries to stay awake, but he is being pulled back into the cold country.

"Mr. Gregory fell trying to get into his wheelchair by himself," Josie says. "He should have waited for his nurse, but she was out of the room and he wanted to visit you."

But Stephen does not hear a word she says.

There were rumors that the camp was going to be liberated. It was late, but no one was asleep. The shadows in the barrack seemed larger tonight.

"It's better for us if the Allies don't come," Viktor said to Stephen.

"Why do you say that?"

"Haven't you noticed that the ovens are going day and night? The Nazis are in a hurry."

"I'm going to try to sleep," Stephen said.

"Look around you, even the *Musselmänner* are agitated," Viktor said. "Animals become nervous before the slaughter. I've worked with animals. People are not so different."

"Shut up and let me sleep," Stephen said, and he dreamed that he could hear the crackling of distant gunfire.

"Attention," shouted the guards as they stepped into the barrack. There were more guards than usual, and each one had two Alsatian dogs. "Come on, form a line. Hurry."

"They're going to kill us," Viktor said, "then they'll evacuate the camp and save themselves."

The guards marched the prisoners toward the north section of the camp. Although it was still dark, it was hot and humid, without a trace of the usual morning chill. The ovens belched fire and turned the sky aglow. Everyone was quiet, for there was nothing to be done. The guards were nervous and would cut down anyone who uttered a sound, as an example for the rest.

The booming of big guns could be heard in the distance. If I'm going to die, Stephen thought, I might as well go now and take a Nazi with me. Suddenly, all of his buried fear, aggression, and revulsion surfaced; his face became hot and his heart felt as if it were pumping in his throat. But Stephen argued with himself. There was always a chance. He had once heard of some women who were waiting in line for the ovens; for no apparent reason the guards sent them back to their barracks. Anything could happen. There was always a chance. But to attack a guard would mean certain death.

The guns became louder. Stephen could not be sure, but he thought the noise was coming from the west. The thought passed through his mind that everyone would be better off dead. That would stop all the guns and screaming voices, the clenched fists and wildly beating hearts. The Nazis should kill everyone, and then themselves, as a favor to humanity.

The guards stopped the prisoners in an open field surrounded on three sides by forestland. Sunrise was moments away; purple-black clouds drifted across the sky, touched by grey in the east. It promised to be a hot, gritty day.

Half-step Walter, a Judenrat sympathizer who worked for the guards, handed out shovel heads to everyone.

"He's worse than the Nazis," Viktor said to Stephen.

"The Judenrat thinks he will live," said Berek, "but he will die like a Jew with the rest of us."

"Now, when it's too late, the *Musselmänn* regains consciousness," Viktor said.

"Hurry," shouted the guards, "or you'll die now. As long as you dig, you'll live."

Stephen hunkered down on his knees and began to dig with the shovel head.

"Do you think we might escape?" Berek whined.

"Shut up and dig," Stephen said. "There is no escape, just stay alive as long as you can. Stop whining, are you becoming a *Musselmänn* again?" Stephen noticed that other prisoners were gathering up twigs and branches. So the Nazis plan to cover us up, he thought.

"That's enough," shouted a guard. "Put your shovels down in front of you and stand in a line."

The prisoners stood shoulder to shoulder along the edge of the mass grave. Stephen stood between Viktor and Berek. Someone screamed and ran and was shot immediately.

I don't want to see trees or guards or my friends, Stephen thought as he stared into the sun. I only want to see the sun, let it burn out my eyes, fill up my head with light. He was shaking uncontrollably, quaking with fear.

Guns were booming in the background.

Maybe the guards won't kill us, Stephen thought, even as he heard the crackcrack of their rifles. Men were screaming and begging for life. Stephen turned his head, only to see someone's face blown away.

Screaming, tasting vomit in his mouth, Stephen fell backward, pulling Viktor and Berek into the grave with him.

Darkness, Stephen thought. His eyes were open, yet it was dark, I must be dead, this must be death. . . .

He could barely move. Corpses can't move, he thought. Something brushed against his face; he stuck out his tongue, felt something spongy. It tasted bitter. Lifting first one arm and then the other, Stephen moved some branches away. Above, he could see a few dim stars; the clouds were lit like lanterns by a quarter moon.

He touched the body beside him; it moved. That must be Viktor, he thought. "Viktor, are you alive, say something if you're alive," Stephen whispered, as if in fear of disturbing the dead.

Viktor groaned and said, "Yes, I'm alive, and so is Berek."

"And the others?"

"All dead. Can't you smell the stink? You, at least, were unconscious all day."

"They can't *all* be dead," Stephen said, then he began to cry.

"Shut up," Viktor said, touching Stephen's face to comfort him. "We're alive, that's something. They could have fired a volley into the pit."

"I thought I was dead," Berek said. He was a shadow among shadows.

"Why are we still here?" Stephen asked.

"We stayed in here because it is safe," Viktor said.

"But they're all dead," Stephen whispered, amazed that there could be speech and reason inside a grave.

"Do you think it's safe to leave now?" Berek asked Viktor.

"Perhaps. I think the killing has stopped. By now the Americans or English or whoever they are have taken over the camp. I heard gunfire and screaming. I think it's best to wait a while longer."

"Here?" asked Stephen. "Among the dead?"

"It's best to be safe."

It was late afternoon when they climbed out of the grave. The air was thick with flies. Stephen could see bodies sprawled in awkward positions beneath the covering of twigs and branches. "How can I live when all the others are dead?" he asked himself aloud.

"You live, that's all," answered Viktor.

They kept close to the forest and worked their way back toward the camp.

"Look there," Viktor said, motioning Stephen and Berek to take cover. Stephen could see trucks moving toward the camp compound.

"Americans," whispered Berek.

"No need to whisper now," Stephen said. "We're safe."

"Guards could be hiding anywhere," Viktor said. "I haven't slept in the grave to be shot now."

They walked into the camp through a large break in the barbed-wire fence, which had been hit by an artillery shell. When they reached the compound, they found nurses, doctors, and army personnel bustling about.

"You speak English," Viktor said to Stephen, as they walked past several quonsets. "Maybe you can speak for us."

"I told you, I can't speak English."

"But I've heard you!"

"Wait," shouted an American army nurse. "You fellows are going the wrong way." She was stocky and spoke perfect German. "You must check in at the hospital; it's back that way."

"No," said Berek, shaking his head. "I won't go in there."

"There's no need to be afraid now," she said. "You're free. Come along, I'll take you to the hospital."

Something familiar about her, Stephen thought. He felt dizzy and everything turned grey.

"Josie," he murmured, as he fell to the ground.

"What is it?" Josie asks. "Everything is all right, Josie is here."

"Josie," Stephen mumbles.

"You're all right."

"How can I live when they're all dead?" he asks.

"It was a dream," she says as she wipes the sweat from his forehead. "You see, your fever has broken, you're getting well."

"Did you know about the grave?"

"It's all over now, forget the dream."

"Did you know?"

"Yes," Josie says. "Viktor told me how he survived the grave, but that was so long ago, before you were even born. Dr. Volk tells me you'll be going home soon."

"I don't want to leave, I want to stay with you."

"Stop that talk, you've got a whole life ahead of you. Soon, you'll forget all about this, and you'll forget me, too."

"Josie," Stephen asks, "let me see that old photograph again. Just one last time."

"Remember, this is the last time," she says as she hands him the faded photograph.

He recognizes Viktor and Berek, but the young man standing between them is not Stephen. "That's not me," he says, certain that he will never return to the camp.

Yet the shots still echo in his mind.

GEORGE R. R. MARTIN

❧ *Sandkings*

George R. R. Martin, an ex-college journalism instructor, first caught the attention of science-fiction readers with a series of stories published from 1971 through 1975 in *Analog,* notably "With Morning Comes Mistfall," a Hugo finalist, and "The Storms of Windhaven" (with Lisa Tuttle), also a Hugo finalist. His first novel, *Dying of the Light,* which appeared in 1977 (titled *After the Festival* when serialized in *Analog*), was a Hugo winner and attracted intense critical attention for its narrative strength. Another Hugo winner and probably Martin's most popular novella, "A Song for Lya," is a showcase for his romantic style, and was the title story for a collection of his work. Another collection, *Songs of Stars and Shadows,* was published in 1977. He edited the first of the *New Voices* series of original anthologies featuring stories by John Campbell Award nominees. His Nebula-winning story in this volume has already been cited by leading critics for its literary effectiveness.

❧ Winner, Nebula, for Best Novelette of 1979.

Simon Kress lived alone in a sprawling manor house among the dry, rocky hills fifty kilometers from the city. So, when he was called away unexpectedly on business, he had no neighbors he could conveniently impose on to take his pets. The carrion hawk was no problem; it roosted in the unused belfry and customarily fed itself anyway. The shambler Kress simply shooed outside and left to fend for itself; the little monster would gorge on slugs and birds and rockjocks. But the fish tank, stocked with genuine Earth piranha, posed a difficulty. Kress finally just threw a haunch of beef into the huge tank. The piranha could always eat each other if he were detained longer than expected. They'd done it before. It amused him.

Unfortunately, he was detained *much* longer than expected this time. When he finally returned, all the fish were dead. So was the carrion hawk. The shambler had climbed up to the belfry and eaten it. Simon Kress was vexed.

The next day he flew his skimmer to Asgard, a journey of some two hundred kilometers. Asgard was Baldur's largest city and boasted the oldest and largest starport as well. Kress liked to impress his friends with animals that were unusual, entertaining, and expensive; Asgard was the place to buy them.

This time, though, he had poor luck. Xenopets had closed its doors, t'Etherane the Petseller tried to foist another carrion hawk off on him, and Strange Waters offered nothing more exotic than piranha, glowsharks, and spider-squids. Kress had had all those; he wanted something new.

Near dusk, he found himself walking down the Rainbow Boulevard, looking for places he had not patronized before. So close to the starport, the street was lined by importers' marts. The big corporate emporiums had impressive long windows, where rare and costly alien artifacts reposed on felt cushions against dark drapes that made the interiors of the stores a mystery. Between them were the junk shops; narrow, nasty little places whose display areas were crammed with all manner of offworld bric-a-brac. Kress tried both kinds of shop, with equal dissatisfaction.

Then he came across a store that was different.

It was quite close to the port. Kress had never been there before. The shop occupied a small, single-story building of moderate size, set between a euphoria bar and a temple-brothel of the Secret Sisterhood. Down this far, the Rainbow Boulevard grew tacky. The shop itself was unusual. Arresting.

The windows were full of mist; now a pale red, now the grey of true fog, now sparkling and golden. The mist swirled and eddied and glowed faintly from within. Kress glimpsed objects in the window—machines, pieces of art, other things he could not recognize—but he could not get a good look at any of them. The mists flowed sensuously around them, displaying a bit of first one thing and then another, then cloaking all. It was intriguing.

As he watched, the mist began to form letters. One word at a time. Kress stood and read.

WO AND SHADE, IMPORTERS
ARTIFACTS · ART · LIFEFORMS · MISC.

The letters stopped. Through the fog, Kress saw something moving. That was enough for him, that and the "Lifeforms" in their advertisement. He swept his walking cloak over his shoulder and entered the store.

Inside, Kress felt disoriented. The interior seemed vast, much larger than he would have guessed from the relatively modest frontage. It was dimly lit, peaceful. The ceiling was a starscape, complete with spiral nebulae, very dark and realistic, very nice.

The counters all shone faintly, to better display the merchandise within. The aisles were carpeted with ground fog. It came almost to his knees in places, and swirled about his feet as he walked.

"Can I help you?"

She almost seemed to have risen from the fog. Tall and gaunt and pale, she wore a practical grey jumpsuit and a strange little cap that rested well back on her head.

"Are you Wo or Shade?" Kress asked. "Or only sales help?"

"Jala Wo, ready to serve you," she replied. "Shade does not see customers. We have no sales help."

"You have quite a large establishment," Kress said. "Odd that I have never heard of you before."

"We have only just opened this shop on Baldur," the woman said. "We have franchises on a number of other worlds, however. What can I sell you? Art, perhaps? You have the look of a collector. We have some fine Nor T'alush crystal carvings."

"No," Simon Kress said. "I own all the crystal carvings I desire. I came to see about a pet."

"A lifeform?"

"Yes."

"Alien?"

"Of course."

"We have a mimic in stock. From Celia's World. A clever little simian. Not only will it learn to speak, but eventually it will mimic your voice, inflections, gestures, even facial expressions."

"Cute," said Kress. "And common. I have no use for either, Wo. I want something exotic. Unusual. And not cute. I detest cute animals. At the moment I own a shambler. Imported from Cotho, at no mean expense. From time to time I feed him a litter of unwanted kittens. That is what I think of *cute*. Do I make myself understood?"

Wo smiled enigmatically. "Have you ever owned an animal that worshipped you?" she asked.

Kress grinned. "Oh, now and again. But I don't require worship, Wo. Just entertainment."

"You misunderstand me," Wo said, still wearing her strange smile. "I meant worship literally."

"What are you talking about?"

"I think I have just the thing for you," Wo said. "Follow me."

She led Kress between the radiant counters and down a long, fog-shrouded aisle beneath false starlight. They passed through a wall of mist into another section of the store, and stopped before a large plastic tank. An aquarium, thought Kress.

Wo beckoned. He stepped closer and saw that he was wrong. It was a terrarium. Within lay a miniature desert about two meters square. Pale sand bleached scarlet by wan red light. Rocks: basalt and quartz and granite. In each corner of the tank stood a castle.

Kress blinked, and peered, and corrected himself; actually only three castles stood. The fourth leaned; a crumbled, broken ruin. The other three were crude but intact, carved of stone and sand. Over their battlements and through their rounded porticos, tiny creatures climbed and scrambled. Kress pressed his face against the plastic. "Insects?" he asked.

"No," Wo replied. "A much more complex lifeform. More intelligent as well. Smarter than your shambler by a considerable amount. They are called sandkings."

"Insects," Kress said, drawing back from the tank. "I don't care how complex they are." He frowned. "And kindly don't try to gull me with this talk of intelligence. These things are far too small to have anything but the most rudimentary brains."

"They share hiveminds," Wo said. "Castle minds, in this case. There are only three organisms in the tank, actually. The fourth died. You see how her castle has fallen."

Kress looked back at the tank. "Hiveminds, eh? Interesting." He frowned again. "Still, it is only an oversized ant farm. I'd hoped for something better."

"They fight wars."

"Wars? Hmmm." Kress looked again.

"Note the colors, if you will," Wo told him. She pointed to the creatures that swarmed over the nearest castle. One was scrabbling at the tank wall. Kress studied it. It still looked like an insect to his eyes. Barely as long as his fingernail, six-limbed, with six tiny eyes set all around its body. A wicked set of mandibles clacked visibly, while two long fine antennae wove patterns in the air. Antennae, mandibles, eyes and legs were sooty black, but the dominant color was the burnt orange of its armor plating. "It's an insect," Kress repeated.

"It is not an insect," Wo insisted calmly. "The armored exoskeleton is shed when the sandking grows larger. *If* it grows larger. In a tank this size, it won't." She took Kress by the elbow and led him around the tank to the next castle. "Look at the colors here."

He did. They were different. Here the sandkings had bright red armor; antennae, mandibles, eyes and legs were yellow. Kress glanced across the tank. The denizens of the third live castle were off-white, with red trim. "Hmmm," he said.

"They war, as I said," Wo told him. "They even have truces and alliances. It was an alliance that destroyed the fourth castle in this tank. The blacks were getting too numerous, so the others joined forces to destroy them."

Kress remained unconvinced. "Amusing, no doubt. But insects fight wars too."

"Insects do not worship," Wo said.

"Eh?"

Wo smiled and pointed at the castle. Kress stared. A face had been carved into the wall of the highest tower. He recognized it. It was Jala Wo's face. "How . . . ?"

"I projected a holograph of my face into the tank, kept it there for a few days. The face of god, you see? I feed them, I am always close. The sandkings have a rudimentary psionic sense. Proximity telepathy. They sense me, and worship me by using my face to decorate their buildings. All the castles have them, see." They did.

On the castle, the face of Jala Wo was serene and peaceful, and very lifelike. Kress marveled at the workmanship. "How do they do it?"

"The foremost legs double as arms. They even have fingers of a sort; three small, flexible tendrils. And they cooperate well, both in building and in battle. Remember, all the mobiles of one color share a single mind."

"Tell me more," Kress said.

Wo smiled. "The maw lives in the castle. Maw is my name for her. A pun, if you will; the thing is mother and stomach both. Female, large as your fist, immobile. Actually, sandking is a bit of a misnomer. The mobiles are peasants and warriors, the real ruler is a queen. But that analogy is faulty as well. Considered as a whole, each castle is a single hermaphroditic creature."

"What do they eat?"

"The mobiles eat pap, predigested food obtained inside the castle. They get it from the maw after she has worked on it for several days. Their stomachs can't handle anything else, so if the maw dies, they soon die as well. The maw . . . the maw eats anything. You'll have no special expense there. Table scraps will do excellently."

"Live food?" Kress asked.

Wo shrugged. "Each maw eats mobiles from the other castles, yes."

"I am intrigued," he admitted. "If only they weren't so small."

"Yours can be larger. These sandkings are small because their tank is small. They seem to limit their growth to fit available space. If I moved these to a larger tank, they'd start growing again."

"Hmmmm. My piranha tank is twice this size, and vacant. It could be cleaned out, filled with sand. . . ."

"Wo and Shade would take care of the installation. It would be our pleasure."

"Of course," said Kress, "I would expect four intact castles."

"Certainly," Wo said.

They began to haggle about the price.

Three days later Jala Wo arrived at Simon Kress' estate, with dormant sandkings and a work crew to take charge of the installation. Wo's assistants were aliens unlike any Kress was familiar with; squat, broad bipeds with four arms and bulging, multifaceted eyes. Their skin was thick and leathery, and twisted into horns and spines and protrusions at odd spots upon their bodies. But they were very strong, and good workers. Wo ordered them about in a musical tongue that Kress had never heard.

In a day it was done. They moved his piranha tank to the center of his spacious living room, arranged couches on either side of it for better viewing, scrubbed it clean and filled it two-thirds of the way up with sand and rock. Then they installed a special lighting system, both to provide the dim red illumination the sandkings preferred and to project holographic images into the tank. On top they mounted a sturdy plastic cover, with a feeder mechanism built in. "This way you can feed your sandkings without removing the top of the tank," Wo explained. "You would not want to take any chances on the mobiles escaping."

The cover also included climate control devices, to condense just the right amount of moisture from the air. "You want it dry, but not too dry," Wo said.

Finally one of the four-armed workers climbed into the tank and dug deep pits in the four corners. One of his companions handed the dormant maws over to him, removing them one-by-one from their frosted cryonic traveling cases. They were nothing to look it. Kress decided they resembled nothing so much as a mottled, half-spoiled chunk of raw meat. With a mouth.

The alien buried them, one in each corner of the tank. Then they sealed it all up and took their leave.

"The heat will bring the maws out of dormancy," Wo said. "In less than a week, mobiles will begin to hatch and burrow to the surface. Be certain to give them plenty of food. They will need all their strength until they are well established. I would estimate that you will have castles rising in about three weeks."

"And my face? When will they carve my face?"

"Turn on the hologram after about a month," she advised him. "And be patient. If you have any questions, please call. Wo and Shade are at your service." She bowed and left.

Kress wandered back to the tank and lit a joy stick. The desert was still and empty. He drummed his fingers impatiently against the plastic, and frowned.

On the fourth day, Kress thought he glimpsed motion beneath the sand, subtle subterranean stirrings.

On the fifth day, he saw his first mobile, a lone white.

On the sixth day, he counted a dozen of them, whites and reds and blacks. The oranges were tardy. He cycled through a bowl of half-decayed table scraps. The mobiles sensed it at once, rushed to it, and began to drag pieces back to their respective corners. Each color group was very organized. They did not fight. Kress was a bit disappointed, but he decided to give them time.

The oranges made their appearance on the eighth day. By then the other sandkings had begun to carry small stones and erect crude fortifications. They still did not war. At the moment they were only half the size of those he had seen at Wo and Shade's, but Kress thought they were growing rapidly.

The castles began to rise midway through the second week.

Organized battalions of mobiles dragged heavy chunks of sandstone and granite back to their corners, where other mobiles were pushing sand into place with mandibles and tendrils. Kress had purchased a pair of magnifying goggles so he could watch them work, wherever they might go in the tank. He wandered around and around the tall plastic walls, observing. It was fascinating. The castles were a bit plainer than Kress would have liked, but he had an idea about that. The next day he cycled through some obsidian and flakes of colored glass along with the food. Within hours, they had been incorporated into the castle walls.

The black castle was the first completed, followed by the white and red fortresses. The oranges were last, as usual. Kress took his meals into the living room and ate seated on the couch, so he could watch. He expected the first war to break out any hour now.

He was disappointed. Days passed, the castles grew taller and more grand, and Kress seldom left the tank except to attend to his sanitary needs and answer critical business calls. But the sandkings did not war. He was getting upset.

Finally he stopped feeding them.

Two days after the table scraps had ceased to fall from their desert sky, four black mobiles surrounded an orange and dragged it back to their maw. They maimed it first, ripping off its mandibles and antennae and limbs, and carried it through the shadowed main gate of their miniature castle. It never emerged. Within an hour, more than forty orange mobiles marched across the sand and attacked the blacks' corner. They were outnumbered by the blacks that came rushing up from the depths. When the fighting was over, the attackers had been slaughtered. The dead and dying were taken down to feed the black maw.

Kress, delighted, congratulated himself on his genius.

When he put food into the tank the following day, a three-cornered battle broke out over its possession. The whites were the big winners.

After that, war followed war.

Almost a month to the day after Jala Wo had delivered the sandkings, Kress turned on the holographic projector, and his face materialized in the tank. It turned, slowly, around and around, so his gaze fell on all four castles equally. Kress thought it rather a good likeness; it had his impish grin, wide mouth, full cheeks. His blue eyes sparkled, his grey hair was carefully arrayed in a fashionable sidesweep, his eyebrows were thin and sophisticated.

Soon enough, the sandkings set to work. Kress fed them lavishly while his image beamed down at them from their sky. Temporarily, the wars stopped. All activity was directed towards worship.

His face emerged on the castle walls.

At first all four carvings looked alike to him, but as the work continued and Kress studied the reproductions, he began to detect subtle differences in technique and execution. The reds were the most creative, using tiny flakes of slate to put the grey in his hair. The white idol seemed young and mischievous to him, while the face shaped by the blacks—although virtually the same, line for line—struck him as wise and beneficent. The orange sandkings, as ever, were last and least. The wars had not gone well for them, and their castle was sad compared to the others. The image they carved was crude and cartoonish and they seemed to intend to leave it that way. When they stopped work on the face, Kress grew quite piqued with them, but there was really nothing he could do.

When all of the sandkings had finished their Kress-faces, he turned off the holograph and decided that it was time to have a party. His friends would be impressed. He could even stage a war for them, he thought. Humming happily to himself, he began to draw up a guest list.

The party was a wild success.

Kress invited thirty people; a handful of close friends who shared his amusements, a few former lovers, and a collection of business and social rivals who could not afford to ignore his summons. He knew some of them would be discomfited and even offended by his sandkings. He counted on it. Simon Kress customarily considered his parties a failure unless at least one guest walked out in high dudgeon.

On impulse he added Jala Wo's name to his list. "Bring Shade if you like," he added when dictating her invitation.

Her acceptance surprised him just a bit. "Shade, alas, will be unable to attend. He does not go to social functions," Wo added.

"As for myself, I look forward to the chance to see how your sandkings are doing."

Kress ordered them up a sumptuous meal. And when at last the conversation had died down, and most of his guests had gotten silly on wine and joy sticks, he shocked them by personally scraping their table leavings into a large bowl. "Come, all of you," he told them. "I want to introduce you to my newest pets." Carrying the bowl, he conducted them into his living room.

The sandkings lived up to his fondest expectations. He had starved them for two days in preparation, and they were in a fighting mood. While the guests ringed the tank, looking through the magnifying glasses Kress had thoughtfully provided, the sandkings waged a glorious battle over the scraps. He counted almost sixty dead mobiles when the struggle was over. The reds and whites, who had recently formed an alliance, emerged with most of the food.

"Kress, you're disgusting," Cath m'Lane told him. She had lived with him for a short time two years before, until her soppy sentimentality almost drove him mad. "I was a fool to come back here. I thought perhaps you'd changed, wanted to apologize." She had never forgiven him for the time his shambler had eaten an excessively cute puppy of which she had been fond. "Don't *ever* invite me here again, Simon." She strode out, accompanied by her current lover and a chorus of laughter.

His other guests were full of questions.

Where did the sandkings come from? they wanted to know. "From Wo and Shade, Importers," he replied, with a polite gesture towards Jala Wo, who had remained quiet and apart through most of the evening.

Why did they decorate their castles with his likeness? "Because I am the source of all good things. Surely you know that?" That brought a round of chuckles.

Will they fight again? "Of course, but not tonight. Don't worry. There will be other parties."

Jad Rakkis, who was an amateur xenologist, began talking about other social insects and the wars they fought. "These sandkings are amusing, but nothing really. You ought to read about Terran soldier ants, for instance."

"Sandkings are not insects," Jala Wo said sharply, but Jad was off and running, and no one paid her the slightest attention. Kress smiled at her and shrugged.

Malada Blane suggested a betting pool the next time they got together to watch a war, and everyone was taken with the idea. An animated discussion about rules and odds ensued. It lasted for almost an hour. Finally the guests began to take their leave.

Jala Wo was the last to depart. "So," Kress said to her when they were alone, "it appears my sandkings are a hit."

"They are doing well," Wo said. "Already they are larger than my own."

"Yes," Kress said, "except for the oranges."

"I had noticed that," Wo replied. "They seem few in number, and their castle is shabby."

"Well, someone must lose," Kress said. "The oranges were late to emerge and get established. They have suffered for it."

"Pardon," said Wo, "but might I ask if you are feeding your sandkings sufficiently?"

Kress shrugged. "They diet from time to time. It makes them fiercer."

She frowned. "There is no need to starve them. Let them war in their own time, for their own reasons. It is their nature, and you will witness conflicts that are delightfully subtle and complex. The constant war brought on by hunger is artless and degrading."

Simon Kress repaid Wo's frown with interest. "You are in my house, Wo, and here I am the judge of what is degrading. I fed the sandkings as you advised, and they did not fight."

"You must have patience."

"No," Kress said. "I am their master and their god, after all. Why should I wait on their impulses? They did not war often enough to suit me. I corrected the situation."

"I see," said Wo. "I will discuss the matter with Shade."

"It is none of your concern, or his," Kress snapped.

"I must bid you good night, then," Wo said with resignation. But as she slipped into her coat to depart, she fixed him with a final disapproving stare. "Look to your faces, Simon Kress," she warned him. "Look to your faces."

Puzzled, he wandered back to the tank and stared at the castles

after she had taken her departure. His faces were still there, as
ever. Except—he snatched up his magnifying goggles and slipped
them on. Even then it was hard to make out. But it seemed to him
that the expression on the face of his images had changed slightly,
that his smile was somehow twisted so that it seemed a touch
malicious. But it was a very subtle change, if it was a change at all.
Kress finally put it down to his suggestibility, and resolved not to
invite Jala Wo to any more of his gatherings.

Over the next few months, Kress and about a dozen of his
favorites got together weekly for what he liked to call his "war
games." Now that his initial fascination with the sandkings was
past, Kress spent less time around his tank and more on his business affairs and his social life, but he still enjoyed having a few
friends over for a war or two. He kept the combatants sharp on
a constant edge of hunger. It had severe effects on the orange
sandkings, who dwindled visibly until Kress began to wonder if
their maw was dead. But the others did well enough.

Sometimes at night, when he could not sleep, Kress would take
a bottle of wine into the darkened living room, where the red
gloom of his miniature desert was the only light. He would drink
and watch for hours, alone. There was usually a fight going on
somewhere, and when there was not he could easily start one by
dropping in some small morsel of food.

They took to betting on the weekly battles, as Malada Blane had
suggested. Kress won a good amount by betting on the whites,
who had become the most powerful and numerous colony in the
tank, with the grandest castle. One week he slid the corner of the
tank top aside, and dropped the food close to the white castle
instead of on the central battleground as usual, so the others had
to attack the whites in their stronghold to get any food at all. They
tried. The whites were brilliant in defense. Kress won a hundred
standards from Jad Rakkis.

Rakkis, in fact, lost heavily on the sandkings almost every week.
He pretended to a vast knowledge of them and their ways, claim-
ing that he had studied them after the first party, but he had no
luck when it came to placing his bets. Kress suspected that Jad's
claims were empty boasting. He had tried to study the sandkings

a bit himself, in a moment of idle curiosity, tying in to the library to find out what world his pets were native to. But there was no listing for them. He wanted to get in touch with Wo and ask her about it, but he had other concerns, and the matter kept slipping his mind.

Finally, after a month in which his losses totalled more than a thousand standards, Jad Rakkis arrived at the war games carrying a small plastic case under his arm. Inside was a spider-like thing covered with fine golden hair.

"A sand spider," Rakkis announced. "From Cathaday. I got it this afternoon from t'Etherane the Petseller. Usually they remove the poison sacs, but this one is intact. Are you game, Simon? I want my money back. I'll bet a thousand standards, sand spider against sandkings."

Kress studied the spider in its plastic prison. His sandkings had grown—they were twice as large as Wo's, as she'd predicted—but they were still dwarfed by this thing. It was venomed, and they were not. Still, there were an awful lot of them. Besides, the endless sandking wars had begun to grow tiresome lately. The novelty of the match intrigued him. "Done," Kress said. "Jad, you are a fool. The sandkings will just keep coming until this ugly creature of yours is dead."

"You are the fool, Simon," Rakkis replied, smiling. "The Cathadayn sand spider customarily feeds on burrowers that hide in nooks and crevices and—well, watch—it will go straight into those castles, and eat the maws."

Kress scowled amid general laughter. He hadn't counted on that. "Get on with it," he said irritably. He went to freshen his drink.

The spider was too large to cycle conveniently through the food chamber. Two of the others helped Rakkis slide the tank top slightly to one side, and Malada Blane handed him up his case. He shook the spider out. It landed lightly on a miniature dune in front of the red castle, and stood confused for a moment, mouth working, legs twitching menacingly.

"Come on," Rakkis urged. They all gathered round the tank. Simon Kress found his magnifiers and slipped them on. If he was going to lose a thousand standards, at least he wanted a good view of the action.

The sandkings had seen the invader. All over the castle, activity had ceased. The small scarlet mobiles were frozen, watching.

The spider began to move towards the dark promise of the gate. On the tower above, Simon Kress' countenance stared down impassively.

At once there was a flurry of activity. The nearest red mobiles formed themselves into two wedges and streamed over the sand towards the spider. More warriors erupted from inside the castle and assembled in a triple line to guard the approach to the underground chamber where the maw lived. Scouts came scuttling over the dunes, recalled to fight.

Battle was joined.

The attacking sandkings washed over the spider. Mandibles snapped shut on legs and abdomen, and clung. Reds raced up the golden legs to the invader's back. They bit and tore. One of them found an eye, and ripped it loose with tiny yellow tendrils. Kress smiled and pointed.

But they were *small,* and they had no venom, and the spider did not stop. Its legs flicked sandkings off to either side. Its dripping jaws found others, and left them broken and stiffening. Already a dozen of the reds lay dying. The sand spider came on and on. It strode straight through the triple line of guardians before the castle. The lines closed around it, covered it, waging desperate battle. A team of sandkings had bitten off one of the spider's legs, Kress saw. Defenders leapt from atop the towers to land on the twitching, heaving mass.

Lost beneath the sandkings, the spider somehow lurched down into the darkness and vanished.

Jad Rakkis let out a long breath. He looked pale. "Wonderful," someone else said. Malada Blane chuckled deep in her throat.

"Look," said Idi Noreddian, tugging Kress by the arm.

They had been so intent on the struggle in the corner that none of them had noticed the activity elsewhere in the tank. But now the castle was still, the sands empty save for dead red mobiles, and now they saw.

Three armies were drawn up before the red castle. They stood quite still, in perfect array, rank after rank of sandkings, orange and white and black. Waiting to see what emerged from the depths.

Simon Kress smiled. "A *cordon sanitaire*," he said. "And glance at the other castles, if you will, Jad."

Rakkis did, and swore. Teams of mobiles were sealing up the gates with sand and stone. If the spider somehow survived this encounter, it would find no easy entrance at the other castles. "I should have brought four spiders," Jad Rakkis said. "Still, I've won. My spider is down there right now, eating your damned maw."

Kress did not reply. He waited. There was motion in the shadows.

All at once, red mobiles began pouring out of the gate. They took their positions on the castle, and began repairing the damage the spider had wrought. The other armies dissolved and began to retreat to their respective corners.

"Jad," said Simon Kress, "I think you are a bit confused about who is eating who."

The following week Rakkis brought four slim silver snakes. The sandkings dispatched them without much trouble.

Next he tried a large black bird. It ate more than thirty white mobiles, and its thrashing and blundering virtually destroyed that castle, but ultimately its wings grew tired, and the sandkings attacked in force wherever it landed.

After that it was a case of insects, armored beetles not too unlike the sandkings themselves. But stupid, stupid. An allied force of oranges and blacks broke their formation, divided them, and butchered them.

Rakkis began giving Kress promissory notes.

It was around that time that Kress met Cath m'Lane again, one evening when he was dining in Asgard at his favorite restaurant. He stopped at her table briefly and told her about the war games, inviting her to join them. She flushed, then regained control of herself and grew icy. "Someone has to put a stop to you, Simon. I guess it's going to be me," she said. Kress shrugged and enjoyed a lovely meal and thought no more about her threat.

Until a week later, when a small, stout woman arrived at his door and showed him a police wristband. "We've had complaints," she said. "Do you keep a tank full of dangerous insects, Kress?"

"Not insects," he said, furious. "Come, I'll show you."

When she had seen the sandkings, she shook her head. "This will never do. What do you know about these creatures, anyway? Do you know what world they're from? Have they been cleared by the ecological board? Do you have a license for these things? We have a report that they're carnivores, possibly dangerous. We also have a report that they are semi-sentient. Where did you get these creatures, anyway?"

"From Wo and Shade," Kress replied.

"Never heard of them," the woman said. "Probably smuggled them in, knowing our ecologists would never approve them. No, Kress, this won't do. I'm going to confiscate this tank and have it destroyed. And you're going to have to expect a few fines as well."

Kress offered her a hundred standards to forget all about him and his sandkings.

She *tsk*ed. "Now I'll have to add attempted bribery to the charges against you."

Not until he raised the figure to two thousand standards was she willing to be persuaded. "It's not going to be easy, you know," she said. "There are forms to be altered, records to be wiped. And getting a forged license from the ecologists will be time-consuming. Not to mention dealing with the complainant. What if she calls again?"

"Leave her to me," Kress said. "Leave her to me."

He thought about it for a while. That night he made some calls.

First he got t'Etherane the Petseller. "I want to buy a dog," he said. "A puppy."

The round-faced merchant gawked at him. "A puppy? That is not like you, Simon. Why don't you come in? I have a lovely choice."

"I want a very specific *kind* of puppy," Kress said. "Take notes. I'll describe to you what it must look like."

Afterwards he punched for Idi Noreddian. "Idi," he said, "I want you out here tonight with your holo equipment. I have a notion to record a sandking battle. A present for one of my friends."

The night after they made the recording, Simon Kress stayed up late. He absorbed a controversial new drama in his sensorium, fixed himself a small snack, smoked a joy stick or two, and broke out a bottle of wine. Feeling very happy with himself, he wandered into the living room, glass in hand.

The lights were out. The red glow of the terrarium made the shadows flushed and feverish. He walked over to look at his domain, curious as to how the blacks were doing in the repairs on their castle. The puppy had left it in ruins.

The restoration went well. But as Kress inspected the work through his magnifiers, he chanced to glance closely at the face. It startled him.

He drew back, blinked, took a healthy gulp of wine, and looked again.

The face on the walls was still his. But it was all wrong, all *twisted*. His cheeks were bloated and piggish, his smile was a crooked leer. He looked impossibly malevolent.

Uneasy, he moved around the tank to inspect the other castles. They were each a bit different, but ultimately all the same.

The oranges had left out most of the fine detail, but the result still seemed monstrous, crude—a brutal mouth and mindless eyes.

The reds gave him a satanic, twitching kind of smile. His mouth did odd, unlovely things at its corners.

The whites, his favorites, had carved a cruel idiot god.

Simon Kress flung his wine across the room in rage. "You *dare*," he said under his breath. "Now you won't eat for a week, you damned . . ." His voice was shrill. "I'll teach you." He had an idea. He strode out of the room, returned a moment later with an antique iron throwing-sword in his hand. It was a meter long, and the point was still sharp. Kress smiled, climbed up and moved the tank cover aside just enough to give him working room, opening one corner of the desert. He leaned down, and jabbed the sword at the white castle below him. He waved it back and forth, smashing towers and ramparts and walls. Sand and stone collapsed, burying the scrambling mobiles. A flick of his wrist obliterated the features of the insolent, insulting caricature the sandkings had made of his face. Then he poised the point of the sword above the dark mouth that opened down into the maw's chamber, and thrust with all his strength. He heard a soft, squishing sound, and met resistance. All of the mobiles trembled and collapsed. Satisfied, Kress pulled back.

He watched for a moment, wondering whether he'd killed the maw. The point of the throwing-sword was wet and slimy. But finally the white sandkings began to move again. Feebly, slowly, but they moved.

He was preparing to slide the cover back in place and move on to a second castle when he felt something crawling on his hand.

He screamed and dropped the sword, and brushed the sandking from his flesh. It fell to the carpet, and he ground it beneath his heel, crushing it thoroughly long after it was dead. It had crunched when he stepped on it. After that, trembling, he hurried to seal the tank up again, and rushed off to shower and inspect himself carefully. He boiled his clothing.

Later, after several fresh glasses of wine, he returned to the living room. He was a bit ashamed of the way the sandking had terrified him. But he was not about to open the tank again. From now on, the cover stayed sealed permanently. Still, he had to punish the others.

Kress decided to lubricate his mental processes with another glass of wine. As he finished it, an inspiration came to him. He went to the tank smiling, and made a few adjustments to the humidity controls.

By the time he fell asleep on the couch, his wine glass still in his hand, the sand castles were melting in the rain.

Kress woke to angry pounding on his door.

He sat up, groggy, his head throbbing. Wine hangovers were always the worst, he thought. He lurched to the entry chamber.

Cath m'Lane was outside. "You monster," she said, her face swollen and puffy and streaked by tears. "I cried all night, damn you. But no more, Simon, no more."

"Easy," he said, holding his head. "I've got a hangover."

She swore and shoved him aside and pushed her way into his house. The shambler came peering round a corner to see what the noise was. She spat at it and stalked into the living room, Kress trailing ineffectually after her. "Hold on," he said, "where do you

. . . you can't . . ." He stopped, suddenly horrorstruck. She was carrying a heavy sledgehammer in her left hand. "No," he said.

She went directly to the sandking tank. "You like the little charmers so much, Simon? Then you can live with them."

"Cath!" he shrieked.

Gripping the hammer with both hands, she swung as hard as she could against the side of the tank. The sound of the impact set his head to screaming, and Kress made a low blubbering sound of despair. But the plastic held.

She swung again. This time there was a *crack*, and a network of thin lines sprang into being.

Kress threw himself at her as she drew back her hammer for a third swing. They went down flailing, and rolled. She lost her grip on the hammer and tried to throttle him, but Kress wrenched free and bit her on the arm, drawing blood. They both staggered to their feet, panting.

"You should see yourself, Simon," she said grimly. "Blood dripping from your mouth. You look like one of your pets. How do you like the taste?"

"Get out," he said. He saw the throwing-sword where it had fallen the night before, and snatched it up. "Get out," he repeated, waving the sword for emphasis. "Don't go near that tank again."

She laughed at him. "You wouldn't dare," she said. She bent to pick up her hammer.

Kress shrieked at her, and lunged. Before he quite knew what was happening, the iron blade had gone clear through her abdomen. Cath m'Lane looked at him wonderingly, and down at the sword. Kress fell back whimpering. "I didn't mean . . . I only wanted . . ."

She was transfixed, bleeding, dead, but somehow she did not fall. "You monster," she managed to say, though her mouth was full of blood. And she whirled, impossibly, the sword in her, and swung with her last strength at the tank. The tortured wall shattered, and Cath m'Lane was buried beneath an avalanche of plastic and sand and mud.

Kress made small hysterical noises and scrambled up on the couch.

Sandkings were emerging from the muck on his living room

floor. They were crawling across Cath's body. A few of them ventured tentatively out across the carpet. More followed.

He watched as a column took shape, a living, writhing square of sandkings, bearing something, something slimy and featureless, a piece of raw meat big as a man's head. They began to carry it away from the tank. It pulsed.

That was when Kress broke and ran.

It was late afternoon before he found the courage to return.

He had run to his skimmer and flown to the nearest city, some fifty kilometers away, almost sick with fear. But once safely away, he had found a small restaurant, put down several mugs of coffee and two anti-hangover tabs, eaten a full breakfast, and gradually regained his composure.

It had been a dreadful morning, but dwelling on that would solve nothing. He ordered more coffee and considered his situation with icy rationality.

Cath m'Lane was dead at his hand. Could he report it, plead that it had been an accident? Unlikely. He had run her through, after all, and he had already told that policer to leave her to him. He would have to get rid of the evidence, and hope that she had not told anyone where she was going this morning. That was probable. She could only have gotten his gift late last night. She said that she had cried all night, and she had been alone when she arrived. Very well, he had one body and one skimmer to dispose of.

That left the sandkings. They might prove more of a difficulty. No doubt they had all escaped by now. The thought of them around his house, in his bed and his clothes, infesting his food— it made his flesh crawl. He shuddered and overcame his revulsion. It really shouldn't be too hard to kill them, he reminded himself. He didn't have to account for every mobile. Just the four maws, that was all. He could do that. They were large, as he'd seen. He would find them and kill them.

Simon Kress went shopping before he flew back to his home. He bought a set of skinthins that would cover him from head to foot, several bags of poison pellets for rockjock control, and a spray cannister of illegally strong pesticide. He also bought a magnalock towing device.

When he landed, he went about things methodically. First he hooked Cath's skimmer to his own with the magnalock. Searching it, he had his first piece of luck. The crystal chip with Idi Noreddian's holo of the sandking fight was on the front seat. He had worried about that.

When the skimmers were ready, he slipped into his skinthins and went inside for Cath's body.

It wasn't there.

He poked through the fast-drying sand carefully, but there was no doubt of it; the body was gone. Could she have dragged herself away? Unlikely, but Kress searched. A cursory inspection of his house turned up neither the body nor any sign of the sandkings. He did not have time for a more thorough investigation, not with the incriminating skimmer outside his front door. He resolved to try later.

Some seventy kilometers north of Kress' estate was a range of active volcanoes. He flew there, Cath's skimmer in tow. Above the glowering cone of the largest, he released the magnalock and watched it vanish in the lava below.

It was dusk when he returned to his house. That gave him pause. Briefly he considered flying back to the city and spending the night there. He put the thought aside. There was work to do. He wasn't safe yet.

He scattered the poison pellets around the exterior of his house. No one would find that suspicious. He'd always had a rockjock problem. When that task was completed, he primed the cannister of pesticide and ventured back inside.

Kress went through the house room by room, turning on lights everywhere he went until he was surrounded by a blaze of artificial illumination. He paused to clean up in the living room, shoveling sand and plastic fragments back into the broken tank. The sandkings were all gone, as he'd feared. The castles were shrunken and distorted, slagged by the watery bombardment Kress had visited upon them, and what little remained was crumbling as it dried.

He frowned and searched on, the cannister of pest spray strapped across his shoulders.

Down in his deepest wine cellar, he came upon Cath m'Lane's corpse.

It sprawled at the foot of a steep flight of stairs, the limbs twisted as if by a fall. White mobiles were swarming all over it, and as Kress watched, the body moved jerkily across the hard-packed dirt floor.

He laughed and twisted the illumination up to maximum. In the far corner, a squat little earthen castle and a dark hole were visible between two wine racks. Kress could make out a rough outline of his face on the cellar wall.

The body shifted once again, moving a few centimeters towards the castle. Kress had a sudden vision of the white maw waiting hungrily. It might be able to get Cath's foot in its mouth, but no more. It was too absurd. He laughed again, and started down into the cellar, finger poised on the trigger of the hose that snaked down his right arm. The sandkings—hundreds of them moving as one—deserted the body and formed battle lines, a field of white between him and their maw.

Suddenly Kress had another inspiration. He smiled and lowered his firing hand. "Cath was always hard to swallow," he said, delighted at his wit. "Especially for one your size. Here, let me give you some help. What are gods for, after all?"

He retreated upstairs, returning shortly with a cleaver. The sandkings, patient, waited and watched while Kress chopped Cath m'Lane into small, easily digestible pieces.

Simon Kress slept in his skinthins that night, the pesticide close at hand, but he did not need it. The whites, sated, remained in the cellar, and he saw no sign of the others.

In the morning, he finished clean-up in the living room. After he was through, no trace of the struggle remained except for the broken tank.

He ate a light lunch, and resumed his hunt for the missing sandkings. In full daylight, it was not too difficult. The blacks had located in his rock garden, and built a castle heavy with obsidian and quartz. The reds he found at the bottom of his long-disused swimming pool, which had partially filled with wind-blown sand over the years. He saw mobiles of both colors ranging about his grounds, many of them carrying poison pellets back to their maws.

Kress decided his pesticide was unnecessary. No use risking a fight when he could just let the poison do its work. Both maws should be dead by evening.

That left only the burnt orange sandkings unaccounted for. Kress circled his estate several times, in ever-widening spirals, but found no trace of them. When he began to sweat in his skinthins —it was a hot, dry day—he decided it was not important. If they were out here, they were probably eating the poison pellets along with the reds and blacks.

He crunched several sandkings underfoot, with a certain degree of satisfaction, as he walked back to the house. Inside he removed his skinthins, settled down to a delicious meal, and finally began to relax. Everything was under control. Two of the maws would soon be defunct, the third was safely located where he could dispose of it after it had served his purposes, and he had no doubt that he would find the fourth. As for Cath, all trace of her visit had been obliterated.

His reverie was interrupted when his viewscreen began to blink at him. It was Jad Rakkis, calling to brag about some cannibal worms he was bringing to the war games tonight.

Kress had forgotten about that, but he recovered quickly. "Oh, Jad, my pardons. I neglected to tell you. I grew bored with all that, and got rid of the sandkings. Ugly little things. Sorry, but there'll be no party tonight."

Rakkis was indignant. "But what will I do with my worms?"

"Put them in a basket of fruit and send them to a loved one," Kress said, signing off. Quickly he began calling the others. He did not need anyone arriving at his doorstep now, with the sandkings alive and about the estate.

As he was calling Idi Noreddian, Kress became aware of an annoying oversight. The screen began to clear, indicating that someone had answered at the other end. Kress flicked off.

Idi arrived on schedule an hour later. She was surprised to find the party cancelled, but perfectly happy to share an evening alone with Kress. He delighted her with his story of Cath's reaction to the holo they had made together. While telling it, he managed to ascertain that she had not mentioned the prank to anyone. He nodded, satisfied, and refilled their wine glasses. Only a trickle was

left. "I'll have to get a fresh bottle," he said. "Come with me to my
wine cellar, and help me pick out a good vintage. You've always
had a better palate than I."

She came along willingly enough, but balked at the top of the
stairs when Kress opened the door and gestured for her to precede
him. "Where are the lights?" she said. "And that smell—what's
that peculiar smell, Simon?"

When he shoved her, she looked briefly startled. She screamed
as she tumbled down the stairs. Kress closed the door and began
to nail it shut with the boards and air-hammer he had left for that
purpose. As he was finishing, he heard Idi groan. "I'm hurt," she
called. "Simon, what is this?" Suddenly she squealed, and shortly
after that the screaming started.

It did not cease for hours. Kress went to his sensorium and dialed
up a saucy comedy to blot it out of his mind.

When he was sure she was dead, Kress flew her skimmer north
to his volcanoes and discarded it. The magnalock was proving a
good investment.

Odd scrabbling noises were coming from beyond the wine cellar door the next morning when Kress went down to check it out.
He listened for several uneasy moments, wondering if Idi Noreddian could possibly have survived and be scratching to get out. It
seemed unlikely; it had to be the sandkings. Kress did not like the
implications of that. He decided that he would keep the door
sealed, at least for the moment, and went outside with a shovel to
bury the red and black maws in their own castles.

He found them very much alive.

The black castle was glittering with volcanic glass, and sandkings were all over it, repairing and improving. The highest tower
was up to his waist, and on it was a hideous caricature of his face.
When he approached, the blacks halted in their labors, and
formed up into two threatening phalanxes. Kress glanced behind
him and saw others closing off his escape. Startled, he dropped the
shovel and sprinted out of the trap, crushing several mobiles beneath his boots.

The red castle was creeping up the walls of the swimming pool.

The maw was safely settled in a pit, surrounded by sand and concrete and battlements. The reds crept all over the bottom of the pool. Kress watched them carry a rockjock and a large lizard into the castle. He stepped back from the poolside, horrified, and felt something crunch. Looking down, he saw three mobiles climbing up his leg. He brushed them off and stamped them to death, but others were approaching quickly. They were larger than he remembered. Some were almost as big as his thumb.

He ran. By the time he reached the safety of the house, his heart was racing and he was short of breath. The door closed behind him, and Kress hurried to lock it. His house was supposed to be pest-proof. He'd be safe in here.

A stiff drink steadied his nerve. So poison doesn't faze them, he thought. He should have known. Wo had warned him that the maw could eat anything. He would have to use the pesticide. Kress took another drink for good measure, donned his skinthins, and strapped the cannister to his back. He unlocked the door.

Outside, the sandkings were waiting.

Two armies confronted him, allied against the common threat. More than he could have guessed. The damned maws must be breeding like rockjocks. They were everywhere, a creeping sea of them.

Kress brought up the hose and flicked the trigger. A grey mist washed over the nearest rank of sandkings. He moved his hand side to side.

Where the mist fell, the sandkings twitched violently and died in sudden spasms. Kress smiled. They were no match for him. He sprayed in a wide arc before him and stepped forward confidently over a litter of black and red bodies. The armies fell back. Kress advanced, intent on cutting through them to their maws.

All at once the retreat stopped. A thousand sandkings surged toward him.

Kress had been expecting the counterattack. He stood his ground, sweeping his misty sword before him in great looping strokes. They came at him and died. A few got through; he could not spray everywhere at once. He felt them climbing up his legs, sensed their mandibles biting futilely at the reinforced plastic of his skinthins. He ignored them, and kept spraying.

Then he began to feel soft impacts on his head and shoulders. Kress trembled and spun and looked up above him. The front of his house was alive with sandkings. Blacks and reds, hundreds of them. They were launching themselves into the air, raining down on him. They fell all around him. One landed on his face-plate, its mandibles scraping at his eyes for a terrible second before he plucked it away.

He swung up his hose and sprayed the air, sprayed the house, sprayed until the airborne sandkings were all dead and dying. The mist settled back on him, making him cough. He coughed, and kept spraying. Only when the front of the house was clean did Kress turn his attention back to the ground.

They were all around him, on him, dozens of them scurrying over his body, hundreds of others hurrying to join them. He turned the mist on them. The hose went dead. Kress heard a loud *hiss* and the deadly fog rose in a great cloud from between his shoulders, cloaking him, choking him, making his eyes burn and blur. He felt for the hose, and his hand came away covered with dying sandkings. The hose was severed; they'd eaten it through. He was surrounded by a shroud of pesticide, blinded. He stumbled and screamed, and began to run back to the house, pulling sand-kings from his body as he went.

Inside, he sealed the door and collapsed on the carpet, rolling back and forth until he was sure he had crushed them all. The cannister was empty by then, hissing feebly. Kress stripped off his skinthins and showered. The hot spray scalded him and left his skin reddened and sensitive, but it made his flesh stop crawling.

He dressed in his heaviest clothing, thick workpants and leath-ers, after shaking them out nervously. "Damn," he kept mutter-ing, "damn." His throat was dry. After searching the entry hall thoroughly to make certain it was clean, he allowed himself to sit and pour a drink. "Damn," he repeated. His hand shook as he poured, slopping liquor on the carpet.

The alcohol settled him, but it did not wash away the fear. He had a second drink, and went to the window furtively. Sandkings were moving across the thick plastic pane. He shuddered and retreated to his communications console. He had to get help, he thought wildly. He would punch through a call to the authorities, and policers would come out with flamethrowers and . . .

Simon Kress stopped in mid-call, and groaned. He couldn't call in the police. He would have to tell them about the whites in his cellar, and they'd find the bodies there. Perhaps the maw might have finished Cath m'Lane by now, but certainly not Idi Noreddian. He hadn't even cut her up. Besides, there would be bones. No, the police could be called in only as a last resort.

He sat at the console, frowning. His communications equipment filled a whole wall; from here he could reach anyone on Baldur. He had plenty of money, and his cunning; he had always prided himself on his cunning. He would handle this somehow.

Briefly he considered calling Wo, but he soon dismissed the idea. Wo knew too much, and she would ask questions, and he did not trust her. No, he needed someone who would do as he asked *without* questions.

His frown faded, and slowly turned into a smile. Simon Kress had contacts. He put through a call to a number he had not used in a long time.

A woman's face took shape on his viewscreen; white-haired, bland of expression, with a long hook nose. Her voice was brisk and efficient. "Simon," she said. "How is business?"

"Business is fine, Lissandra," Kress replied. "I have a job for you."

"A removal? My price has gone up since last time, Simon. It has been ten years, after all."

"You will be well paid," Kress said. "You know I'm generous. I want you for a bit of pest control."

She smiled a thin smile. "No need to use euphemisms, Simon. The call is shielded."

"No, I'm serious. I have a pest problem. Dangerous pests. Take care of them for me. No questions. Understood?"

"Understood."

"Good. You'll need . . . oh, three or four operatives. Wear heat-resistant skinthins, and equip them with flamethrowers or lasers, something on that order. Come out to my place. You'll see the problem. Bugs, lots and lots of them. In my rock garden and the old swimming pool you'll find castles. Destroy them, kill everything inside them. Then knock on the door, and I'll show you what else needs to be done. Can you get out here quickly?"

Her face was impassive. "We'll leave within the hour."

Lissandra was true to her word. She arrived in a lean black skimmer with three operatives. Kress watched them from the safety of a second-story window. They were all faceless in dark plastic skinthins. Two of them wore portable flamethrowers; a third carried lasercannon and explosives. Lissandra carried nothing; Kress recognized her by the way she gave orders.

Their skimmer passed low overhead first, checking out the situation. The sandkings went mad. Scarlet and ebon mobiles ran everywhere, frenetic. Kress could see the castle in the rock garden from his vantage point. It stood tall as a man. Its ramparts were crawling with black defenders, and a steady stream of mobiles flowed down into its depths.

Lissandra's skimmer came down next to Kress' and the operatives vaulted out and unlimbered their weapons. They looked inhuman, deadly.

The black army drew up between them and the castle. The reds —Kress suddenly realized that he could not see the reds. He blinked. Where had they gone?

Lissandra pointed and shouted, and her two flamethrowers spread out and opened up on the black sandkings. Their weapons coughed dully and began to roar, long tongues of blue-and-scarlet fire licking out before them. Sandkings crisped and blackened and died. The operatives began to play the fire back and forth in an efficient, interlocking pattern. They advanced with careful, measured steps.

The black army burned and disintegrated, the mobiles fleeing in a thousand different directions, some back towards the castle, others towards the enemy. None reached the operatives with the flamethrowers. Lissandra's people were very professional.

Then one of them stumbled.

Or seemed to stumble. Kress looked again, and saw that the ground had given way beneath the man. Tunnels, he thought with a tremor of fear; tunnels, pits, traps. The flamer was sunk in sand up to his waist, and suddenly the ground around him seemed to erupt, and he was covered with scarlet sandkings. He dropped the flamethrower and began to claw wildly at his own body. His screams were horrible to hear.

His companion hesitated, then swung and fired. A blast of flame swallowed human and sandkings both. The screaming stopped abruptly. Satisfied, the second flamer turned back to the castle and took another step forward, and recoiled as his foot broke through the ground and vanished up to the ankle. He tried to pull it back and retreat, and the sand all around him gave way. He lost his balance and stumbled, flailing, and the sandkings were everywhere, a boiling mass of them, covering him as he writhed and rolled. His flamethrower was useless and forgotten.

Kress pounded wildly on the window, shouting for attention. "The castle! Get the castle!"

Lissandra, standing back by her skimmer, heard and gestured. Her third operative sighted with the lasercannon and fired. The beam throbbed across the grounds and sliced off the top of the castle. He brought it down sharply, hacking at the sand and stone parapets. Towers fell. Kress' face disintegrated. The laser bit into the ground, searching round and about. The castle crumbled; now it was only a heap of sand. But the black mobiles continued to move. The maw was buried too deeply; they hadn't touched her.

Lissandra gave another order. Her operative discarded the laser, primed an explosive, and darted forward. He leapt over the smoking corpse of the first flamer, landed on solid ground within Kress' rock garden, and heaved. The explosive ball landed square atop the ruins of the black castle. White-hot light seared Kress' eyes, and there was a tremendous gout of sand and rock and mobiles. For a moment dust obscured everything. It was raining sandkings and pieces of sandkings.

Kress saw that the black mobiles were dead and unmoving.

"The pool," he shouted down through the window. "Get the castle in the pool."

Lissandra understood quickly; the ground was littered with motionless blacks, but the reds were pulling back hurriedly and reforming. Her operative stood uncertain, then reached down and pulled out another explosive ball. He took one step forward, but Lissandra called him and he sprinted back in her direction.

It was all so simple then. He reached the skimmer, and Lissandra took him aloft. Kress rushed to another window in another room to watch. They came swooping in just over the pool, and the operative pitched his bombs down at the red castle from the safety of the skimmer. After the fourth run, the castle was unrecognizable, and the sandkings stopped moving.

Lissandra was thorough. She had him bomb each castle several additional times. Then he used the lasercannon, crisscrossing methodically until it was certain that nothing living could remain intact beneath those small patches of ground.

Finally they came knocking at his door. Kress was grinning manically when he let them in. "Lovely," he said, "lovely."

Lissandra pulled off the mask of her skinthins. "This will cost you, Simon. Two operatives gone, not to mention the danger to my own life."

"Of course," Kress blurted. "You'll be well paid, Lissandra. Whatever you ask, just so you finish the job."

"What remains to be done?"

"You have to clean out my wine cellar," Kress said. "There's another castle down there. And you'll have to do it without explosives. I don't want my house coming down around me."

Lissandra motioned to her operative. "Go outside and get Rajk's flamethrower. It should be intact."

He returned armed, ready, silent. Kress led them down to the wine cellar.

The heavy door was still nailed shut, as he had left it. But it bulged outward slightly, as if warped by some tremendous pressure. That made Kress uneasy, as did the silence that held reign about them. He stood well away from the door as Lissandra's operative removed his nails and planks. "Is that safe in here?" he found himself muttering, pointing at the flamethrower. "I don't want a fire, either, you know."

"I have the laser," Lissandra said. "We'll use that for the kill. The flamethrower probably won't be needed. But I want it here just in case. There are worse things than fire, Simon."

He nodded.

The last plank came free of the cellar door. There was still no sound from below. Lissandra snapped an order, and her underling fell back, took up a position behind her, and leveled the flamethrower square at the door. She slipped her mask back on, hefted the laser, stepped forward, and pulled open the door.

No motion. No sound. It was dark down there.

"Is there a light?" Lissandra asked.

"Just inside the door," Kress said. "On the right-hand side. Mind the stairs, they're quite steep."

She stepped into the doorway, shifted the laser to her left hand, and reached up with her right, fumbling inside for the light panel. Nothing happened. "I feel it," Lissandra said, "but it doesn't seem to . . ."

Then she was screaming, and she stumbled backward. A great white sandking had clamped itself around her wrist. Blood welled through her skinthins where its mandibles had sunk in. It was fully as large as her hand.

Lissandra did a horrible little jig across the room and began to smash her hand against the nearest wall. Again and again and again. It landed with a heavy, meaty thud. Finally the sandking fell away. She whimpered and fell to her knees. "I think my fingers are broken," she said softly. The blood was still flowing freely. She had dropped the laser near the cellar door.

"I'm not going down there," her operative announced in clear firm tones.

Lissandra looked up at him. "No," she said. "Stand in the door and flame it all. Cinder it. Do you understand?"

He nodded.

Simon Kress moaned. "My *house*," he said. His stomach churned. The white sandking had been so *large*. How many more were down there? "Don't," he continued. "Leave it alone. I've changed my mind. Leave it alone."

Lissandra misunderstood. She held out her hand. It was covered with blood and greenish-black ichor. "Your little friend bit clean through my glove, and you saw what it took to get it off. I don't care about your house, Simon. Whatever is down there is going to die."

Kress hardly heard her. He thought he could see movement in the shadows beyond the cellar door. He imagined a white army bursting forth, all as large as the sandking that had attacked Lissandra. He saw himself being lifted by a hundred tiny arms, and dragged down into the darkness where the maw waited hungrily. He was afraid. "Don't," he said.

They ignored him.

Kress darted forward, and his shoulder slammed into the back of Lissandra's operative just as the man was bracing to fire. He grunted and unbalanced and pitched forward into the black. Kress listened to him fall down the stairs. Afterwards there were other noises, scuttlings and snaps and soft squishing sounds.

Kress swung around to face Lissandra. He was drenched in cold sweat, but a sickly kind of excitement was on him. It was almost sexual.

Lissandra's calm cold eyes regarded him through her mask. "What are you doing?" she demanded as Kress picked up the laser she had dropped. *"Simon!"*

"Making a peace," he said, giggling. "They won't hurt god, no, not so long as god is good and generous. I was cruel. Starved them. I have to make up for it now, you see."

"You're insane," Lissandra said. It was the last thing she said. Kress burned a hole in her chest big enough to put his arm through. He dragged the body across the floor and rolled it down the cellar stairs. The noises were louder; chitinous clackings and scrapings and echoes that were thick and liquid. Kress nailed up the door once again.

As he fled, he was filled with a deep sense of contentment that coated his fear like a layer of syrup. He suspected it was not his own.

He planned to leave his home, to fly to the city and take a room for a night, or perhaps for a year. Instead Kress started drinking. He was not quite sure why. He drank steadily for hours, and retched it all up violently on his living room carpet. At some point he fell asleep. When he woke, it was pitch dark in the house.

He cowered against the couch. He could hear *noises*. Things were moving in the walls. They were all around him. His hearing was extraordinarily acute. Every little creak was the footstep of a sandking. He closed his eyes and waited, expecting to feel their terrible touch, afraid to move lest he brush against one.

Kress sobbed, and was very still.

After a while, nothing happened.

He opened his eyes again. He trembled. Slowly the shadows began to soften and dissolve. Moonlight was filtering through the high windows. His eyes adjusted.

The living room was empty. Nothing there, nothing, nothing. Only his drunken fears.

Simon Kress steeled himself, and rose, and went to a light. Nothing there. The room was quiet, deserted.

He listened. Nothing. No sound. Nothing in the walls. It had all been his imagination, his fear.

The memories of Lissandra and the thing in the cellar returned to him unbidden. Shame and anger washed over him. Why had he done that? He could have helped her burn it out, kill it. *Why* . . . he knew why. The maw had done it to him, put fear in him. Wo had said it was psionic, even when it was small. And now it was large, so large. It had feasted on Cath, and Idi, and now it had two more bodies down there. It would keep growing. And it had learned to like the taste of human flesh, he thought.

He began to shake, but he took control of himself again and stopped. It wouldn't hurt him; he was god; the whites had always been his favorites.

He remembered how he had stabbed it with his throwing-sword. That was before Cath came. Damn her anyway.

He couldn't stay here. The maw would grow hungry again. Large as it was, it wouldn't take long. Its appetite would be terrible. What would it do then? He had to get away, back to the safety of the city while it was still contained in his wine cellar. It was only plaster and hard-packed earth down there, and the mobiles could dig and tunnel. When they got free . . . Kress didn't want to think about it.

He went to his bedroom and packed. He took three bags. Just a single change of clothing, that was all he needed; the rest of the space he filled with his valuables, with jewelry and art and other things he could not bear to lose. He did not expect to return.

His shambler followed him down the stairs, staring at him from its baleful glowing eyes. It was gaunt. Kress realized that it had been ages since he had fed it. Normally it could take care of itself, but no doubt the pickings had grown lean of late. When it tried to clutch at his leg, he snarled at it and kicked it away, and it scurried off, offended.

Kress slipped outside, carrying his bags awkwardly, and shut the door behind him.

For a moment he stood pressed against the house, his heart thudding in his chest. Only a few meters between him and his skimmer. He was afraid to take them. The moonlight was bright, and the front of his house was a scene of carnage. The bodies of Lissandra's two flamers lay where they had fallen, one twisted and burned, the other swollen beneath a mass of dead sandkings. And the mobiles, the black and red mobiles, they were all around him. It was an effort to remember that they were dead. It was almost as if they were simply waiting, as they had waited so often before.

Nonsense, Kress told himself. More drunken fears. He had seen the castles blown apart. They were dead, and the white maw was trapped in his cellar. He took several deep and deliberate breaths, and stepped forward onto the sandkings. They crunched. He ground them into the sand savagely. They did not move.

Kress smiled, and walked slowly across the battleground, listening to the sounds, the sounds of safety.

Crunch. Crackle. Crunch.

He lowered his bags to the ground and opened the door to his skimmer.

Something moved from shadow into light. A pale shape on the seat of his skimmer. It was as long as his forearm. Its mandibles clacked together softly, and it looked up at him from six small eyes set all around its body.

Kress wet his pants and backed away slowly.

There was more motion from inside the skimmer. He had left the door open. The sandking emerged and came toward him, cautiously. Others followed. They had been hiding beneath his seats, burrowed into the upholstery. But now they emerged. They formed a ragged ring around the skimmer.

Kress licked his lips, turned, and moved quickly to Lissandra's skimmer.

He stopped before he was halfway there. Things were moving inside that one too. Great maggoty things half-seen by the light of the moon.

Kress whimpered and retreated back towards the house. Near the front door, he looked up.

He counted a dozen long white shapes creeping back and forth across the walls of the building. Four of them were clustered close together near the top of the unused belfry where the carrion hawk had once roosted. They were carving something. A face. A very recognizable face.

Simon Kress shrieked and ran back inside.

A sufficient quantity of drink brought him the easy oblivion he sought. But he woke. Despite everything, he woke. He had a terrific headache, and he smelled, and he was hungry. Oh so very hungry. He had never been so hungry.

Kress knew it was not his *own* stomach hurting.

A white sandking watched him from atop the dresser in his bedroom, its antennae moving faintly. It was as big as the one in the skimmer the night before. He tried not to shrink away. "I'll . . . I'll feed you," he said to it. "I'll feed you." His mouth was horribly dry, sandpaper dry. He licked his lips and fled from the room.

The house was full of sandkings; he had to be careful where he put his feet. They all seemed busy on errands of their own. They were making modifications in his house, burrowing into or out of his walls, carving things. Twice he saw his own likeness staring out at him from unexpected places. The faces were warped, twisted, livid with fear.

He went outside to get the bodies that had been rotting in the yard, hoping to appease the white maw's hunger. They were gone, both of them. Kress remembered how easily the mobiles could carry things many times their own weight.

It was terrible to think that the maw was *still* hungry after all of that.

When Kress reentered the house, a column of sandkings was wending its way down the stairs. Each carried a piece of his shambler. The head seemed to look at him reproachfully as it went by.

Kress emptied his freezers, his cabinets, everything, piling all the food in the house in the center of his kitchen floor. A dozen whites waited to take it away. They avoided the frozen food, leaving it to thaw in a great puddle, but they carried off everything else.

When all the food was gone, Kress felt his own hunger pangs abate just a bit, though he had not eaten a thing. But he knew the respite would be short-lived. Soon the maw would be hungry again. He had to feed it.

Kress knew what to do. He went to his communicator. "Malada," he began casually when the first of his friends answered, "I'm having a small party tonight. I realize this is terribly short notice, but I hope you can make it. I really do."

He called Jad Rakkis next, and then the others. By the time he had finished, nine of them had accepted his invitation. Kress hoped that would be enough.

Kress met his guests outside—the mobiles had cleaned up remarkably quickly, and the grounds looked almost as they had before the battle—and walked them to his front door. He let them enter first. He did not follow.

When four of them had gone through, Kress finally worked up his courage. He closed the door behind his latest guest, ignoring the startled exclamations that soon turned into shrill gibbering, and sprinted for the skimmer the man had arrived in. He slid in safely, thumbed the startplate, and swore. It was programmed to lift only in response to its owner's thumbprint, of course.

Jad Rakkis was the next to arrive. Kress ran to his skimmer as it set down, and seized Rakkis by the arm as he was climbing out. "Get back in, quickly," he said, pushing. "Take me to the city. Hurry, Jad. *Get out of here!*"

But Rakkis only stared at him, and would not move. "Why, what's wrong, Simon? I don't understand. What about your party?"

And then it was too late, because the loose sand all around them was stirring, and the red eyes were staring at them, and the mandibles were clacking. Rakkis made a choking sound, and moved to get back in his skimmer, but a pair of mandibles snapped shut about his ankle, and suddenly he was on his knees. The sand seemed to boil with subterranean activity. Jad thrashed and cried terribly as they tore him apart. Kress could hardly bear to watch.

After that, he did not try to escape again. When it was all over, he cleaned out what remained in his liquor cabinet, and got extremely drunk. It would be the last time he would enjoy that luxury, he knew. The only alcohol remaining in the house was stored down in the wine cellar.

Kress did not touch a bite of food the entire day, but he fell asleep feeling bloated, sated at last, the awful hunger vanquished. His last thoughts before the nightmares took him were on who he could ask out tomorrow.

Morning was hot and dry. Kress opened his eyes to see the white sandking on his dresser again. He shut them again quickly, hoping the dream would leave him. It did not, and he could not go back to sleep, and soon he found himself staring at the thing.

He stared for almost five minutes before the strangeness of it dawned on him; the sandking was not moving.

The mobiles could be preternaturally still, to be sure. He had seen them wait and watch a thousand times. But always there was some motion about them; the mandibles clacked, the legs twitched, the long fine antennae stirred and swayed.

But the sandking on his dresser was completely still.

Kress rose, holding his breath, not daring to hope. Could it be dead? Could something have killed it? He walked across the room.

The eyes were glassy and black. The creature seemed swollen, somehow; as if it were soft and rotting inside, filling up with gas that pushed outward at the plates of white armor.

Kress reached out a trembling hand and touched it.

It was warm; hot even, and growing hotter. But it did not move.

He pulled his hand back, and as he did, a segment of the sandking's white exoskeleton fell away from it. The flesh beneath was the same color, but softer-looking, swollen and feverish. And it almost seemed to throb.

Kress backed away, and ran to the door.

Three more white mobiles lay in his hall. They were all like the one in his bedroom.

He ran down the stairs, jumping over sandkings. None of them moved. The house was full of them, all dead, dying, comatose,

whatever. Kress did not care what was wrong with them. Just so
they could not move.

He found four of them inside his skimmer. He picked them up
one by one, and threw them as far as he could. Damned monsters.
He slid back in, on the ruined half-eaten seats, and thumbed the
startplate.

Nothing happened.

Kress tried again, and again. Nothing. It wasn't fair. This was
his skimmer, it ought to start, why wouldn't it lift, he didn't understand.

Finally he got out and checked, expecting the worst. He found
it. The sandkings had torn apart his gravity grid. He was trapped.
He was still trapped.

Grimly Kress marched back into the house. He went to his
gallery and found the antique axe that had hung next to the throw-
ing sword he had used on Cath m'Lane. He set to work. The
sandkings did not stir even as he chopped them to pieces. But they
splattered when he made the first cut, the bodies almost bursting.
Inside was awful: strange half-formed organs, a viscous reddish
ooze that looked almost like human blood, and the yellow ichor.

Kress destroyed twenty of them before he realized the futility
of what he was doing. The mobiles were nothing, really. Besides,
there were so *many* of them. He could work for a day and night
and still not kill them all.

He had to go down into the wine cellar and use the axe on the
maw.

Resolute, he started down. He got within sight of the door, and
stopped.

It was not a door any more. The walls had been eaten away, so
the hole was twice the size it had been, and round. A pit, that was
all. There was no sign that there had ever been a door nailed shut
over that black abyss.

A ghastly choking foetid odor seemed to come from below.

And the walls were wet and bloody and covered with patches
of white fungus.

And worst, it was *breathing*.

Kress stood across the room and felt the warm wind wash over
him as it exhaled, and he tried not to choke, and when the wind
reversed direction, he fled.

Back in the living room, he destroyed three more mobiles, and collapsed. What was *happening?* He didn't understand.

Then he remembered the only person who might understand. Kress went to his communicator again, stepped on a sandking in his haste, and prayed fervently that the device still worked.

When Jala Wo answered, he broke down and told her everything.

She let him talk without interruption, no expression save for a slight frown on her gaunt, pale face. When Kress had finished, she said only, "I ought to leave you there."

Kress began to blubber. "You can't. Help me. I'll pay . . ."

"I ought to," Wo repeated, "but I won't."

"Thank you," Kress said. "Oh, thank . . ."

"Quiet," said Wo. "Listen to me. This is your own doing. Keep your sandkings well, and they are courtly ritual warriors. You turned yours into something else, with starvation and torture. You were their god. You made them what they are. That maw in your cellar is sick, still suffering from the wound you gave it. It is probably insane. Its behavior is . . . unusual.

"You have to get out of there quickly. The mobiles are not dead, Kress. They are dormant. I told you the exoskeleton falls off when they grow larger. Normally, in fact, it falls off much earlier. I have never heard of sandkings growing as large as yours while still in the insectoid stage. It is another result of crippling the white maw, I would say. That does not matter.

"What matters is the metamorphosis your sandkings are now undergoing. As the maw grows, you see, it gets progressively more intelligent. Its psionic powers strengthen, and its mind becomes more sophisticated, more ambitious. The armored mobiles are useful enough when the maw is tiny and only semi-sentient, but now it needs better servants, bodies with more capabilities. Do you understand? The mobiles are all going to give birth to a new breed of sandking. I can't say exactly what it will look like. Each maw designs its own, to fit its perceived needs and desires. But it will be biped, with four arms, and opposable thumbs. It will be able to construct and operate advanced machinery. The individual sandkings will not be sentient. But the maw will be very sentient indeed."

Simon Kress was gaping at Wo's image on the viewscreen. "Your

workers," he said, with an effort. "The ones who came out here
. . . who installed the tank . . ."

Jala Wo managed a faint smile. "Shade," she said.

"Shade is a sandking," Kress repeated numbly. "And you sold
me a tank of . . . of . . . infants, ah . . ."

"Do not be absurd," Wo said. "A first-stage sandking is more like
a sperm than an infant. The wars temper and control them in
nature. Only one in a hundred reaches second stage. Only one in
a thousand achieves the third and final plateau, and becomes like
Shade. Adult sandkings are not sentimental about the small maws.
There are too many of them, and their mobiles are pests." She
sighed. "And all this talk wastes time. That white sandking is going
to waken to full sentience soon. It is not going to need you any
longer, and it hates you, and it will be very hungry. The transfor-
mation is taxing. The maw must eat enormous amounts both before and after. So you have to get out of there. Do you understand?"

"I *can't*," Kress said. "My skimmer is destroyed, and I can't get
any of the others to start. I don't know how to reprogram them.
Can you come out for me?"

"Yes," said Wo. "Shade and I will leave at once, but it is more
than two hundred kilometers from Asgard to you, and there is
equipment we will need to deal with the deranged sandking
you've created. You cannot wait there. You have two feet. Walk.
Go due east, as near as you can determine, as quickly as you can.
The land out there is pretty desolate. We can find you easily with
an aerial search, and you'll be safely away from the sandkings. Do
you understand?"

"Yes," said Simon Kress. "Yes, oh, yes."

They signed off, and he walked quickly towards the door. He
was halfway there when he heard the noise; a sound halfway
between a pop and a crack.

One of the sandkings had split open. Four tiny hands covered
with pinkish-yellow blood came up out of the gap, and began to
push the dead skin aside.

Kress began to run.

He had not counted on the heat.

The hills were dry and rocky. Kress ran from the house as quickly as he could, ran until his ribs ached and his breath was coming in gasps. Then he walked, but as soon as he had recovered he began to run again. For almost an hour he ran and walked, ran and walked, beneath the fierce hot sun. He sweated freely, and wished that he had thought to bring some water, and he watched the sky in hopes of seeing Wo and Shade.

He was not made for this. It was too hot, and too dry, and he was in no condition. But he kept himself going with the memory of the way the maw had breathed, and the thought of the wriggling little things that by now were surely crawling all over his house. He hoped Wo and Shade would know how to deal with them.

He had his own plans for Wo and Shade. It was all their fault, Kress had decided, and they would suffer for it. Lissandra was dead, but he knew others in her profession. He would have his revenge. He promised himself that a hundred times as he struggled and sweated his way east.

At least he hoped it was east. He was not that good at directions, and he wasn't certain which way he had run in his initial panic, but since then he had made an effort to bear due east, as Wo had suggested.

When he had been running for several hours, with no sign of rescue, Kress began to grow certain that he had gone wrong.

When several more hours passed, he began to grow afraid. What if Wo and Shade could not find him? He would die out here. He hadn't eaten in two days, he was weak and frightened, his throat was raw for want of water. He couldn't keep going. The sun was sinking now, and he'd be completely lost in the dark. What was wrong? Had the sandking eaten Wo and Shade? The fear was on him again, filling him, and with it a great thirst and a terrible hunger. But Kress kept going. He stumbled now when he tried to run, and twice he fell. The second time he scraped his hand on a rock, and it came away bloody. He sucked at it as he walked, and worried about infection.

The sun was on the horizon behind him. The ground grew a little cooler, for which Kress was grateful. He decided to walk until last light and settle in for the night. Surely he was far enough from the sandkings to be safe, and Wo and Shade would find him come morning.

When he topped the next rise, he saw the outline of a house in front of him.

It wasn't as big as his own house, but it was big enough. It was habitation, safety. Kress shouted and began to run towards it. Food and drink, he had to have nourishment, he could taste the meal now. He was aching with hunger. He ran down the hill towards the house, waving his arms and shouting to the inhabitants. The light was almost gone now, but he could still make out a half-dozen children playing in the twilight. "Hey there," he shouted. "Help, help."

They came running towards him.

Kress stopped suddenly. "No," he said, "oh, no. Oh, no." He backpedaled, slipped on the sand, got up and tried to run again. They caught him easily. They were ghastly little things with bulging eyes and dusky orange skin. He struggled, but it was useless. Small as they were, each of them had four arms, and Kress had only two.

They carried him toward the house. It was a sad, shabby house built of crumbling sand, but the door was quite large, and dark, and it breathed. That was terrible, but it was not the thing that set Simon Kress to screaming. He screamed because of the others, the little orange children who came crawling out from the castle, and watched impassive as he passed.

All of them had his face.

VONDA N. McINTYRE

The Straining Your Eyes
Through the Viewscreen Blues

It is difficult to present Vonda N. McIntyre to you here because she is a longtime friend and I find it hard to write about friends. The anecdotes keep intruding and this is supposed to be serious stuff. I promised her that I would not tell about the "silent party" because I, too, have had irascible landladies. And you see? I haven't told you about it. Be still, my tongue!

Vonda is what is meant when someone is described as "a talent"—no mean label. She sold her first story when she was 20 and has been a professional writer for more than ten years. Her novels include *The Exile Waiting* and *Dreamsnake* (Hugo and Nebula in 1979). Her short-story collection, *Fireflood,* is used as a teaching tool in writing classes. She coedited with Susan Janice Anderson a collection of original science-fiction stories, *Aurora: Beyond Equality.* Her novelette "Of Mist, and Grass, and Sand" won the 1973 Nebula, and her work is regularly on the Hugo and Nebula finalist lists.

Vonda did graduate work in genetics at the University of Washington but left graduate school because, as she puts it, "As a research scientist I made a very good science-fiction writer." She attended the Clarion, Pennsylvania, writers' workshop in 1970 and has paid her dues to her profession many times over. She ran the Clarion/West workshop for three years, from 1971 through 1973, and taught a writers' workshop in Melbourne, Australia, in 1977. This should alert new writers to what they will find in this essay. It reflects the many valuable discoveries Vonda has made on her way up—a priceless assembly of advice learned the hard way—and she shares it, as usual, with open generosity.

The techniques, hints, rules, and sneaky tricks in this article are designed to help keep the new writer from stumbling into the pitfalls unique to science fiction, as well as to give some pointers on professional presentation of stories. It is all too easy to make egregious mistakes out of ignorance: I know this from personal, embarrassing experience. Experience can keep you from screwing up, and fortunately the experience need not be your own. There is no particular reason why anyone should have to repeat the same error, the sort of error every new writer makes at one point or another—until some overworked but momentarily charitable editor happens to scrawl, at the bottom of a form reject slip, that a story typed on blue paper with a purple ribbon does indeed draw attention—but the wrong kind of attention.

I can give you a foolproof recipe for turning out a professional-looking manuscript, but I cannot offer a foolproof recipe for writing science fiction. If such a recipe existed, there would not be so much bad sf, and the form would not have such a terrible literary reputation. The belief seems to be that sf and fantasy are both easy: in every writer's workshop where I have ever spoken, at least one student has expressed the opinion that it will be easy to break into print by writing "a crappy thud and blunder story." Why anyone would want to break into print this way is beyond me: setting out deliberately to do something badly is soul-deadening.

The truth is that sf and fantasy both are extremely difficult to do well, and doing them well (while making the task *look* easy) is the main job of the writer.

You want to be a writer. More to the point, you want to write: you want to write science fiction and you think you would be good at it. But you write a story you feel is outstanding and it keeps coming back with frustratingly impersonal rejection slips. Assuming you have not chosen to retell one of the standard cliché stories (the one editors most dread seeing again is the two-character end-of-the-world story, in which He and She turned out to be Adam and Eve), nor peopled your tale with characters of the purest cardboard, you may have made one of the equally serious but more subtle errors peculiar to science fiction.

The first and probably most frequently committed mistake is the perpetration of the expository lump. The sf writer must be quite explicit with information that is tacit in realistic fiction. Readers live in the world of mainstream fiction; its texture need only be implied for them, not completely created. But in sf, the creation of a world's texture, its reality, is one of the most important goals the writer has. If you create a world you must make the reader experience its sights and sounds and smells. If you create a language you must get across the meanings of the words. If your characters are in a fix impossible to get into on earth, you must make it not only comprehensible but believable.

If you convey all this necessary information gracelessly, you will end up with an expository lump. The lump comes in two forms.

First is the narrative lump, in which the writer drags the story to a screeching halt and explains at length what is going on. This technique violates the first principle of fiction writing: "show, don't tell."

The second and even clumsier species is the dialog lump, in which one character lectures another (the brilliant scientist's beautiful but dumb daughter generally filled the post of listener in pulp fiction), or in which two characters tell each other things they both know already: ("Hi, Fred, how are you this morning?" "Fine, George, even though—as you know—the space station we're living on is in a decaying orbit and will crash into the Pacific Ocean tomorrow. But we don't have to worry about that, since, as

I'm sure you recall, our oxygen will run out in eight hours.") All this lecturing is ostensibly for the benefit of the reader, but few readers will sit still for it: they will either skip over it and find the rest of the story flat or downright incomprehensible; or they will skip over the rest of the story period.

No easy solution to the expository lump exists. Writers have used all sorts of methods to convey necessary information: the invented-encyclopedia excerpt, the newspaper-clipping sidebar, even the footnote. But the only truly satisfactory way around the expository lump is by way of good writing. Envision your world so clearly that when you write about it you show it to us. After that, if you have technical information that *must* be included, don't dump it out in one huge mass. Spin it out to us, gracefully.

The second most serious problem, and the one with the most potential to make you look silly, is what Samuel R. Delany calls "subjunctive tension," the ambiguity between what your words say and all the possibilities of their meaning. Subjunctive tension is little noted in realistic fiction because certain phrases have certain set meanings which a reader will understand unconsciously. Good examples are "she threw her eyes down the road" and "the sun came in the window." If those lines attracted attention in mainstream fiction it would only be because they were clumsy, not because they were ridiculous. But in a science-fiction story it might be perfectly possible for a character to physically throw her eyes down the road, if she were a robot, an android, or a cybernetic spy; or for the sun to come in the window, if it were going nova or if a spaceship were falling into it. My favorite example of subjunctive tension is "he strained his eyes through the viewscreen," a line suitable only for a very bad horror movie.

One can get away with thoughtless awkwardness in mainstream fiction; in sf, though, an ambiguous phrase may have your readers rolling hysterically on the floor during a highly serious and emotional scene. Other good examples (courtesy of David White) are "his eyes fell on the papers" (boing! boing!) and "he walked through the door" (teleportation, obviously). The problem in all these cases is that the writer has substituted a less precise word for one that is more precise. The sunlight, not the sun, came through the window; his gaze, not his eyes, fell on the papers; and unless you are writing about the Incredible Hulk, he probably walked through the doorway rather than the door itself.

Some other fairly serious problems seem to be the result of American sf's antecedents in pulp magazines. Even now, writers are often paid by the word, and the temptation is to pad mercilessly with adjectives, adverbs, and polysyllabic substitutions for perfectly adequate, but short, words. Fortunately for the quality of today's work, the days in which a writer could turn in ten thousand words per week and have them published with hardly an editorial reading are long gone, and the quality of current writing is high enough that a heavily padded story is likely to be recognized, and rejected, for what it is. Still, some of the conventions remain. One of the most noticeable is what James Blish called the "said-bookism." I have never seen a said-book, and I have spells of believing it is apocryphal, but (it is claimed) one used to be able to buy a book that contained nothing but lists of supposed synonyms for "said." Tom Swifties are a highly developed version of the said-bookism, deliberately including a pun; the classical said-bookism is funniest in its innocence. Characters have been known to hiss sentences containing not a single sibilant, to growl lines consisting mostly of vowels, to ejaculate, to effuse, to smile entire conversations. Once one becomes aware of the said-bookism, its use becomes hilarious.

I disagree with writers who say one must never use any word *but* "said," though I agree that one need not worry too much about its overuse, as it tends to vanish into the page. But words that really do describe ways of speaking are useful: whisper, shout, scream, *et cetera;* and despite my general advice to avoid adverbs whenever possible, "said" with an occasional modifier is perfectly appropriate. " 'Good morning,' he grated" is a physical impossibility; " 'Good morning,' he said grimly," or " 'Good morning.' His expression was grim" are, if not scintillating prose, at least literate.

Another pulp sf convention is the capitalization of words referring to an Invented Philosophy, Important Personage, Significant Place, or Very Large Physical Structure. This can get you into a great deal of trouble; almost inevitably you will end up somewhere with a paragraph that is 50 percent capitalized words. This looks ridiculous (see sentence one of this paragraph); worse, it looks like

exactly what it is: an attempt to make one's inventions important
by typographical tricks rather than by the power of the descrip-
tive words themselves. Words are very powerful; if you use them
right, they do not need to be punched up. If you do not use them
right, you are in the wrong profession.

Sometimes it is necessary to create an alien language. When this
is done well, it is lovely—several contemporary writers do it so
beautifully that they can get away with paragraphs studded with
italicized alien words to a level of complexity requiring a glossary.
(C. J. Cherryh carries this off brilliantly; she is also a linguist.) To
invent a language (or future slang) you must have a feel for the way
language flows and forms. If you do not, you will end up with a
story littered with random sounds that serve little purpose and
confuse the reader as well. Writers of far more experience than I
have been heard to recommend using typographical errors as
alien words. My advice is that this advice is wrong: unless you have
exceedingly inventive fingers, typos *look* like typos. One can generally even figure out what the original word was, and this rather
tends to drain the verisimilitude out of your alien creations.

Science-fiction writers have a bad habit of using neologisms to
describe familiar objects. This is a slightly less blatant version of
the game of space opera, in which one writes a western, then
trades earth for Omega Orion XI, trades the six-guns for lasers,
masers, rasers, phasers, or occasionally for broadswords and cross-
bows (in a high-tech civilization, mind you); the horses transmute
to FTL starcruisers, the cleancut collegiate-type good guys in
white hats turn into cleancut collegiate-type good guys in mylar
jumpsuits, and the squinty-eyed bad guys in black hats turn into
clones, giant ambulatory carrots, humanoids, virusoids, or insect-
oids (or vice-versa, depending on one's level of xenophobia). A
writer in one tv series appears to be under the impression that the
way to make something sound "sci-fi" is to add "-on" to quite
ordinary words. No character ever pulled a chairon up to a ta-
bleon, but they came close. TV science fiction is not alone in
employing this convention. When I was a kid I used to wonder
why people in sf stories always wrote with a stylus; I was curious
about what a stylus was and what made it different from a pencil
or a pen. Imagine the damage to my sense of wonder when I

realized that a stylus *was* a pencil or a pen, that all those exotic-sounding cold drinks were martinis or beer, that all those interesting hot drinks were coffee or tea. Coffee is probably the thing most often transformed into some weird cute word. But coffee has been around a couple of hundred years and the caffeine fix shows no sign of falling out of fashion. If your people are drinking something hot with cream and sugar out of styrofoam cups, you might as well give in and admit that it is coffee.

Just as the "fiction" part of sf conceals some unique problems, so does the "science" part. SF writers are often asked if writing sf requires a heavy hard science background. The answer is no, though it doesn't hurt. If you *do* have a science background, you must not let it take over your story; you are, after all, writing fiction, and fiction is about people, be they humans or aliens.

The hierarchy of rules for science in sf is as follows: if you can make it right, you should; if you can't make it right, at least make it plausible; if you can't make it right *or* plausible, you had better make it fun. (Rubber science is a grand tradition of sf.)

One of the lovely things about the science-fiction community is that you can almost always find someone whose brains you can pick for information, someone who will help you out with any given subject. Then you are left with the delicate philosophical question of how to thank them. My own personal opinion is that someone who spends a significant amount of time helping you out should be acknowledged in print: if they help you to invent a new FTL drive, for instance, you might name it after them. (You might also check with them before you do, just in case their department head loathes sf.) If you use someone's recent formal research or speculation as a basis for your further speculation, I feel you should acknowledge them somehow: if you set a story in a Dyson sphere, for heaven's sake *call* it a Dyson sphere. Someone who advises you out of a minor tight spot ought, at the very least, be given a copy of your book.

It is impossible to keep up with all fields of science; in fact, it is even impossible to keep up with any single field. It is possible, however, to stay aware of current developments. The best way of doing this that I know about is a weekly magazine called *Science News* (231 W. Center St., Marion, OH 43302). It is sort of a cross between *Time* magazine and *Scientific American*, written with the general reader very much in mind. It is never written down; neither is it written in the impenetrable jargon of most scientific journals. A somewhat more technical magazine is the British journal *New Scientist*, which is entertaining (they recently reprinted the *Analog* piece on building your own atomic bomb; and one article was a killer review of an advertisement printed opposite the review) and informative, but rather expensive.

Those are some of the major problems to be aware of before you start writing. The writing itself is up to you: no one can teach you how to do it beyond a few pointers.

After you have finished an inventive, original, literate sf story, the next step is to prepare it for publication. This step is by no means trivial. The appearance of your manuscript is your introduction to an editor, so it is worth your while to spend some time and trouble making it look right. You can present yourself as a professional, or as a rank amateur. Many of the apparently arbitrary rules for manuscript preparation (often ignored by novices) exist for very good reasons. I will try to include the reasons with the rules.

When you are ready to type a fair copy of your story, start with good quality opaque white paper, clean typeface, and a black typewriter ribbon new enough not to have faded to gray. If you have a choice of type sizes, pica (ten spaces to the inch) is more readable than elite (twelve spaces to the inch). A serif typeface is more readable than sans-serif. (Typeface and size are ideals; clean type and a black ribbon are essentials.)

Set up your page so your margins are generous—an inch at least, top, bottom, and sides, or, better, twelve spaces (pica) or fifteen (elite) on either side.

A cover page is optional. It offers a bit of protection from random coffee stains. Most cover pages follow one of two styles: identical to the first page of the story but omitting the text; or with the author's name and address and the approximate word-count transposed to the lower half of the page.

It does not matter very much what style you choose for your cover page, for it will simply be discarded if the story sells. It is not set in type; it is a distraction for copyeditor and typesetter. For this reason a manuscript with a cover page still must follow formal manuscript style, particularly on page one of the text.

On page one, the author's name and address (telephone number optional) should appear in the upper left-hand corner. This is the only place in your manuscript that may be single-spaced (even if you include extensive indented quotations in the text). In the upper right-hand corner show the approximate word-count, rounded off to the nearest hundred words. Count two or three average pages and estimate: it is not necessary to count every word of the story. (One of the signs of the novice is a heading such as "6458 words," rather than "About 6500 words.") The word-count indicates to the editor how much space the story will take, and, often, how much you will be paid, so accuracy is important. You will not impress an editor if you underestimate and you will get a very bad rep if you severely overestimate.

After the heading, space down half a page. (The editor needs room on page one for directions to the typesetter.) Center the title and type it using standard rules of capitalization. Do not type it all in caps, or underline it, or put it in quotation marks (unless it *is* a quotation). If you do any of these typographical tricks you will give a copyeditor the opportunity to put a blue pencil to your manuscript. This is to be avoided. Most copyeditors are frustrated writers who appear to believe that one necessary correction entitles them to two utterly gratuitous changes in your text. (A good copyeditor is worth gold, though: I wish you the same luck I've had on my last two books.)

A quick bit of empirical advice about titles: never give a story a title that is impossible to pronounce or embarrassing to say. Everyone can think of books they never discuss because they are afraid they will mispronounce some weird word. As for embarrassing titles, I once called a story "Screwtop" and I have been sorry ever since.

Your byline goes, centered, one double-space beneath the story title. The name in the upper left-hand corner will get the money; the name beneath the title will get the recognition, as it is the name the story will be published under. Whether to use a pseudonym or not is up to you. My own observation has been that most people who choose a name other than their birth-name (assuming

their parents did not perpetrate some outrageous cruelty on them)
are eventually sorry. One new writer of the seventies chose a
"cute" pseudonym and had to build up his momentum all over
again when he went back to his real name.

After your byline, double-space twice, indent at least five spaces
(the division between paragraphs must be clear: two or three
spaces make it look as if your typewriter hiccupped; on the other
hand, ten or fifteen spaces can break the rhythm of reading), and
begin the story. The text *must* be double-spaced. A single-spaced
manuscript is too difficult to read and too difficult for the typesetter to follow. Out of pure self-defense most editors will return a
single-spaced manuscript without even reading it. Some typewriters permit 1½ vertical spacing; this is, if anything, even harder to
read than single-space, and should be avoided.

The second and subsequent pages should all carry some kind of
identification, in case the pages are separated in an editorial office.
Your last name, or the title (if it is short), or a phrase or distinctive
word from a longer title are all acceptable. (I generally use my last
name, on the grounds that it will not change while I am typing
clean copy, while the title very likely could.) The page number
should also appear, as: McIntyre/3. Most style guides recommend
putting the identification in the upper left-hand corner. I think the
upper right is more efficient and less distracting. However, as
recommendations go that one is fairly minor. After the identification, space down one or two double-spaces and continue the text.

Use the page two form through to the end, where many older
guides recommend that you type —30— , which is journalese for
"the end." Unless you actually are a journalist (and one pre-dating
VDTs), using —30— will only serve to announce that you learned
what you know about writing from an old style guide. Actually
there is no particular objection to it; it is not actively offensive as
far as I know. But it is not fashionable, either.

You would be amazed at the heated arguments relatively ratio-
nal people who happen to be writers will get into over totally
trivial points of manuscript preparation. This is *an* acceptable
form; I do not claim it is the only or even the best form. It is the
one I use, so, obviously, I prefer it. (I also prefer a very long or very
short line over ever hyphenating a word: a hyphenated word gives

the copyeditor another excuse to write on the manuscript.) But one of the best-known writers in the field insists on putting his titles all in caps *and* underlining them, as if his name on a manuscript would not be enough to call attention to the story; and one of the best writers and editors the field ever had would not have been caught dead typing on a pica typewriter. One's own taste counts.

After you have typed your story, proofread the manuscript carefully. The copyeditor's rule of gratuitous changes applies when they correct typos and spelling errors, too; besides, copyeditors cannot be trusted to know spelling, grammar, or usage. I recently read a friend's novel in copyedited manuscript form and found more typos than the copyeditor caught. Sending in the cleanest manuscript possible is to your benefit.

If you are unsure of the spelling or usage of a word, look it up. Do not contribute to the degeneration of the language. Do not use "decimate" to mean "totally destroyed," or "energy-intensive" to mean "efficient," or "situation" to mean *anything*. If you change a point of grammar or usage (as I have in this article), do it for a reason that you feel is important enough to fight for.

An occasional missed typo does not mean the whole page must be retyped. If you can re-insert the paper in the typewriter to make the correction, bravo; but crossing out a word and making a neat correction in black ink (blue does not photocopy well, and even if you do not photocopy your manuscript it is likely that the publisher will, eventually) is acceptable. One should not be able to read the crossed-out words; that is distracting. Once you get to three visible corrections on a single page, you should consider retyping it. No rule exists here, just basic courtesy: the page should be legible and neat.

If you use the original manuscript as your submission copy, be sure to make a carbon or photocopy to keep. I prefer to keep the original and send out a photocopy (*not* a carbon). Most editors will not object to receiving good-quality photocopies of manuscripts, as long as you mention that you are mailing out a copy for some other reason than submitting the story to every editor in the field simultaneously. (Simultaneous submissions, also called multiple submissions, are frowned upon: this is rather too bad from the writer's point of view, but it is the way it is.) You should not send copies on that slick gray photocopy paper that feels almost as slimy as erasable bond (which is also frowned upon: it makes your skin crawl, it is slippery, and it smudges). So, for those of you whose typewriters cannot spell, or for those of you who are sick of getting back original manuscripts in such a ruined state that they must be retyped, or for those of you like me who fit both categories: many errors can be repaired on the original manuscript in such a way that they do not even show on a photocopy. Beyond correction fluid, correct-type, or erasing (does anyone ever erase anymore? Your typewriter will last much longer if you do not get crumbs of rubber in it), even a careful cut and paste job can turn out to be invisible. In fact a good photocopy on decent paper will often come out looking better than the original.

Do not bind or staple the finished manuscript. Use a paperclip. Most editors take work home; a bound manuscript will snap shut on the nose of anyone trying to read in bed. A stapled manuscript cannot help but have its corners bent and folded. A removable paperclip generally assures that the pages will remain in their relatively planar state.

Your story is ready to send out. How do you decide where to send it? It helps to know the field: read the magazines and anthologies. Several writers' magazines list potential markets, but because of the active nature of the genre, their sf listings are generally incomplete and out of date. A far better way to get details of the markets is to subscribe to one of the sf newsletters, *Locus* (which has been a staple in the field for years), or *Science Fiction Chronicle* or *Science Fiction Times* (relative newcomers). These publications can often be found in the magazine section of larger bookstores. They contain market reports from magazine and anthology editors and from editors looking for novels (as well as other news of interest in the sf community, such as convention listings, awards, and book publication dates).

A query is a letter you send to an editor asking if they would like to see your story. There is some disagreement about the usefulness of query letters. It is very difficult to describe a short story; for an sf story sent to a market that accepts unsolicited work (which is most of them), a query is almost invariably extraneous. For a novel, the general consensus seems to be that a query won't hurt, but will almost always be answered by "Please send the manuscript," unless the editor's schedule is filled for the forseeable future.

Many writers' guides recommend trying to sell a novel on the basis of three chapters and an outline. This can be done—it is a common occurrence with established writers—but it is very difficult for new writers. It probably will not damage your chances of selling the novel to try to sell it before it is finished; you might luck out and get an offer. Ordinarily, though, editors prefer to see completed first novels. My experience has been that one gets a *better* offer for a completed manuscript, but I am prejudiced. I prefer to finish a book before trying to sell it. This is a personal quirk not shared by most writers who make a living in the field.

Your story is finished and in proper manuscript form and you have sought out and found the perfect market. You are ready to put your story in the mail. Put it in a manila envelope, and enclose another manila envelope bearing your name and address and sufficient return postage. The advice generally offered is to stiffen the package with a sheet of cardboard. Someone recently pointed out to me, though, that cardboard almost forces the mail carrier to fold the envelope and crease the manuscript. A "naked" manuscript, on the other hand, will bend. My own compromise is to use a manila folder, which will protect the corners of the manuscript yet permit it to bend without creasing.

One of the most frequent "bad-example" stories told by professional editors concerns the new writer who wants to be certain their story has been read all the way through: two pages stuck together or a page turned upside-down, halfway through the story, are the most common techniques. This is one of the few things that will mark you as an absolute and possibly unregenerate amateur; most editors who encounter this test will leave the pages stuck together or the page reversed, just out of pure irritation, even if they do read your story all the way through. And if they do *not* finish your story: if you have not caught the reader's interest by page five, or ten, you have either started the story in the wrong place or you have told the wrong story.

Always send manuscripts flat. Even a short manuscript, if folded, must be beaten with a stick before it will lie flat enough to read.

Send your story first class; anything else is folly.

Do not try to paperclip together the pages of a novel. Send the manuscript loose in a box; enclose return postage and an address label.

A cover letter, especially with a short story, is optional. (It should be in one or another business form, always including your address in the heading: this, as in any correspondence with an editor, is simple courtesy.) A cover letter must be short and to the point. It must not beg the editor to buy the story and it should not explain the story. If the editor has said nice things about your work in the past, by all means mention that in a tactful way. If a published writer has recommended that you send a story to a particular editor, it is perfectly proper to say so if you have permission. If you have special training that pertains to the subject of your story, mention that; however, if you have done your research properly it will not be necessary to apologize for (or even mention) *not* having a degree in a field related to your subject. The work will stand on its own.

After you send your story out, do not be *too* impatient about a reply. Most editors are conscientious and will accept or reject your work in a reasonable time, say, one to two months. After eight or ten weeks it is not unreasonable to drop the editor a polite note asking if your story arrived. (It is courteous to enclose a stamped return envelope.) It is unreasonable, and definitely not courteous, to demand to know what the hell the editor is doing with your story a week after you mailed it. Believe it or not, this does happen.

If the perfect market sends your story back, send it to the next-most-perfect market. And so on. I sent my first story out twenty-two times before it was accepted. (And then the editor emigrated to New Zealand and the magazine never appeared.)

I have given you a lot of rules here, some of them important and some apparently trivial. (Sometimes the trivia make the difference.) All the information has been gained through long experience or other writers or dumb mistakes. Here is the last rule, the most important of all: under some circumstances, anything I have said will be wrong. If you are a good enough writer you can build up such trust in your readers that they will follow you as you blithely shatter every rule in existence. Holding blindly to any rule is a terrible mistake, because the rules are not important. The story is important, the story and its relation to you and the way you write, to your readers and the way they read. If the story demands that you break rules it is quite possible that you have a terrific story brewing. But you need to know what the rules are so you know when you are breaking them, and, more important, *why*. Because if you do something absurd out of ignorance you will destroy the reader's trust in you, the "willing suspension of disbelief" that is even more important in sf than in realistic fiction. The next time you do something absurd, even if it is for the deliberate absurdity and brilliance of it, your reader will not know whether to trust you, and you will have undermined your own work.

Study your craft and respect your art.

Good luck.

BARRY B. LONGYEAR

❧ *Enemy Mine*

Barry Longyear sold his first story, "The Tryouts," to *Isaac Asimov's Science Fiction Magazine* (November/December 1978) and since then has been a regular *IASFM* contributor. Much of his work furthers the chronicle of Momus, the circus world. Until recently, his headquarters was the back room of a tax accountant's office in Farmington, Maine, where he wrote in spite of visits from taxpayers' wandering children. To demonstrate the intensity of his dedication, he has now taken over space in the front room of this office.

Longyear is well known as a conductor of writers' workshops, most recently at the University of Tennessee at Knoxville. He has addressed teachers' associations all over New England on the general topic of persuading children to read more by using science fiction as bait, and he is a frequent and popular visitor to the sixth-grade classroom at Wilton Academy, Wilton, Maine, where he talks about what makes a story and helps the children write their own stories. His book on the problems of beginning writers, *Science Fiction Writer's Workshop I*, was scheduled for release at the World Con '80 in Boston. When you read *Enemy Mine*, you should understand his popularity and why this story won a Nebula.

❧ Winner, Nebula, for Best Novella, 1979.

The Dracon's three-fingered hands flexed. In the thing's yellow eyes I could read the desire to either have those fingers around a weapon or my throat. As I flexed my own fingers, I knew it read the same in my eyes.

"Irkmaan!" the thing spat.

"You piece of Drac slime." I brought my hands up in front of my chest and waved the thing on. "Come on, Drac; come and get it."

"Irkmaan vaa, koruum su!"

"Are you going to talk, or fight? Come on!" I could feel the spray from the sea behind me—a boiling madhouse of white-capped breakers that threatened to swallow me as it had my fighter. I had ridden my ship in. The Drac had ejected when its own fighter had caught one in the upper atmosphere, but not before crippling my power plant. I was exhausted from swimming to the grey, rocky beach and pulling myself to safety. Behind the Drac, among the rocks on the otherwise barren hill, I could see its ejection capsule. Far above us, its people and mine were still at it, slugging out the possession of an uninhabited corner of nowhere. The Drac just stood there and I went over the phrase taught us in training—a phrase calculated to drive any Drac into a frenzy. *"Kiz da yuo-meen, Shizumaat!"* Meaning: Shizumaat, the most revered Drac philosopher, eats kiz excrement. Something on the level of stuffing a Moslem full of pork.

The Drac opened its mouth in horror, then closed it as anger literally changed its color from yellow to reddish-brown. *"Irkmaan, yaa stupid Mickey Mouse is!"*

I had taken an oath to fight and die over many things, but that venerable rodent didn't happen to be one of them. I laughed, and continued laughing until the guffaws in combination with my exhaustion forced me to my knees. I forced open my eyes to keep track of my enemy. The Drac was running toward the high ground, away from me and the sea. I half-turned toward the sea and caught a glimpse of a million tons of water just before they fell on me, knocking me unconscious.

"Kiz da yuomeen, Irkmaan, ne?"

My eyes were gritty with sand and stung with salt, but some part of my awareness pointed out: "Hey, you're alive." I reached to wipe the sand from my eyes and found my hands bound. A straight metal rod had been run through my sleeves and my wrists tied to it. As my tears cleared the sand from my eyes, I could see the Drac sitting on a smooth black boulder looking at me. It must have pulled me out of the drink. "Thanks, toad face. What's with the bondage?"

"Ess?"

I tried waving my arms and wound up giving an impression of an atmospheric fighter dipping its wings. "Untie me, you Drac slime!" I was seated on the sand, my back against a rock.

The Drac smiled, exposing the upper and lower mandibles that looked human—except that instead of separate teeth, they were solid. *"Eh, ne, Irkmaan."* It stood, walked over to me, and checked my bonds.

"Untie me!"

The smile disappeared. *"Ne!"* It pointed at me with a yellow finger. *"Kos son va?"*

"I don't speak Drac, toad face. You speak Esper or English?"

The Drac delivered a very human-looking shrug, then pointed at its own chest. *"Kos va son Jeriba Shigan."* It pointed again at me. *"Kos son va?"*

"Davidge. My name is Willis E. Davidge."

"Ess?"

I tried my tongue on the unfamiliar syllables. *"Kos va son Willis Davidge."*

"Eh." Jeriba Shigan nodded, then motioned with its fingers. *"Dasu, Davidge."*

"Same to you, Jerry."

"Dasu, dasu!" Jeriba began sounding a little impatient. I shrugged as best I could. The Drac bent over and grabbed the front of my jump suit with both hands and pulled me to my feet. *"Dasu, dasu, kizlode!"*

"All right! So *dasu* is 'get up.' What's a *kizlode?"*

Jerry laughed. *"Gavey 'kiz'?"*

"Yeah, I *gavey."*

Jerry pointed at its head. *"Lode."* It pointed at my head. *"Kizlode, gavey?"*

I got it, then swung my arms around, catching Jerry upside its head with the metal rod. The Drac stumbled back against a rock, looking surprised. It raised a hand to its head and withdrew it covered with that pale pus that Dracs think is blood. It looked at me with murder in its eyes. *"Gefh! Nu Gefh, Davidge!"*

"Come and get it, Jerry, you *kizlode* sonofabitch!"

Jerry dived at me and I tried to catch it again with the rod, but the Drac caught my right wrist in both hands and, using the momentum of my swing, whirled me around, slamming my back against another rock. Just as I was getting back my breath, Jerry picked up a small boulder and came at me with every intention of turning my melon into pulp. With my back against the rock, I lifted a foot and kicked the Drac in the midsection, knocking it to the sand. I ran up, ready to stomp Jerry's melon, but he pointed behind me. I turned and saw another tidal wave gathering steam, and heading our way. *"Kiz!"* Jerry got to its feet and scampered for the high ground with me following close behind.

With the roar of the wave at our backs, we weaved among the water- and sand-ground, black boulders, until we reached Jerry's ejection capsule. The Drac stopped, put its shoulder to the egg-shaped contraption, and began rolling it uphill. I could see Jerry's point. The capsule contained all of the survival equipment and food either of us knew about. "Jerry!" I shouted above the rumble of the fast approaching wave. "Pull out this damn rod and I'll help!" The Drac frowned at me. "The rod, *kizlode,* pull it out!" I cocked my head toward my outstretched arm.

Jerry placed a rock beneath the capsule to keep it from rolling back, then quickly untied my wrists and pulled out the rod. Both of us put our shoulders to the capsule, and we quickly rolled it to higher ground. The wave hit and climbed rapidly up the slope until it came up to our chests. The capsule bobbed like a cork, and it was all we could do to keep control of the thing until the water receded, wedging the capsule between three big boulders. I stood there, puffing.

Jerry dropped to the sand, its back against one of the boulders, and watched the water rush back out to sea. *"Magasienna!"*

"You said it, brother." I sank down next to the Drac; we agreed by eye to a temporary truce, and promptly passed out.

My eyes opened on a sky boiling with blacks and greys. Letting my head loll over on my left shoulder, I checked out the Drac. It was still out. First, I thought that this would be the perfect time to get the drop on Jerry. Second, I thought about how silly our insignificant scrap seemed compared to the insanity of the sea that surrounded us. Why hadn't the rescue team come? Did the Dracon fleet wipe us out? Why hadn't the Dracs come to pick up Jerry? Did they wipe out each other? I didn't even know where I was. An island. I had seen that much coming in, but where and in relation to what? Fyrine IV: the planet didn't even rate a name, but was important enough to die over.

With an effort, I struggled to my feet. Jerry opened its eyes and quickly pushed itself to a defensive crouching position. I waved my hand and shook my head. "Ease off, Jerry. I'm just going to look around." I turned my back on it and trudged off between the boulders. I walked uphill for a few minutes until I reached level ground.

It was an island, all right, and not a very big one. By eyeball estimation, height from sea level was only eighty meters, while the island itself was about two kilometers long and less than half that wide. The wind whipping my jump suit against my body was at least drying it out, but as I looked around at the smooth-ground boulders on top of the rise, I realized that Jerry and I could expect bigger waves than the few puny ones we had seen.

A rock clattered behind me and I turned to see Jerry climbing up the slope. When it reached the top, the Drac looked around. I squatted next to one of the boulders and passed my hand over it to indicate the smoothness, then I pointed toward the sea. Jerry nodded. *"Ae, Gavey."* It pointed downhill toward the capsule, then to where we stood. *"Echey masu, nasesay."*

I frowned, then pointed at the capsule. *"Nasesay?* The capsule?"

"Ae, capsule *nasesay. Echey masu."* Jerry pointed at its feet.

I shook my head. "Jerry, if you *gavey* how these rocks got smooth"—I pointed at one—"then you *gavey* that *masu*ing the *nasesay* up here isn't going to do a damned bit of good." I made a sweeping up and down movement with my hands. "Waves." I pointed at the sea below. "Waves, up here." I pointed to where we stood. "Waves, *echey.*"

"Ae, gavey." Jerry looked around the top of the rise, then rubbed the side of its face. The Drac squatted next to some small rocks and began piling one on top of another. *"Viga, Davidge."*

I squatted next to it and watched while its nimble fingers constructed a circle of stones that quickly grew into a dollhouse-sized arena. Jerry stuck one of its fingers in the center of the circle. *"Echey, nasesay."*

The days on Fyrine IV seemed to be three times longer than any I had seen on any other habitable planet. I use the designation 'habitable' with reservations. It took us most of the first day to painfully roll Jerry's *nasesay* up to the top of the rise. The night was too black to work and was bone-cracking cold. We removed the couch from the capsule, which made just enough room for both of us to fit inside. The body heat warmed things up a bit; and we killed time between sleeping, nibbling on Jerry's supply of ration bars (they taste a bit like fish mixed with cheddar cheese), and trying to come to some agreement about language.

"Eye."

"Thuyo."

"Finger."

"Zurath."

"Head."

The Drac laughed. *"Lode."*

"Ho, ho, very funny."
"Ho, ho."

At dawn on the second day, we rolled and pushed the capsule into the center of the rise and wedged it between two large rocks, one of which had an overhang that we hoped would hold down the capsule when one of those big soakers hit. Around the rocks and capsule, we laid a foundation of large stones and filled in the cracks with smaller stones. By the time the wall was knee high, we discovered that building with those smooth, round stones and no mortar wasn't going to work. After some experimentation, we figured out how to break the stones to give us flat sides with which to work. It's done by picking up one stone and slamming it down on top of another. We took turns, one slamming and one building. The stone was almost a volcanic glass, and we also took turns extracting rock splinters from each other. It took nine of those endless days and nights to complete the walls, during which waves came close many times and once washed us ankle deep. For six of those nine days, it rained. The capsule's survival equipment included a plastic blanket, and that became our roof. It sagged in at the center, and the hole we put in it there allowed the water to run out, keeping us almost dry and giving us a supply of fresh water. If a wave of any determination came along, we could kiss the roof good-bye; but we both had confidence in the walls, which were almost two meters thick at the bottom and at least a meter thick at the top.

After we finished, we sat inside and admired our work for about an hour, until it dawned on us that we had just worked ourselves out of jobs. "What now, Jerry?"

"Ess?"

"What do we do now?"

"Now wait, we." The Drac shrugged. "Else what, *ne?"*

I nodded. *"Gavey."* I got to my feet and walked to the passage-way we had built. With no wood for a door, where the walls would have met, we bent one out and extended it about three meters around the other wall with the opening away from the prevailing winds. The never-ending winds were still at it, but the rain had stopped. The shack wasn't much to look at, but looking at it stuck there in the center of that deserted island made me feel good. As

Shizumaat observed: "Intelligent life making its stand against the universe." Or, at least, that's the sense I could make out of Jerry's hamburger of English. I shrugged and picked up a sharp splinter of stone and made another mark in the large standing rock that served as my log. Ten scratches in all, and under the seventh, a small x to indicate the big wave that just covered the top of the island.

I threw down the splinter. "Damn, I hate this place!"

"Ess?" Jerry's head poked around the edge of the opening. "Who talking at, Davidge?"

I glared at the Drac, then waved my hand at it. "Nobody."

"Ess va, 'nobody'?"

"Nobody. Nothing."

"Ne gavey, Davidge."

I poked at my chest with my finger. "Me! I'm talking to myself! You *gavey* that stuff, toad face!"

Jerry shook its head. "Davidge, now I sleep. Talk not so much nobody, *ne?"* It disappeared back into the opening.

"And so's your mother!" I turned and walked down the slope. *Except, strictly speaking, toad face, you don't have a mother—or father. "If you had your choice, who would you like to be trapped on a desert island with?"* I wondered if anyone ever picked a wet freezing corner of Hell shacked up with a hermaphrodite.

Half of the way down the slope, I followed the path I had marked with rocks until I came to my tidal pool, that I had named "Rancho Sluggo." Around the pool were many of the water-worn rocks, and underneath those rocks, below the pool's waterline, lived the fattest orange slugs either of us had ever seen. I made the discovery during a break from house building and showed them to Jerry.

Jerry shrugged. "And so?"

"And so what? Look, Jerry, those ration bars aren't going to last forever. What are we going to eat when they're all gone?"

"Eat?" Jerry looked at the wriggling pocket of insect life and grimaced. *"Ne,* Davidge. Before then pickup. Search us find, then pickup."

"What if they don't find us? What then?"

Jerry grimaced again and turned back to the half-completed

house. "Water we drink, then until pickup." He muttered something about kiz excrement and my tastebuds, then walked out of
sight.

Since then I had built up the pool's walls, hoping the increased
protection from the harsh environment would increase the herd.
I looked under several rocks, but no increase was apparent. I
wondered if I could bring myself to swallow one of the things. I
replaced the rock I was looking under, stood, and looked out to the
sea. Although the eternal cloud cover still denied the surface the
drying rays of Fyrine, there was no rain and the usual haze had
lifted.

In the direction past where I had pulled myself up on the beach,
the sea continued to the horizon. In the spaces between the whitecaps, the water was as grey as a loan officer's heart. Parallel lines
of rollers formed approximately five kilometers from the island.
The center, from where I was standing, would smash on the island,
while the remainder steamed on. To my right, in line with the
breakers, I could just make out another small island perhaps ten
kilometers away. Following the path of the rollers, I looked far to
my right, and where the grey-white of the sea should have met the
lighter grey of the sky, there was a black line on the horizon.

The harder I tried to remember the briefing charts on Fyrine
IV's land masses, the less clear it became. Jerry couldn't remember
anything either—at least nothing it would tell me. Why should we
remember? The battle was supposed to be in space, each one
trying to deny the other an orbital staging area in the Fyrine
system. Neither side wanted to set foot on Fyrine, much less fight
a battle there. Still, whatever it was called, it was land and considerably larger than the sand-and-rock bar we were occupying.

How to get there was the problem. Without wood, fire, leaves,
or animal skins, Jerry and I were destitute compared to the average poverty-stricken caveman. The only thing we had that would
float was the *nasesay*. The capsule. Why not? The only real problem to overcome was getting Jerry to go along with it.

That evening, while the greyness made its slow transition to
black, Jerry and I sat outside the shack nibbling our quarter por-
tions of ration bars. The Drac's yellow eyes studied the dark line
on the horizon, then it shook its head. "*Ne*, Davidge. Dangerous
is."

I popped the rest of my ration bar into my mouth and talked around it. "Any more dangerous than staying here?"

"Soon pickup, *ne?*"

I studied those yellow eyes. "Jerry, you don't believe that any more than I do." I leaned forward on the rock and held out my hands. "Look, our chances will be a lot better on a larger land mass. Protection from the big waves, maybe food. . . ."

"Not maybe, *ne?*" Jerry pointed at the water. "How *nasesay* steer, Davidge? In that, how steer? *Ess eh* soakers, waves, beyond land take, *gavey? Bresha,*" Jerry's hands slapped together. "*Ess eh bresha* rocks on, *ne?* Then we death."

I scratched my head. "The waves are going in that direction from here, and so is the wind. If the land mass is large enough, we don't have to steer, *gavey?*"

Jerry snorted. "*Ne* large enough; then?"

"I didn't say it was a sure thing."

"*Ess?*"

"A sure thing; certain, *gavey?*" Jerry nodded. "As for smashing up on the rocks, it probably has a beach like this one."

"Sure thing, *ne?*"

I shrugged. "No, it's not a sure thing, but what about staying here? We don't know how big those waves can get. What if one just comes along and washes us off the island? What then?"

Jerry looked at me, its eyes narrowed. "What there, Davidge? *Irkmaan* base, *ne?*"

I laughed. "I told you, we don't have any bases on Fyrine IV."

"Why want go, then?"

"Just what I said, Jerry. I think our chances would be better."

"Ummm." The Drac folded its arms. "*Viga,* Davidge, *nasesay* stay. I know."

"Know what?"

Jerry smirked then stood and went into the shack. After a moment it returned and threw a two-meter-long metal rod at my feet. It was the one the Drac had used to bind my arms. "Davidge, I know."

I raised my eyebrows and shrugged. "What are you talking about? Didn't that come from your capsule?"

"*Ne, Irkmaan.*"

I bent down and picked up the rod. Its surface was uncorroded and at one end were Arabic numerals—a part number. For a moment a flood of hope washed over me, but it drained away when I realized it was a civilian part number. I threw the rod on the sand. "There's no telling how long that's been here, Jerry. It's a civilian part number and no civilian missions have been in this part of the galaxy since the war. Might be left over from an old seeding operation or exploratory mission. . . . "

The Drac nudged it with the toe of his boot. "New, *gavey?*"

I looked up at it. "You *gavey* stainless steel?"

Jerry snorted and turned back toward the shack. "I stay, *nasesay* stay; where you want, you go, Davidge!"

With the black of the long night firmly bolted down on us, the wind picked up, shrieking and whistling in and through the holes in the walls. The plastic roof flapped, pushed in and sucked out with such violence it threatened to either tear or sail off into the night. Jerry sat on the sand floor, its back leaning against the *nasesay* as if to make clear that both Drac and capsule were staying put, although the way the sea was picking up seemed to weaken Jerry's argument.

"Sea rough now is, Davidge, *ne?*"

"It's too dark to see, but with this wind. . . . " I shrugged more for my own benefit than the Drac's, since the only thing visible inside the shack was the pale light coming through the roof. Any minute we could be washed off that sandbar. "Jerry, you're being silly about that rod. You know that."

"*Surda.*" The Drac sounded contrite if not altogether miserable.

"*Ess?*"

"*Ess eh 'Surda'?*"

"*Ae.*"

Jerry remained silent for a moment. "Davidge, *gavey* 'not certain not is'?"

I sorted out the negatives. "You mean 'possible,' 'maybe,' 'perhaps'?"

"*Ae,* possiblemaybeperhaps. Dracon fleet Irkmaan ships have. Before war buy; after war capture. Rod possiblemaybeperhaps Dracon is."

"So, if there's a secret base on the big island, *surda* it's a Dracon base?"

"Possiblemaybeperhaps, Davidge."

"Jerry, does that mean you want to try it? The *nasesay?*"

"*Ne.*"

"*Ne?* Why, Jerry? If it might be a Drac base—"

"*Ne! Ne* talk!" The Drac seemed to choke on the words.

"Jerry, we talk, and you better *believe* we talk! If I'm going to death it on this island, I have a right to know why."

The Drac was quiet for a long time. "Davidge."

"*Ess?*"

"*Nasesay,* you take. Half ration bars you leave. I stay."

I shook my head to clear it. "You want me to take the capsule alone?"

"What you want is, *ne?*"

"*Ae,* but why? You must realize there won't be any pickup."

"Possiblemaybeperhaps."

"*Surda,* nothing. You know there isn't going to be a pickup. What is it? You afraid of the water? If that's it, we have a better chance—"

"Davidge, up your mouth shut. *Nasesay* you have. Me *ne* you need, *gavey?*"

I nodded in the dark. The capsule was mine for the taking; what did I need a grumpy Drac along for—especially since our truce could expire at any moment? The answer made me feel a little silly —human. Perhaps it's the same thing. The Drac was all that stood between me and utter aloneness. Still, there was the small matter of staying alive. "We should go together, Jerry."

"Why?"

I felt myself blush. If humans have this need for companionship, why are they also ashamed to admit it? "We just should. Our chances would be better."

"Alone your chances better are, Davidge. Your enemy I am."

I nodded again and grimaced in the dark. "Jerry, you *gavey* 'loneliness'?"

"*Ne gavey.*"

"Lonely. Being alone, by myself."

"*Gavey* you alone. Take *nasesay;* I stay."

"That's it . . . see, *viga,* I don't want to."

"You want together go?" A low, dirty chuckle came from the other side of the shack. "You Dracon like? You me death, *Irk-*

maan." Jerry chuckled some more. *"Irkmaan poorzhab* in head, *poorzhab."*

"Forget it!" I slid down from the wall, smoothed out the sand and curled up with my back toward the Drac. The wind seemed to die down a bit and I closed my eyes to try and sleep. In a bit, the snap, crack of the plastic roof blended in with the background of shrieks and whistles and I felt myself drifting off, when my eyes opened wide at the sound of footsteps in the sand. I tensed, ready to spring.

"Davidge?" Jerry's voice was very quiet.

"What?"

I heard the Drac sit on the sand next to me. "You loneliness, Davidge. About it hard you talk, *ne?"*

"So what?" The Drac mumbled something that was lost in the wind. "What?" I turned over and saw Jerry looking through a hole in the wall.

"Why I stay. Now, you I tell, *ne?"*

I shrugged. "Okay; why not?"

Jerry seemed to struggle with the words, then opened its mouth to speak. Its eyes opened wide. *"Magasienna!"*

I sat up. *"Ess?"*

Jerry pointed at the hole. "Soaker!"

I pushed it out of the way and looked through the hole. Steaming toward our island was an insane mountainous fury of white-capped rollers. It was hard to tell in the dark, but the one in front looked taller than the one that had wet our feet a few days before. The ones following it were bigger. Jerry put a hand on my shoulder and I looked into the Drac's eyes. We broke and ran for the capsule. We heard the first wave rumbling up the slope as we felt around in the dark for the recessed doorlatch. I just got my finger on it when the wave smashed against the shack, collapsing the roof. In half a second we were under water, the currents inside the shack agitating us like socks in a washing machine.

The water receded, and as I cleared my eyes, I saw that the windward wall of the shack had caved in. "Jerry!"

Through the collapsed wall, I saw the Drac staggering around outside. *"Irkmaan?"* Behind him I could see the second roller gathering speed.

"*Kizlode,* what'n the hell you doing out there? Get in here!"

I turned to the capsule, still lodged firmly between the two rocks, and found the handle. As I opened the door, Jerry stumbled through the missing wall and fell against me. "Davidge . . . forever soakers go on! Forever!"

"Get in!" I helped the Drac through the door and didn't wait for it to get out of the way. I piled in on top of Jerry and latched the door just as the second wave hit. I could feel the capsule lift a bit and rattle against the overhang of the one rock.

"Davidge, we float?"

"No. The rocks are holding us. We'll be all right once the breakers stop."

"Over you move."

"Oh." I got off Jerry's chest and braced myself against one end of the capsule. After a bit, the capsule came to rest and we waited for the next one. "Jerry?"

"*Ess?*"

"What was it that you were about to say?"

"Why I stay?"

"Yeah."

"About it hard me talk, *gavey?*"

"I know, I know."

The next breaker hit and I could feel the capsule rise and rattle against the rock. "Davidge, *gavey 'vi nessa'?*"

"Ne gavey."

"Vi nessa . . . little me, *gavey?*"

The capsule bumped down the rock and came to rest. "What about little you?"

"Little me . . . little Drac. From me, *gavey?*"

"Are you telling me you're *pregnant?*"

"Possiblemaybeperhaps."

I shook my head. "Hold on, Jerry. I don't want any misunderstandings. Pregnant . . . are you going to be a parent?"

"*Ae,* parent, two-zero-zero in line, very important is, *ne?*"

"Terrific. What's this got to do with you not wanting to go to the other island?"

"Before, me *vi nessa, gavey? Tean* death."

"Your child, it died?"

"Ae!" The Drac's sob was torn from the lips of the universal mother. "I in fall hurt. *Tean* death. *Nasesay* in sea us bang. *Tean* hurt, *gavey?"*

"Ae, I *gavey."* So, Jerry was afraid of losing another child. It was almost certain that the capsule trip would bang us around a lot, but staying on the sandbar didn't appear to be improving our chances. The capsule had been at rest for quite a while, and I decided to risk a peek outside. The small canopy windows seemed to be covered with sand, and I opened the door. I looked around, and all of the walls had been smashed flat. I looked toward the sea, but could see nothing. "It looks safe, Jerry . . ." I looked up, toward the blackish sky, and above me towered the white plume of a descending breaker. *"Maga* damn *sienna!"* I slammed the hatch door.

"Ess, Davidge?"

"Hang on, Jerry!"

The sound of the water hitting the capsule was beyond hearing. We banged once, twice against the rock, then we could feel ourselves twisting, shooting upward. I made a grab to hang on, but missed as the capsule took a sickening lurch downward. I fell into Jerry, then was flung to the opposite wall where I struck my head. Before I went blank, I heard Jerry cry *"Tean! Vi tean!"*

. . . the lieutenant pressed his hand control and a figure—tall, humanoid, yellow—appeared on the screen.

"Dracslime!" shouted the auditorium of seated recruits.

The lieutenant faced the recruits. "Correct. This is a Drac. Note that the Drac race is uniform as to color; they are all yellow." The recruits chuckled politely. The officer preened a bit, then with a light wand began pointing out various features. "The three-fingered hands are distinctive, of course, as is the almost noseless face, which gives the Drac a toadlike appearance. On average, eyesight is slightly better than human, hearing about the same, and smell . . ." the lieutenant paused. "The smell is terrible!" The officer beamed at the uproar from the recruits. When the auditorium quieted down, he pointed his light wand at a fold in the figure's belly. "This is where the Drac keeps its family jewels—all of them." Another chuckle. "That's right, Dracs are hermaphrodites, with both male and female reproductive organs contained

in the same individual." The lieutenant faced the recruits. "You
go tell a Drac to go boff himself, then watch out, because he can!"
The laughter died down, and the lieutenant held out a hand toward the screen. "You see one of these things, what do you do?"

"KILL IT. . . ."

. . . I cleared the screen and computer sighted on the next Drac
fighter, looking like a double x in the screen's display. The Drac
shifted hard to the left, then right again. I felt the autopilot pull
my ship after the fighter, sorting out and ignoring the false images,
trying to lock its electronic crosshairs on the Drac. "Come on, toad
face . . . a little bit to the left. . . ." The double-cross image moved
into the ranging rings on the display and I felt the missile attached
to the belly of my fighter take off. "Gotcha!" Through my canopy
I saw the flash as the missile detonated. My screen showed the
Drac fighter out of control, spinning toward Fyrine IV's cloud-
shrouded surface. I dived after it to confirm the kill . . . skin
temperature increasing as my ship brushed the upper atmosphere. "Come on, dammit, blow!" I shifted the ship's systems
over for atmospheric flight when it became obvious that I'd have
to follow the Drac right to the ground. Still above the clouds, the
Drac stopped spinning and turned. I hit the auto override and
pulled the stick into my lap. The fighter wallowed as it tried to pull
up. Everyone knows the Drac ships work better in atmosphere
. . . heading toward me on an interception course . . . why doesn't
the slime fire . . . just before the collision, the Drac ejects . . . power
gone; have to deadstick it in. I track the capsule as it falls through
the muck intending to find that Dracslime and finish the
job. . . .

It could have been for seconds or years that I groped into the
darkness around me. I felt touching, but the parts of me being
touched seemed far, far away. First chills, then fever, then chills
again, my head being cooled by a gentle hand. I opened my eyes
to narrow slits and saw Jerry hovering over me, blotting my forehead with something cool. I managed a whisper. "Jerry."

The Drac looked into my eyes and smiled. "Good is, Davidge.
Good is."

The light on Jerry's face flickered and I smelled smoke. "Fire."

Jerry got out of the way and pointed toward the center of the room's sandy floor. I let my head roll over and realized that I was lying on a bed of soft, springy branches. Opposite my bed was another bed, and between them crackled a cheery campfire. "Fire now we have, Davidge. And wood." Jerry pointed toward the roof made of wooden poles thatched with broad leaves.

I turned and looked around, then let my throbbing head sink down and closed my eyes. "Where are we?"

"Big island, Davidge. Soaker off sandbar us washed. Wind and waves us here took. Right you were."

"I . . . I don't understand; *ne gavey.* It'd take days to get to the big island from the sandbar."

Jerry nodded and dropped what looked like a sponge into a shell of some sort filled with water. "Nine days. You I strap to *nasesay,* then here on beach we land."

"Nine days? I've been out for nine days?"

Jerry shook his head. "Seventeen. Here we land eight days . . ." The Drac waved its hand behind itself.

"Ago . . . eight days ago."

"Ae."

Seventeen days on Fyrine IV was better than a month on Earth. I opened my eyes again and looked at Jerry. The Drac was almost bubbling with excitement. "What about *tean,* your child?"

Jerry patted its swollen middle. "Good is, Davidge. You more *nasesay* hurt."

I overcame an urge to nod. "I'm happy for you." I closed my eyes and turned my face toward the wall, a combination of wood poles and leaves. "Jerry?"

"Ess?"

"You saved my life."

"Ae."

"Why?"

Jerry sat quietly for a long time. "Davidge. On sandbar you talk. Loneliness now *gavey.*" The Drac shook my arm. "Here, now you eat."

I turned and looked into a shell filled with a steaming liquid. "What is it; chicken soup?"

"Ess?"

"Ess va?" I pointed at the bowl, realizing for the first time how weak I was.

Jerry frowned. "Like slug, but long."

"An eel?"

"Ae, but eel on land, *gavey?"*

"You mean 'snake'?"

"Possiblemaybeperhaps."

I nodded and put my lips to the edge of the shell. I sipped some of the broth, swallowed and let the broth's healing warmth seep through my body. "Good."

"You *custa* want?"

"Ess?"

"Custa." Jerry reached next to the fire and picked up a squareish chunk of clear rock. I looked at it, scratched it with my thumbnail, then touched it with my tongue.

"Halite! Salt!"

Jerry smiled. *"Custa* you want?"

I laughed. "All the comforts. By all means, let's have *custa."*

Jerry took the halite, knocked off a corner with a small stone, then used the stone to grind the pieces against another stone. He held out the palm of his hand with a tiny mountain of white granules in the center. I took two pinches, dropped them into my snake soup, and stirred it with my finger. Then I took a long swallow of the delicious broth. I smacked my lips. "Fantastic."

"Good, *ne?"*

"Better than good; fantastic." I took another swallow, making a big show of smacking my lips and rolling my eyes.

"Fantastic, Davidge, *ne?"*

"Ae." I nodded at the Drac. "I think that's enough. I want to sleep."

"Ae, Davidge, *gavey."* Jerry took the bowl and put it beside the fire. The Drac stood, walked to the door and turned back. Its yellow eyes studied me for an instant, then it nodded, turned, and went outside. I closed my eyes and let the heat from the campfire coax the sleep over me.

In two days I was up in the shack trying my legs, and in two more days, Jerry helped me outside. The shack was located at the top of a long, gentle rise in a scrub forest; none of the trees were any taller than five or six meters. At the bottom of the slope, better than eight kilometers from the shack, was the still-rolling sea. The Drac had carried me. Our trusty *nasesay* had filled with water and had been dragged back into the sea soon after Jerry pulled me to dry land. With it went the remainder of the ration bars. Dracs are very fussy about what they eat, but hunger finally drove Jerry to sample some of the local flora and fauna—hunger and the human lump that was rapidly drifting away from lack of nourishment. The Drac had settled on a bland, starchy type of root, a green bushberry that when dried made an acceptable tea, and snakemeat. Exploring, Jerry had found a partly eroded salt dome. In the days that followed, I grew stronger and added to our diet with several types of sea mollusk and a fruit resembling a cross between a pear and a plum.

As the days grew colder, the Drac and I were forced to realize that Fyrine IV had a winter. Given that, we had to face the possibility that the winter would be severe enough to prevent the gathering of food—and wood. When dried next to the fire, the berrybush and roots kept well, and we tried both salting and smoking snakemeat. With strips of fiber from the berrybush for thread, Jerry and I pieced together the snakeskins for winter clothing. The design we settled on involved two layers of skins with the down from berrybush seed pods stuffed between and then held in place by quilting the layers.

We agreed that the house would never do. It took three days of searching to find our first cave, and another three days before we found one that suited us. The mouth opened onto a view of the eternally tormented sea, but was set in the face of a low cliff well above sea level. Around the cave's entrance we found great quantities of dead wood and loose stone. The wood we gathered for heat; and the stone we used to wall up the entrance, leaving only space enough for a hinged door. The hinges were made of snake leather and the door of wooden poles tied together with berrybush fibre. The first night after completing the door, the sea winds blew it to pieces; and we decided to go back to the original door design we had used on the sandbar.

Deep inside the cave, we made our living quarters in a chamber with a wide, sandy floor. Still deeper, the cave had natural pools of water, which were fine for drinking but too cold for bathing. We used the pool chamber for our supply room. We lined the walls of our living quarters with piles of wood and made new beds out of snakeskins and seed-pod down. In the center of the chamber we built a respectable fireplace with a large, flat stone over the coals for a griddle. The first night we spent in our new home, I discovered that, for the first time since ditching on that damned planet, I couldn't hear the wind.

During the long nights, we would sit at the fireplace making things—gloves, hats, packbags—out of snake leather, and we would talk. To break the monotony, we alternated days between speaking Drac and English, and by the time the winter hit with its first ice storm, each of us was comfortable in the other's language.

We talked of Jerry's coming child:

"What are you going to name it, Jerry?"

"It already has a name. See, the Jeriba line has five names. My name is Shigan; before me came my parent, Gothig; before Gothig was Haesni; before Haesni was Ty, and before Ty was Zammis. The child is named Jeriba Zammis."

"Why only the five names? A human child can have just about any name its parents pick for it. In fact, once a human becomes an adult, he or she can pick any name he or she wants."

The Drac looked at me, its eyes filled with pity. "Davidge, how lost you must feel. You humans—how lost you must feel."

"Lost?"

Jerry nodded. "Where do you come from, Davidge?"

"You mean my parents?"

"Yes."

I shrugged. "I remember my parents."

"And their parents?"

"I remember my mother's father. When I was young we used to visit him."

"Davidge, what do you know about this grandparent?"

I rubbed my chin. "It's kind of vague . . . I think he was in some kind of agriculture—I don't know."

"And his parents?"

I shook my head. "The only thing I remember is that somewhere along the line, English and Germans figured. *Gavey* Germans and English?"

Jerry nodded. "Davidge, I can recite the history of my line back to the founding of my planet by Jeriba Ty, one of the original settlers, one hundred and ninety-nine generations ago. At our line's archives on Draco, there are the records that trace the line across space to the racehome planet, Sindie, and there back seventy generations to Jeriba Ty, the founder of the Jeriba line."

"How does one become a founder?"

"Only the firstborn carries the line. Products of second, third, or fourth births must found their own lines."

I nodded, impressed. "Why only the five names? Just to make it easier to remember them?"

Jerry shook its head. "No. The names are things to which we add distinction; they are the same, commonplace five so that they do not overshadow the events that distinguish their bearers. The name I carry, Shigan, has been served by great soldiers, scholars, students of philosophy, and several priests. The name my child will carry has been served by scientists, teachers, and explorers."

"You remember all of your ancestor's occupations?"

Jerry nodded. "Yes, and what they each did and where they did it. You must recite your line before the line's archives to be admitted into adulthood as I was twenty-two of my years ago. Zammis will do the same, except the child must begin its recitation—" Jerry smiled—"with my name, Jeriba Shigan."

"You can recite almost two hundred biographies from memory?"

"Yes."

I went over to my bed and stretched out. As I stared up at the smoke being sucked through the crack in the chamber's ceiling, I began to understand what Jerry meant by feeling lost. A Drac with several dozens of generations under its belt knew who it was and what it had to live up to. "Jerry?"

"Yes, Davidge?"

"Will you recite them for me?" I turned my head and looked at the Drac in time to see an expression of utter surprise melt into joy. It was only after many years had passed that I learned I had done Jerry a great honor in requesting his line. Among the Dracs, it is a rare expression of respect, not only of the individual, but of the line.

Jerry placed the hat he was sewing on the sand, stood, and began.

"Before you here I stand, Shigan of the line of Jeriba, born of Gothig, the teacher of music. A musician of high merit, the students of Gothig included Datzizh of the Nem line, Perravane of the Tuscor line, and many lesser musicians. Trained in music at the Shimuram, Gothig stood before the archives in the year 11,051 and spoke of its parent Haesni, the manufacturer of ships. . . ."

As I listened to Jerry's singsong of formal Dracon, the backward biographies—beginning with death and ending with adulthood—I experienced a sense of time-binding, of being able to know and touch the past. Battles, empires built and destroyed, discoveries made, great things done—a tour through twelve thousand years of history, but perceived as a well-defined, living continuum.

Against this: I, Willis of the Davidge line, stand before you, born of Sybil the housewife and Nathan the second-rate civil engineer, one of them born of Grandpop, who probably had something to do with agriculture, born of nobody in particular. . . . Hell, I wasn't even that! My older brother carried the line; not me. I listened and made up my mind to memorize the line of Jeriba.

We talked of war:

"That was a pretty neat trick, suckering me into the atmosphere, then ramming me."

Jerry shrugged. "Dracon fleet pilots are best; this is well known."

I raised my eyebrows. "That's why I shot your tail feathers off, huh?"

Jerry shrugged, frowned, and continued sewing on the scraps of snake leather. "Why do the Earthmen invade this part of the galaxy, Davidge? We had thousands of years of peace before you came."

"Hah! Why do the Dracs invade? We were at peace, too. What are you doing here?"

"We settle these planets. It is the Drac tradition. We are explorers and founders."

"Well, toad face, what do you think we are, a bunch of homebodies? Humans have had space travel for less than two hundred years, but we've settled almost twice as many planets as the Dracs—"

Jerry held up a finger. "Exactly! You humans spread like a disease. Enough! We don't want you here!"

"Well, we're here, and here to stay. Now, what are you going to do about it?"

"You see what we do, *Irkmaan*, we fight!"

"Phooey! You call that little scrap we were in a fight? Hell, Jerry, we were kicking you junk jocks out of the sky—"

"Haw, Davidge! That's why you sit here sucking on smoked snakemeat!"

I pulled the little rascal out of my mouth and pointed it at the Drac. "I notice your breath has a snake flavor, too, Drac!"

Jerry snorted and turned away from the fire. I felt stupid, first because we weren't going to settle an argument that had plagued a hundred worlds for over a century. Second, I wanted to have Jerry check my recitation. I had over a hundred generations memorized. The Drac's side was toward the fire, leaving enough light falling on its lap to see its sewing.

"Jerry, what are you working on?"

"We have nothing to talk about, Davidge."

"Come on, what is it?"

Jerry turned its head toward me, then looked back into its lap and picked up a tiny snakeskin suit. "For Zammis." Jerry smiled and I shook my head, then laughed.

We talked of philosophy:

"You studied Shizumaat, Jerry; why won't you tell me about its teachings?"

Jerry frowned. "No, Davidge."

"Are Shizumaat's teachings secret or something?"

Jerry shook its head. "No. But we honor Shizumaat too much for talk."

I rubbed my chin. "Do you mean too much to talk about it, or to talk about it with a human?"

"Not with humans, Davidge; just not with you."

"Why?"

Jerry lifted its head and narrowed its yellow eyes. "You know what you said . . . on the sandbar."

I scratched my head and vaguely recalled the curse I laid on the Drac about Shizumaat eating it. I held out my hands. "But, Jerry, I was mad, angry. You can't hold me accountable for what I said then."

"I do."

"Will it change anything if I apologize?"

"Not a thing."

I stopped myself from saying something nasty and thought back to that moment when Jerry and I stood ready to strangle each other. I remembered something about that meeting and screwed the corners of my mouth in place to keep from smiling. "Will you tell me Shizumaat's teachings if I forgive you . . . for what you said about Mickey Mouse?" I bowed my head in an appearance of reverence, although its chief purpose was to suppress a cackle.

Jerry looked up at me, its face pained with guilt. "I have felt bad about that, Davidge. If you forgive me, I will talk about Shizumaat."

"Then, I forgive you, Jerry."

"One more thing."

"What?"

"You must tell me of the teachings of Mickey Mouse."

"I'll . . . uh, do my best."

We talked of Zammis:

"Jerry, what do you want little Zammy to be?"

The Drac shrugged. "Zammis must live up to its own name. I want it to do that with honor. If Zammis does that, it is all I can ask."

"Zammy will pick its own trade?"

"Yes."

"Isn't there anything special you want, though?"

Jerry nodded. "Yes, there is."

"What's that?"

"That Zammis will, one day, find itself off this miserable planet."

I nodded. "Amen."

"Amen."

The winter dragged on until Jerry and I began wondering if we had gotten in on the beginning of an ice age. Outside the cave, everything was coated with a thick layer of ice, and the low temperature combined with the steady winds made venturing outside a temptation of death by falls or freezing. Still, by mutual agreement, we both went outside to relieve ourselves. There were several isolated chambers deep in the cave; but we feared polluting our water supply, not to mention the air inside the cave. The main risk outside was dropping one's drawers at a wind chill factor that froze breath vapor before it could be blown through the thin face muffs we had made out of our flight suits. We learned not to dawdle.

One morning, Jerry was outside answering the call, while I stayed by the fire mashing up dried roots with water for griddle cakes. I heard Jerry call from the mouth of the cave. "Davidge!"

"What?"

"Davidge, come quick!"

A ship! It had to be! I put the shell bowl on the sand, put on my hat and gloves, and ran through the passage. As I came close to the door, I untied the muff from around my neck and tied it over my mouth and nose to protect my lungs. Jerry, its head bundled in a similar manner, was looking through the door, waving me on. "What is it?"

Jerry stepped away from the door to let me through. "Come, look!"

Sunlight. Blue sky and sunlight. In the distance, over the sea, new clouds were piling up; but above us the sky was clear. Neither of us could look at the sun directly, but we turned our faces to it and felt the rays of Fyrine on our skins. The light glared and sparkled off the ice-covered rocks and trees. "Beautiful."

"Yes." Jerry grabbed my sleeve with a gloved hand. "Davidge, you know what this means?"

"What?"

"Signal fires at night. On a clear night, a large fire could be seen from orbit, *ne?*"

I looked at Jerry, then back at the sky. "I don't know. If the fire were big enough, and we get a clear night, and if anybody picks that moment to look . . ." I let my head hang down. "That's always supposing that there's someone in orbit up there to do the looking." I felt the pain begin in my fingers. "We better go back in."

"Davidge, it's a chance!"

"What are we going to use for wood, Jerry?" I held out an arm toward the trees above and around the cave. "Everything that can burn has at least fifteen centimeters of ice on it."

"In the cave—"

"Our firewood?" I shook my head. "How long is this winter going to last? Can you be sure that we have enough wood to waste on signal fires?"

"It's a chance, Davidge. It's a chance!"

Our survival riding on a toss of the dice. I shrugged. "Why not?"

We spent the next few hours hauling a quarter of our carefully gathered firewood and dumping it outside the mouth of the cave. By the time we were finished and long before night came, the sky was again a solid blanket of grey. Several times each night, we would check the sky, waiting for stars to appear. During the days, we would frequently have to spend several hours beating the ice off the wood pile. Still, it gave both of us hope, until the wood in the cave ran out and we had to start borrowing from the signal pile.

That night, for the first time, the Drac looked absolutely defeated. Jerry sat at the fireplace, staring at the flames. Its hand reached inside its snakeskin jacket through the neck and pulled out a small golden cube suspended on a chain. Jerry held the cube clasped in both hands, shut its eyes, and began mumbling in Drac. I watched from my bed until Jerry finished. The Drac sighed, nodded, and replaced the object within its jacket.

"What's that thing?"

Jerry looked up at me, frowned, then touched the front of its jacket. "This? It is my *Talman*— what you call a Bible."

"A Bible is a book. You know, with pages that you read."

Jerry pulled the thing from its jacket, mumbled a phrase in Drac, then worked a small catch. Another gold cube dropped from the first and the Drac held it out to me. "Be very careful with it, Davidge."

I sat up, took the object, and examined it in the light of the fire.

Three hinged pieces of the golden metal formed the binding of a book two-and-a-half centimeters on an edge. I opened the book in the middle and looked over the double columns of dots, lines, and squiggles. "It's in Drac."

"Of course."

"But I can't read it."

Jerry's eyebrows went up. "You speak Drac so well, I didn't remember . . . would you like me to teach you?"

"To read this?"

"Why not? You have an appointment you have to keep?"

I shrugged. "No." I touched my finger to the book and tried to turn one of the tiny pages. Perhaps fifty pages went at once. "I can't separate the pages."

Jerry pointed at a small bump at the top of the spine. "Pull out the pin. It's for turning the pages."

I pulled out the short needle, touched it against a page, and it slid loose of its companion and flipped. "Who wrote your *Talman*, Jerry?"

"Many. All great teachers."

"Shizumaat?"

Jerry nodded. "Shizumaat is one of them."

I closed the book and held it in the palm of my hand. "Jerry, why did you bring this out now?"

"I needed its comfort." The Drac held out its arms. "This place. Maybe we will grow old here and die. Maybe we will never be found. I see this today as we brought in the signal fire wood." Jerry placed its hands on its belly. "Zammis will be born here. The *Talman* helps me to accept what I cannot change."

"Zammis, how much longer?"

Jerry smiled. "Soon."

I looked at the tiny book. "I would like you to teach me to read this, Jerry."

The Drac took the chain and case from around its neck and handed it to me. "You must keep the *Talman* in this."

I held it for a moment, then shook my head. "I can't keep this, Jerry. It's obviously of great value to you. What if I lost it?"

"You won't. Keep it while you learn. The student must do this."

I put the chain around my neck. "This is quite an honor you do me."

Jerry shrugged. "Much less than the honor you do me by memorizing the Jeriba line. Your recitations have been accurate, and moving." Jerry took some charcoal from the fire, stood, and walked to the wall of the chamber. That night I learned the thirty-one letters and sounds of the Drac alphabet, as well as the additional nine sounds and letters used in formal Drac writings.

The wood eventually ran out. Jerry was very heavy and very, very sick as Zammis prepared to make its appearance, and it was all the Drac could do to waddle outside with my help to relieve itself. Hence, woodgathering, which involved taking our remaining stick and beating the ice off the dead standing trees, fell to me, as did cooking.

On a particularly blustery day, I noticed that the ice on the trees was thinner. Somewhere we had turned winter's corner and were heading for spring. I spent my ice-pounding time feeling great at the thought of spring, and I knew Jerry would pick up some at the news. The winter was really getting the Drac down. I was working the woods above the cave, taking armloads of gathered wood and dropping them down below, when I heard a scream. I froze, then looked around. I could see nothing but the sea and the ice around me. Then, the scream again. "Davidge!" It was Jerry. I dropped the load I was carrying and ran to the cleft in the cliff's face that served as a path to the upper woods. Jerry screamed again; and I slipped, then rolled until I came to the shelf level with the cave's mouth. I rushed through the entrance, down the passage way until I came to the chamber. Jerry writhed on its bed, digging its fingers into the sand.

I dropped on my knees next to the Drac. "I'm here, Jerry. What is it? What's wrong?"

"Davidge!" The Drac rolled its eyes, seeing nothing; its mouth worked silently, then exploded with another scream.

"Jerry, it's me!" I shook the Drac's shoulder. "It's me, Jerry. Davidge!"

Jerry turned its head toward me, grimaced, then clasped the fingers of one hand around my left wrist with the strength of pain.

"Davidge! Zammis . . . something's gone wrong!"

"What? What can I do?"

Jerry screamed again, then its head fell back to the bed in a half-faint. The Drac fought back to consciousness and pulled my head down to its lips. "Davidge, you must swear."

"What, Jerry? Swear what?"

"Zammis . . . on Draco. To stand before the line's archives. Do this."

"What do you mean? You talk like you're dying."

"I am, Davidge. Zammis two hundredth generation . . . very important. Present my child, Davidge. Swear!"

I wiped the sweat from my face with my free hand. "You're not going to die, Jerry. Hang on!"

"Enough! Face truth, Davidge! I die! You must teach the line of Jeriba to Zammis . . . and the book, the *Talman, gavey?*"

"Stop it!" Panic stood over me almost as a physical presence. "Stop talking like that! You aren't going to die, Jerry. Come on; fight, you *kizlode* sonofabitch. . . ."

Jerry screamed. Its breathing was weak, and the Drac drifted in and out of consciousness. "Davidge."

"What?" I realized I was sobbing like a kid.

"Davidge, you must help Zammis come out."

"What . . . how? What in the hell are you talking about?"

Jerry turned its face to the wall of the cave. "Lift my jacket."

"What?"

"Lift my jacket, Davidge. Now!"

I pulled up the snakeskin jacket, exposing Jerry's swollen belly. The fold down the center was bright red and seeping a clear liquid. "What . . . what should I do?"

Jerry breathed rapidly, then held its breath. "Tear it open! You must tear it open, Davidge!"

"No!"

"Do it! Do it, or Zammis dies!"

"What do I care about your goddamn child, Jerry? What do I have to do to save you?"

"Tear it open . . ." whispered the Drac. "Take care of my child, *Irkmaan*. Present Zammis before the Jeriba archives. Swear this to me."

"Oh, Jerry . . ."

"*Swear this!*"

I nodded, hot, fat tears dribbling down my cheeks. "I swear it. . . ." Jerry relaxed its grip on my wrist and closed its eyes. I knelt next to the Drac, stunned. "No. No, no, no, no."

Tear it open! You must tear it open, Davidge!

I reached up a hand and gingerly touched the fold on Jerry's belly. I could feel life struggling beneath it, trying to escape the airless confines of the Drac's womb. I hated it; I hated the damned thing as I never hated anything before. Its struggles grew weaker, then stopped.

Present Zammis before the Jeriba archives. Swear this to me. . . .

I swear it. . . .

I lifted my other hand and inserted my thumbs into the fold and tugged gently. I increased the amount of force, then tore at Jerry's belly like a madman. The fold burst open, soaking the front of my jacket with the clear fluid. Holding the fold open, I could see the still form of Zammis huddled in a well of the fluid, motionless.

I vomited. When I had nothing more to throw up, I reached into the fluid and put my hands under the Drac infant. I lifted it, wiped my mouth on my upper left sleeve, and closed my mouth over Zammis's and pulled the child's mouth open with my right hand. Three times, four times, I inflated the child's lungs, then it coughed. Then it cried. I tied off the two umbilicals with berrybush fibre, then cut them. Jeriba Zammis was freed of the dead flesh of its parent.

I held the rock over my head, then brought it down with all of my force upon the ice. Shards splashed away from the point of impact, exposing the dark green beneath. Again, I lifted the rock and brought it down, knocking loose another rock. I picked it up, stood and carried it to the half-covered corpse of the Drac. "The Drac," I whispered. *Good. Just call it 'the Drac.' Toad face. Dragger.*

The enemy. Call it anything to insulate those feelings against the pain.

I looked at the pile of rocks I had gathered, decided it was sufficient to finish the job, then knelt next to the grave. As I placed the rocks on the pile, unmindful of the gale-blown sleet freezing on my snakeskins, I fought back the tears. I smacked my hands together to help restore the circulation. Spring was coming, but it was still dangerous to stay outside too long. And I had been a long time building the Drac's grave. I picked up another rock and placed it into position. As the rock's weight leaned against the snakeskin mattress cover, I realized that the Drac was already frozen. I quickly placed the remainder of the rocks, then stood.

The wind rocked me and I almost lost my footing on the ice next to the grave. I looked toward the boiling sea, pulled my snakeskins around myself more tightly, then looked down at the pile of rocks. *There should be words. You don't just cover up the dead, then go to dinner. There should be words.* But what words? I was no religionist, and neither was the Drac. Its formal philosophy on the matter of death was the same as my informal rejection of Islamic delights, pagan Valhallas, and Judeo-Christian pies in the sky. Death is death, *finis*, the end; the worms crawl in, the worms crawl out . . . *Still, there should be words.*

I reached beneath my snakeskins and clasped my gloved hand around the golden cube of the *Talman.* I felt the sharp corners of the cube through my glove, closed my eyes and ran through the words of the great Drac philosophers. But there was nothing they had written for this moment.

The *Talman* was a book on life. *Talma* means life, and this occupies Drac philosophy. They spare nothing for death. Death is a fact; the end of life. The *Talman* had no words for me to say. The wind knifed through me, causing me to shiver. Already my fingers were numb and pains were beginning in my feet. Still, there should be words. But the only words I could think of would open the gate, flooding my being with pain—with the realization that the Drac was gone. *Still . . . still, there should be words.*

"Jerry, I . . ." I had no words. I turned from the grave, my tears mixing with the sleet.

With the warmth and silence of the cave around me, I sat on my mattress, my back against the wall of the cave. I tried to lose myself in the shadows and flickers of light cast on the opposite wall by the fire. Images would half-form, then dance away before I could move my mind to see something in them. As a child I used to watch clouds, and in them see faces, castles, animals, dragons, and giants. It was a world of escape—fantasy; something to inject wonder and adventure into the mundane, regulated life of a middle-class boy leading a middle-class life. All I could see on the wall of the cave was a representation of Hell: flames licking at twisted, grotesque representations of condemned souls. I laughed at the thought. We think of Hell as fire, supervised by a cackling sadist in a red union suit. Fyrine IV had taught me this much: Hell is loneliness, hunger, and endless cold.

I heard a whimper, and I looked into the shadows toward the small mattress at the back of the cave. Jerry had made the snakeskin sack filled with seed-pod down for Zammis. It whimpered again, and I leaned forward, wondering if there was something it needed. A pang of fear tickled my guts. What does a Drac infant eat? Dracs aren't mammals. All they ever taught us in training was how to recognize Dracs—that, and how to kill them. Then real fear began working on me. "What in the hell am I going to use for diapers?"

It whimpered again. I pushed myself to my feet, walked the sandy floor to the infant's side, then knelt beside it. Out of the bundle that was Jerry's old flight suit, two chubby three-fingered arms waved. I picked up the bundle, carried it next to the fire, and sat on a rock. Balancing the bundle on my lap, I carefully unwrapped it. I could see the yellow glitter of Zammis's eyes beneath yellow, sleep-heavy lids. From the almost noseless face and solid teeth to its deep yellow color, Zammis was every bit a miniature of Jerry, except for the fat. Zammis fairly wallowed in rolls of fat. I looked and was grateful to find that there was no mess.

I looked into Zammis's face. "You want something to eat?"

"Guh."

Its jaws were ready for business, and I assumed that Dracs must chew solid food from day one. I reached over the fire and picked up a twist of dried snake, then touched it against the infant's lips. Zammis turned its head. "C'mon, eat. You're not going to find anything better around here."

I pushed the snake against its lips again, and Zammis pulled back a chubby arm and pushed it away. I shrugged. "Well, whenever you get hungry enough, it's there."

"Guh meh!" Its head rocked back and forth on my lap, a tiny, three-fingered hand closed around my finger; and it whimpered again.

"You don't want to eat, you don't need to be cleaned up, so what do you want? *Kos va nu?*"

Zammis's face wrinkled, and its hand pulled at my finger. Its other hand waved in the direction of my chest. I picked Zammis up to arrange the flight suit, and the tiny hands reached out, grasped the front of my snakeskins, and held on as the chubby arms pulled the child next to my chest. I held it close; it placed its cheek against my chest and promptly fell asleep. "Well . . . I'll be damned."

Until the Drac was gone, I never realized how closely I had stood near the edge of madness. My loneliness was a cancer—a growth that I fed with hate: hate for the planet with its endless cold, endless winds, and endless isolation; hate for the helpless yellow child with its clawing need for care, food, and an affection that I couldn't give; and hate for myself. I found myself doing things that frightened and disgusted me. To break my solid wall of being alone, I would talk, shout, and sing to myself—uttering curses, nonsense, or meaningless croaks.

Its eyes were open, and it waved a chubby arm and cooed. I picked up a large rock, staggered over to the child's side, and held the weight over the tiny body. "I could drop this thing, kid. Where would you be then?" I felt laughter coming from my lips. I threw the rock aside. "Why should I mess up the cave? Outside. Put you outside for a minute, and you die! You hear me? Die!"

The child worked its three-fingered hands at the empty air, shut its eyes, and cried. "Why don't you eat? Why don't you crap? Why don't you do anything right, but cry?" The child cried more loudly. "Bah! I ought to pick up that rock and finish it! That's what I ought . . ." A wave of revulsion stopped my words, and I went to my mattress, picked up my cap, gloves, and muff, then headed outside.

Before I came to the rocked-in entrance to the cave, I felt the

bite of the wind. Outside I stopped and looked at the sea and sky
—a roiling panorama in glorious black and white, grey and grey.
A gust of wind slapped against me, rocking me back toward the
entrance. I regained my balance, walked to the edge of the cliff
and shook my fist at the sea. "Go ahead! Go ahead and blow, you
kizlode sonofabitch! You haven't killed me yet!"

I squeezed the windburned lids of my eyes shut, then opened
them and looked down. A forty-meter drop to the next ledge, but
if I took a running jump, I could clear it. Then it would be a
hundred and fifty meters to the rocks below. *Jump.* I backed away
from the cliff's edge. "Jump! Sure, jump!" I shook my head at the
sea. "I'm not going to do your job for you! You want me dead,
you're going to have to do it yourself!"

I looked back and up, above the entrance to the cave. The sky
was darkening, and in a few hours, night would shroud the land-
scape. I turned toward the cleft in the rock that led to the scrub
forest above the cave.

I squatted next to the Drac's grave and studied the rocks I had
placed there, already fused together with a layer of ice. "Jerry.
What am I going to do?"

The Drac would sit by the fire, both of us sewing. And we talked.
"You know, Jerry, all this," I held up the Talman, *"I've heard it*
all before. I expected something different."
The Drac lowered its sewing to its lap and studied me for an
instant. Then it shook its head and resumed its sewing. "You are
not a terribly profound creature, Davidge."
"What's that supposed to mean?"
Jerry held out a three-fingered hand. "A universe, Davidge—
there is a universe out there, a universe of life, objects, and events.
There are differences, but it is all the same universe, and we all
must obey the same universal laws. Did you ever think of
that?"
"No."
"That is what I mean, Davidge. Not terribly profound."
I snorted. "I told you, I'd heard this stuff before. So I imagine
that shows humans to be just as profound as Dracs."
Jerry laughed. "You always insist on making something racial

out of my observations. What I said applied to you, not to the race of humans. . . ."

I spat on the frozen ground. "You Dracs think you're so damned smart." The wind picked up, and I could taste the sea salt in it. One of the big blows was coming. The sky was changing to that curious darkness that tricked me into thinking it was midnight blue, rather than black. A trickle of ice found its way under my collar.

"What's wrong with me just being me? Everybody in the universe doesn't have to be a damned philosopher, toadface!" There were millions—billions—like me. More, maybe. "What difference does it make to anything whether I ponder existence or not? It's here; that's all I have to know."

"Davidge, you don't even know your family line beyond your parents, and now you say you refuse to know that of your universe that you can know. How will you know your place in this existence, Davidge? Where are you? Who are you?"

I shook my head and stared at the grave, then I turned and faced the sea. In another hour, or less, it would be too dark to see the whitecaps. "I'm me, that's who." But was that "me" who held the rock over Zammis, threatening a helpless infant with death? I felt my guts curdle as the loneliness I thought I felt grew claws and fangs and began gnawing and slashing at the remains of my sanity. I turned back to the grave, closed my eyes, then opened them. "I'm a fighter pilot, Jerry. Isn't that something?"

"That is what you do, Davidge; that is not who nor what you are."

I knelt next to the grave and clawed at the ice-sheathed rocks with my hands. "You don't talk to me now, Drac! *You're dead!*" I stopped, realizing that the words I had heard were from the *Talman,* processed into my own context. I slumped against the rocks, felt the wind, then pushed myself to my feet. "Jerry, Zammis won't eat. It's been three days. What do I do? Why didn't you tell me anything about Drac brats before you . . ." I held my hands to

my face. "Steady, boy. Keep it up, and they'll stick you in a home."
The wind pressed against my back; I lowered my hands, then
walked from the grave.

I sat in the cave, staring at the fire. I couldn't hear the wind
through the rock, and the wood was dry, making the fire hot and
quiet. I tapped my fingers against my knees, then began humming. Noise, any kind, helped to drive off the oppressive loneliness. "Sonofabitch." I laughed and nodded. "Yea, verily, and *kizlode va nu, dutschaat.*" I chuckled, trying to think of all the
curses and obscenities in Drac that I had learned from Jerry. There
were quite a few. My toe tapped against the sand and my humming started up again. I stopped, frowned, then remembered the
song.

> Highty tighty Christ almighty,
> Who the hell are we?
> Zim zam, Gawd Damn,
> We're in Squadron B.

I leaned back against the wall of the cave, trying to remember
another verse. *A pilot's got a rotten life / no crumpets with our
tea / we have to service the general's wife / and pick fleas from her
knee.* "Damn!" I slapped my knee, trying to see the faces of the
other pilots in the squadron lounge. I could almost feel the whiskey fumes tickling the inside of my nose. Vadik, Wooster, Arnold
. . . the one with the broken nose—Demerest, Kadiz. I hummed
again, swinging an imaginary mug of issue grog by its imaginary
handle.

> And, if he doesn't like it,
> I'll tell you what we'll do:
> We'll fill his ass with broken glass,
> and seal it up with glue.

The cave echoed with the song. I stood, threw up my arms and
screamed. "Yaaaaahoooooo!"
Zammis began crying. I bit my lip and walked over to the bundle on the mattress. "Well? You ready to eat?"
"Unh, unh, weh." The infant rocked its head back and forth. I

went to the fire, picked up a twist of snake, then returned. I knelt next to Zammis and held the snake to its lips. Again, the child pushed it away. "Come on, you. You have to eat." I tried again with the same results. I took the wraps off the child and looked at its body. I could tell it was losing weight, although Zammis didn't appear to be getting weak. I shrugged, wrapped it up again, stood, and began walking back to my mattress.

"Guh, weh."

I turned. "What?"

"Ah, guh, guh."

I went back, stooped over and picked the child up. Its eyes were open and it looked into my face, then smiled.

"What're you laughing at, ugly? You should get a load of your own face."

Zammis barked out a short laugh, then gurgled. I went to my mattress, sat down, and arranged Zammis in my lap. "Gumma, buh, buh." Its hand grabbed a loose flap of snakeskin on my shirt and pulled on it.

"Gumma buh buh to you, too. So, what do we do now? How about I start teaching you the line of Jeriba? You're going to have to learn it sometime, and it might as well be now." The Jeriban line. My recitations of the line were the only things Jerry ever complimented me about. I looked into Zammis's eyes. "When I bring you to stand before the Jeriba archives, you will say this: 'Before you here I stand, Zammis of the line of Jeriba, born of Shigan, the fighter pilot.' " I smiled, thinking of the upraised yellow brows if Zammis continued: "*and, by damn, Shigan was a helluva good pilot, too. Why, I was once told he took a smart round in his tail feathers, then pulled around and rammed the* kizlode *sonofabitch, known to one and all as Willis E. Davidge . . .*" I shook my head. "You're not going to get your wings by doing the line in English, Zammis." I began again:

"*Naatha nu enta va, Zammis zea does Jeriba, estay va Shigan, asaam naa denvadar. . . .*"

For eight of those long days and nights, I feared the child would die. I tried everything—roots, dried berries, dried plumfruit, snakemeat dried, boiled, chewed, and ground. Zammis refused it all. I checked frequently, but each time I looked through the child's wraps, they were as clean as when I had put them on. Zammis lost weight, but seemed to grow stronger. By the ninth day it was crawling the floor of the cave. Even with the fire, the cave wasn't really warm. I feared that the kid would get sick crawling around naked, and I dressed it in the tiny snakeskin suit and cap Jerry had made for it. After dressing it, I stood Zammis up and looked at it. The kid had already developed a smile full of mischief that, combined with the twinkle in its yellow eyes and its suit and cap, made it look like an elf. I was holding Zammis up in a standing position. The kid seemed pretty steady on its legs, and I let go. Zammis smiled, waved its thinning arms about, then laughed and took a faltering step toward me. I caught it as it fell, and the little Drac squealed.

In two more days Zammis was walking and getting into everything that could be gotten into. I spent many an anxious moment searching the chambers at the back of the cave for the kid after coming in from outside. Finally, when I caught him at the mouth of the cave heading full steam for the outside, I had had enough. I made a harness out of snakeskin, attached it to a snake-leather leash, and tied the other end to a projection of rock above my head. Zammis still got into everything, but at least I could find it.

Four days after it learned to walk, it wanted to eat. Drac babies are probably the most convenient and considerate infants in the universe. They live off their fat for about three or four Earth weeks, and don't make a mess the entire time. After they learn to walk, and can therefore make it to a mutually agreed upon spot, then they want food and begin discharging wastes. I showed the kid once how to use the litter box I had made, and never had to again. After five or six lessons, Zammis was handling its own drawers. Watching the little Drac learn and grow, I began to understand those pilots in my squadron who used to bore each other—and everyone else—with countless pictures of ugly children, accompanied by thirty-minute narratives for each snapshot. Before the ice melted, Zammis was talking. I taught it to call me "Uncle."

For lack of a better term, I called the ice-melting season "spring." It would be a long time before the scrub forest showed any green or the snakes ventured forth from their icy holes. The sky maintained its eternal cover of dark, angry clouds, and still the sleet would come and coat everything with a hard, slippery glaze. But the next day the glaze would melt, and the warmer air would push another millimeter into the soil.

I realized that this was the time to be gathering wood. Before the winter hit, Jerry and I working together hadn't gathered enough wood. The short summer would have to be spent putting up food for the next winter. I was hoping to build a tighter door over the mouth of the cave, and I swore that I would figure out some kind of indoor plumbing. Dropping your drawers outside in the middle of winter was dangerous. My mind was full of these things as I stretched out on my mattress watching the smoke curl through a crack in the roof of the cave. Zammis was off in the back of the cave playing with some rocks that it had found, and I must have fallen asleep. I awoke with the kid shaking my arm.

"Uncle?"

"Huh? Zammis?"

"Uncle. Look."

I rolled over on my left side and faced the Drac. Zammis was holding up his right hand, fingers spread out. "What is it, Zammis?"

"Look." It pointed at each of its three fingers in turn. "One, two, three."

"So?"

"Look." Zammis grabbed my right hand and spread out the fingers. "One, two, three, *four, five!*"

I nodded. "So you can count to five."

The Drac frowned and made an impatient gesture with its tiny fists. "Look." It took my outstretched hand and placed its own on top of it. With its other hand, Zammis pointed first at one of its own fingers, then at one of mine. "One, one." The child's yellow eyes studied me to see if I understood.

"Yes."

The child pointed again. "Two, two." It looked at me, then looked back at my hand and pointed. "Three, three." Then he grabbed my two remaining fingers. *"Four, Five!"* It dropped my hand, then pointed to the side of its own hand. "Four, five?"

I shook my head. Zammis, at less than four Earth months old, had detected part of the difference between Dracs and humans. A human child would be—what—five, six, or seven years old before asking questions like that. I sighed. "Zammis."

"Yes, Uncle?"

"Zammis, you are a Drac. Dracs only have three fingers on a hand." I held up my right hand and wiggled the fingers. "I'm a human. I have five."

I swear that tears welled in the child's eyes. Zammis held out its hands, looked at them, then shook its head. "Grow four, five?"

I sat up and faced the kid. Zammis was wondering where its other four fingers had gone. "Look, Zammis. You and I are different . . . different kinds of beings, understand?"

Zammis shook his head. "Grow four, five?"

"You won't. You're a Drac." I pointed at my chest. "I'm a human." This was getting me nowhere. "Your parent, where you came from, was a Drac. Do you understand?"

Zammis frowned. "Drac. What Drac?"

The urge to resort to the timeless standby of "you'll understand when you get older" pounded at the back of my mind. I shook my head. "Dracs have three fingers on each hand. Your parent had three fingers on each hand." I rubbed my beard. "My parent was a human and had five fingers on each hand. That's why I have five fingers on each hand."

Zammis knelt on the sand and studied its fingers. It looked up at me, back to its hands, then back to me. "What parent?"

I studied the kid. It must be having an identity crisis of some kind. I was the only person it had ever seen, and I had five fingers per hand. "A parent is . . . the thing . . ." I scratched my beard again. "Look . . . we all come from someplace. I had a mother and father—two different kinds of humans—that gave me life; that made me, understand?"

Zammis gave me a look that could be interpreted as "Mac, you are full of it." I shrugged. "I don't know if I can explain it."

Zammis pointed at its own chest. "My mother? My father?"

I held out my hands, dropped them into my lap, pursed my lips, scratched my beard, and generally stalled for time. Zammis held an unblinking gaze on me the entire time. "Look, Zammis. You don't have a mother and a father. I'm a human, so I have them; you're a Drac. You have a parent—just one, see?"

Zammis shook its head. It looked at me, then pointed at its own chest. "Drac."

"Right."

Zammis pointed at my chest. "Human."

"Right again."

Zammis removed its hand and dropped it in its lap. "Where Drac come from?"

Sweet Jesus! Trying to explain hermaphroditic reproduction to a kid who shouldn't even be crawling yet! "Zammis . . ." I held up my hands, then dropped them into my lap. "Look. You see how much bigger I am than you?"

"Yes, Uncle."

"Good." I ran my fingers through my hair, fighting for time and inspiration. "Your parent was big, like me. Its name was . . . Jeriba Shigan." Funny how just saying the name was painful. "Jeriba Shigan was like you. It only had three fingers on each hand. It grew you in its tummy." I poked Zammis's middle. "Understand?"

Zammis giggled and held its hands over its stomach. "Uncle, how Dracs grow there?"

I lifted my legs onto the mattress and stretched out. Where do little Dracs come from? I looked over to Zammis and saw the child hanging upon my every word. I grimaced and told the truth. "Damned if I know, Zammis. Damned if I know." Thirty seconds later, Zammis was back playing with its rocks.

Summer, and I taught Zammis how to capture and skin the long grey snakes, and then how to smoke the meat. The child would squat on the shallow bank above a mudpool, its yellow eyes fixed on the snake holes in the bank, waiting for one of the occupants to poke out its head. The wind would blow, but Zammis wouldn't move. Then a flat, triangular head set with tiny blue eyes would appear. The snake would check the pool, turn and check the bank, then check the sky. It would advance out of the hole a bit, then check it all again. Often the snakes would look directly at Zammis, but the Drac could have been carved from rock. Zammis wouldn't move until the snake was too far out of the hole to pull itself back in tail first. Then Zammis would strike, grabbing the snake with both hands just behind the head. The snakes had no fangs and weren't poisonous, but they were lively enough to toss Zammis into the mudpool on occasion.

The skins were spread and wrapped around tree trunks and pegged in place to dry. The tree trunks were kept in an open place near the entrance to the cave, but under an overhang that faced away from the ocean. About two thirds of the skins put up in this manner cured; the remaining third would rot.

Beyond the skin room was the smokehouse: a rock-walled chamber that we would hang with rows of snakemeat. A green-wood fire would be set in a pit in the chamber's floor, then we would fill in the small opening with rocks and dirt.

"Uncle, why doesn't the meat rot after it's smoked?"

I thought upon it. "I'm not sure; I just know it doesn't."

"Why do you know?"

I shrugged. "I just do. I read about it, probably."

"What's read?"

"Reading. Like when I sit down and read the *Talman*."

"Does the *Talman* say why the meat doesn't rot?"

"No. I meant that I probably read it in another book."

"Do we have more books?"

I shook my head. "I meant before I came to this planet."

"Why did you come to this planet?"

"I told you. Your parent and I were stranded here during the battle."

"Why do the humans and Dracs fight?"

"It's very complicated." I waved my hands about for a bit. The human line was that the Dracs were aggressors invading our space. The Drac line was that the humans were aggressors invading their space. The truth? "Zammis, it has to do with the colonization of new planets. Both races are expanding and both races have a tradition of exploring and colonizing new planets. I guess we just expanded into each other. Understand?"

Zammis nodded, then became mercifully silent as it fell into deep thought. The main thing I learned from the Drac child was all of the questions I didn't have answers to. I was feeling very smug, however, at having gotten Zammis to understand about the war, thereby avoiding my ignorance on the subject of preserving meat. "Uncle?"

"Yes, Zammis?"

"What's a planet?"

As the cold, wet summer came to an end, we had the cave jammed with firewood and preserved food. With that out of the way, I concentrated my efforts on making some kind of indoor plumbing out of the natural pools in the chambers deep within the cave. The bathtub was no problem. By dropping heated rocks into one of the pools, the water could be brought up to a bearable—even comfortable—temperature. After bathing, the hollow stems of a bamboo-like plant could be used to siphon out the dirty water. The tub could then be refilled from the pool above. The problem was where to siphon the water. Several of the chambers had holes in their floors. The first three holes we tried drained into our main chamber, wetting the low edge near the entrance. The previous winter, Jerry and I had considered using one of those holes for a toilet that we would flush with water from the pools. Since we didn't know where the goodies would come out, we decided against it.

The fourth hole Zammis and I tried drained out below the entrance to the cave in the face of the cliff. Not ideal, but better than answering the call of nature in the middle of a combination ice-storm and blizzard. We rigged up the hole as a drain for both the tub and toilet. As Zammis and I prepared to enjoy our first hot bath, I removed my snakeskins, tested the water with my toe, then stepped in. "Great!" I turned to Zammis, the child still half-dressed. "Come on in, Zammis. The water's fine." Zammis was staring at me, its mouth hanging open. "What's the matter?"

The child stared wide-eyed, then pointed at me with a three-fingered hand. "Uncle . . . what's that?"

I looked down. "Oh." I shook my head, then looked up at the child. "Zammis, I explained all that, remember? I'm a human."

"But what's it *for?*"

I sat down in the warm water, removing the object of discussion from sight. "It's for the elimination of liquid wastes . . . among other things. Now, hop in and get washed."

Zammis shucked its snakeskins, looked down at its own smooth-surfaced, combined system, then climbed into the tub. The child settled into the water up to its neck, its yellow eyes studying me. "Uncle?"

"Yes?"

"What *other things?*"

Well, I told Zammis. For the first time, the Drac appeared to be trying to decide whether my response was truthful or not, rather than its usual acceptance of my every assertion. In fact, I was convinced that Zammis thought I was lying—probably because I was.

Winter began with a sprinkle of snowflakes carried on a gentle breeze. I took Zammis above the cave to the scrub forest. I held the child's hand as we stood before the pile of rocks that served as Jerry's grave. Zammis pulled its snakeskins against the wind, bowed its head, then turned and looked up into my face. "Uncle, this is the grave of my parent?"

I nodded. "Yes."

Zammis turned back to the grave, then shook its head. "Uncle, how should I feel?"

"I don't understand, Zammis."

The child nodded at the grave. "I can see that you are sad being here. I think you want me to feel the same. Do you?"

I frowned, then shook my head. "No. I don't want you to be sad. I just wanted you to know where it is."

"May I go now?"

"Sure. Are you certain you know the way back to the cave?"

"Yes. I just want to make sure my soap doesn't burn again."

I watched as the child turned and scurried off into the naked trees, then I turned back to the grave. "Well, Jerry, what do you think of your kid? Zammis was using wood ashes to clean the grease off the shells, then it put a shell back on the fire and put water in it to boil off the burnt-on food. Fat and ashes. The next thing, Jerry, we were making soap. Zammis's first batch almost took the hide off us, but the kid's getting better . . ."

I looked up at the clouds, then brought my glance down to the sea. In the distance, low, dark clouds were building up. "See that?

You know what that means, don't you? Ice-storm number one."
The wind picked up and I squatted next to the grave to replace
a rock that had rolled from the pile. "Zammis is a good kid, Jerry.
I wanted to hate it . . . after you died. I wanted to hate it." I
replaced the rock, then looked back toward the sea.

"I don't know how we're going to make it off planet, Jerry—"
I caught a flash of movement out of the corner of my vision. I
turned to the right and looked over the tops of the trees. Against
the grey sky, a black speck streaked away. I followed it with my
eyes until it went above the clouds.

I listened, hoping to hear an exhaust roar, but my heart was
pounding so hard, all I could hear was the wind. Was it a ship? I
stood, took a few steps in the direction the speck was going, then
stopped. Turning my head, I saw that the rocks on Jerry's grave
were already capped with thin layers of fine snow. I shrugged and
headed for the cave. "Probably just a bird."

Zammis sat on its mattress, stabbing several pieces of snakeskin
with a bone needle. I stretched out on my own mattress and
watched the smoke curl up toward the crack in the ceiling. Was
it a bird? Or was it a ship? Damn, but it worked on me. Escape
from the planet had been out of my thoughts, had been buried,
hidden for all that summer. But again, it twisted at me. To walk
where a sun shined, to wear cloth again, experience central heat-
ing, eat food prepared by a chef, to be among . . . people again.

I rolled over on my right side and stared at the wall next to my
mattress. People. Human people. I closed my eyes and swallowed.
Girl human people. Female persons. Images drifted before my
eyes—faces, bodies, laughing couples, the dance after flight training . . . what was her name? Dolora? Dora?

I shook my head, rolled over and sat up, facing the fire. Why did
I have to see whatever it was? All those things I had been able to
bury—to forget—boiling over.

"Uncle?"

I looked up at Zammis. Yellow skin, yellow eyes, noseless toad
face. I shook my head. "What?"

"Is something wrong?"

Is something wrong, hah. "No. I just thought I saw something

today. It probably wasn't anything." I reached to the fire and took
a piece of dried snake from the griddle. I blew on it, then gnawed
on the stringy strip.

"What did it look like?"

"I don't know. The way it moved, I thought it might be a ship.
It went away so fast, I couldn't be sure. Might have been a bird."

"Bird?"

I studied Zammis. It'd never seen a bird; neither had I on Fyrine
IV. "An animal that flies."

Zammis nodded. "Uncle, when we were gathering wood up in
the scrub forest, I saw something fly."

"What? Why didn't you tell me?"

"I meant to, but I forgot."

"Forgot!" I frowned. "In which direction was it going?"

Zammis pointed to the back of the cave. "That way. Away from
the sea." Zammis put down its sewing. "Can we go see where it
went?"

I shook my head. "The winter is just beginning. You don't know
what it's like. We'd die in only a few days."

Zammis went back to poking holes in the snakeskin. To make
the trek in the winter would kill us. But spring would be something else. We could survive with double-layered snakeskins
stuffed with seed-pod down, and a tent. We had to have a tent.
Zammis and I could spend the winter making it, and packs. Boots.
We'd need sturdy walking boots. Have to think on that. . . .

It's strange how a spark of hope can ignite, and spread, until all
desperation is consumed. Was it a ship? I didn't know. If it was, was
it taking off, or landing? I didn't know. If it was taking off, we'd
be heading in the wrong direction. But the opposite direction
meant crossing the sea. Whatever. Come spring we would head
beyond the scrub forest and see what was there.

The winter seemed to pass quickly, with Zammis occupied with
the tent and my time devoted to rediscovering the art of boot
making. I made tracings of both of our feet on snakeskin, and after
some experimentation, I found that boiling the snake leather with
plumfruit made it soft and gummy. By taking several of the
gummy layers, weighting them, then setting them aside to dry,

the result was a tough, flexible sole. By the time I finished Zammis's boots, the Drac needed a new pair.

"They're too small, Uncle."

"Waddaya mean, too small?"

Zammis pointed down. "They hurt. My toes are all crippled up."

I squatted down and felt the tops over the child's toes. "I don't understand. It's only been twenty, twenty-five days since I made the tracings. You sure you didn't move when I made them?"

Zammis shook its head. "I didn't move."

I frowned, then stood. "Stand up, Zammis." The Drac stood and I moved next to it. The top of Zammis's head came to the middle of my chest. Another sixty centimeters and it'd be as tall as Jerry. "Take them off, Zammis. I'll make a bigger pair. Try not to grow so fast."

Zammis pitched the tent inside the cave, put glowing coals inside, then rubbed fat into the leather for waterproofing. It had grown taller, and I had held off making the Drac's boots until I could be sure of the size it would need. I tried to do a projection by measuring Zammis's feet every ten days, then extending the curve into spring. According to my figures, the kid would have feet resembling a pair of attack transports by the time the snow melted. By spring, Zammis would be full grown. Jerry's old flight boots had fallen apart before Zammis had been born, but I had saved the pieces. I used the soles to make my tracings and hoped for the best.

I was busy with the new boots and Zammis was keeping an eye on the tent treatment. The Drac looked back at me.

"Uncle?"

"What?"

"Existence is the first given?"

I shrugged. "That's what Shizumaat says; I'll buy it."

"But, Uncle, how do we *know* that existence is real?"

I lowered my work, looked at Zammis, shook my head, then resumed stitching the boots. "Take my word for it."

The Drac grimaced. "But, Uncle, that is not knowledge; that is faith."

I sighed, thinking back to my sophomore year at the University of Nations—a bunch of adolescents lounging around a cheap flat experimenting with booze, powders, and philosophy. At a little more than one Earth-year old, Zammis was developing into an intellectual bore. "So, what's wrong with faith?"

Zammis snickered. "Come now, Uncle. *Faith?*"

"It helps some of us along this drizzle-soaked coil."

"Coil?"

I scratched my head. "This mortal coil; life. Shakespeare, I think."

Zammis frowned. "It is not in the *Talman.*"

"He, not it. Shakespeare was a human."

Zammis stood, walked to the fire and sat across from me. "Was he a philosopher, like Mistan or Shizumaat?"

"No. He wrote plays—like stories, acted out."

Zammis rubbed its chin. "Do you remember any of Shakespeare?"

I held up a finger. " 'To be, or not to be; that is the question.' "

The Drac's mouth dropped open, then it nodded its head. "Yes. Yes! To be or not to be; that *is* the question!" Zammis held out its hands. "How do we *know* the wind blows outside the cave when we are not there to see it? Does the sea still boil if we are not there to feel it?"

I nodded. "Yes."

"But, Uncle, how do we *know?*"

I squinted at the Drac. "Zammis, I have a question for you. Is the following statement true or false: What I am saying right now is false."

Zammis blinked. "If it is false, then the statement is true. But . . . if it's true . . . the statement is false, but . . ." Zammis blinked again, then turned and went back to rubbing fat into the tent. "I'll think upon it, Uncle."

"You do that, Zammis."

The Drac thought upon it for about ten minutes, then turned back. "The statement is false."

I smiled. "But that's what the statement said, hence it is true, but . . ." I let the puzzle trail off. Oh, smugness, thou temptest even saints.

"No, Uncle. The statement is meaningless in its present context." I shrugged. "You see, Uncle, the statement assumes the existence of truth values that can comment upon themselves devoid of any other reference. I think Lurrvena's logic in the *Talman* is clear on this, and if meaninglessness is equated with falsehood . . ."

I sighed. "Yeah, well—"

"You see, Uncle, you must first establish a context in which your statement has meaning."

I leaned forward, frowned, and scratched my beard. "I see. You mean I was putting Descartes before the horse?"

Zammis looked at me strangely, and even more so when I collapsed on my mattress cackling like a fool.

"Uncle, why does the line of Jeriba have only five names? You say that human lines have many names."

I nodded. "The five names of the Jeriba line are things to which their bearers must add deeds. The deeds are important—not the names."

"Gothig is Shigan's parent as Shigan is my parent."

"Of course. You know that from your recitations."

Zammis frowned. "Then, I *must* name my child Ty when I become a parent?"

"Yes. And Ty must name its child Haesni. Do you see something wrong with that?"

"I would like to name my child Davidge, after you."

I smiled and shook my head. "The Ty name has been served by great bankers, merchants, inventors, and—well, you know your recitation. The name Davidge hasn't been served by much. Think of what Ty would miss by not being Ty."

Zammis thought awhile, then nodded. "Uncle, do you think Gothig is alive?"

"As far as I know."

"What is Gothig like?"

I thought back to Jerry talking about its parent, Gothig. "It taught music, and is very strong. Jerry . . . Shigan said that its parent could bend metal bars with its fingers. Gothig is also very dignified. I imagine that right now Gothig is also very sad. Gothig must think that the line of Jeriba has ended."

Zammis frowned and its yellow brow furrowed. "Uncle, we must make it to Draco. We must tell Gothig the line continues."

"We will."

The winter's ice began thinning, and boots, tent, and packs were ready. We were putting the finishing touches on our new insulated suits. As Jerry had given the *Talman* to me to learn, the golden cube now hung around Zammis's neck. The Drac would drop the tiny golden book from the cube and study it for hours at a time.

"Uncle?"

"What?"

"Why do Dracs speak and write in one language and the humans in another?"

I laughed. "Zammis, the humans speak and write in many languages. English is just one of them."

"How do the humans speak among themselves?"

I shrugged. "They don't always; when they do, they use interpreters—people who can speak both languages."

"You and I speak both English and Drac; does that make us interpreters?"

"I suppose we could be, if you could ever find a human and a Drac who want to talk to each other. Remember, there's a war going on."

"How will the war stop if they do not talk?"

"I suppose they will talk, eventually."

Zammis smiled. "I think I would like to be an interpreter and help end the war." The Drac put its sewing aside and stretched out on its new mattress. Zammis had outgrown even its old mattress, which it now used for a pillow. "Uncle, do you think that we will find anybody beyond the scrub forest?"

"I hope so."

"If we do, will you go with me to Draco?"

"I promised your parent that I would."

"I mean, after. After I make my recitation, what will you do?"

I stared at the fire. "I don't know." I shrugged. "The war might keep us from getting to Draco for a long time."

"After that, what?"

"I suppose I'll go back into the service."

Zammis propped itself up on an elbow. "Go back to being a fighter pilot?"

"Sure. That's about all I know how to do."

"And kill Dracs?"

I put my own sewing down and studied the Drac. Things had changed since Jerry and I had slugged it out—more things than I had realized. I shook my head. "No. I probably won't be a pilot—not a service one. Maybe I can land a job flying commercial ships." I shrugged. "Maybe the service won't give me any choice."

Zammis sat up and was still for a moment; then it stood, walked over to my mattress and knelt before me on the sand. "Uncle, I don't want to leave you."

"Don't be silly. You'll have your own kind around you. Your grandparent, Gothig, Shigan's siblings, their children—you'll forget all about me."

"Will you forget about me?"

I looked into those yellow eyes, then reached out my hand and touched Zammis's cheek. "No. I won't forget about you. But, remember this, Zammis: you're a Drac and I'm a human, and that's how this part of the universe is divided."

Zammis took my hand from his cheek, spread the fingers and studied them. "Whatever happens, Uncle, I will never forget you."

The ice was gone, and the Drac and I stood in the windblown drizzle, packs on our backs, before the grave. Zammis was as tall as I was, which made it a little taller than Jerry. To my relief, the boots fit. Zammis hefted its pack up higher on its shoulders, then turned from the grave and looked out at the sea. I followed Zammis's glance and watched the rollers steam in and smash on the rocks. I looked at the Drac. "What are you thinking about?"

Zammis looked down, then turned toward me. "Uncle, I didn't think of it before, but . . . I will miss this place."

I laughed. "Nonsense! This place?" I slapped the Drac on the shoulder. "Why would you miss this place?"

Zammis looked back out to sea. "I have learned many things here. You have taught me many things here, Uncle. My life happened here."

"Only the beginning, Zammis. You have a life ahead of you." I nodded my head at the grave. "Say good-bye."

Zammis turned toward the grave; stood over it, then knelt to one side and began removing the rocks. After a few moments, it had exposed the hand of a skeleton with three fingers. Zammis nodded, then wept. "I am sorry, Uncle, but I had to do that. This has been nothing but a pile of rocks to me. Now it is more." Zammis replaced the rocks, then stood.

I cocked my head toward the scrub forest. "Go on ahead. I'll catch up in a minute."

"Yes, Uncle."

Zammis moved off toward the naked trees, and I looked down at the grave. "What do you think of Zammis, Jerry? It's bigger than you were. I guess snake agrees with the kid." I squatted next to the grave, picked up a small rock and added it to the pile. "I guess this is it. We're either going to make it to Draco, or die trying." I stood and looked at the sea. "Yeah, I guess I learned a few things here. I'll miss it, in a way." I turned back to the grave and hefted my pack up. *"Ehdevva sahn, Jeriba Shigan.* So long, Jerry."

I turned and followed Zammis into the forest.

The days that followed were full of wonder for Zammis. For me, the sky was still the same, dull grey, and the few variations in plant and animal life that we found were nothing remarkable. Once we got beyond the scrub forest, we climbed a gentle rise for a day, and then found ourselves on a wide, flat, endless plain. It was ankle deep in a purple weed that stained our boots the same color. The nights were still too cold for hiking, and we would hole up in the tent. Both the greased tent and suits worked well keeping out the almost constant rain.

We had been out perhaps two of Fyrine IV's long weeks when we saw it. It screamed overhead, then disappeared over the horizon before either of us could say a word. I had no doubt that the craft I had seen was in landing attitude.

"Uncle! Did it see us?"

I shook my head. "No. I doubt it. But it was landing. Do you hear? It was landing somewhere ahead."

"Uncle?"

"Let's get moving! What is it?"

"Was it a Drac ship, or a human ship?"

I cooled in my tracks. I had never stopped to think about it. I waved my hand. "Come on. It doesn't matter. Either way, you go to Draco. You're a noncombatant, so the USE forces couldn't do anything, and if they're Dracs, you're home free."

We began walking. "But, Uncle, if it's a Drac ship, what will happen to you?"

I shrugged. "Prisoner of war. The Dracs say they abide by the interplanetary war accords, so I should be all right." *Fat chance*, said the back of my head to the front of my head. The big question was whether I preferred being a Drac POW or a permanent resident of Fyrine IV. I had figured that out long ago. "Come on, let's pick up the pace. We don't know how long it will take to get there, or how long it will be on the ground."

Pick 'em up; put 'em down. Except for a few breaks, we didn't stop—even when night came. Our exertion kept us warm. The horizon never seemed to grow nearer. The longer we slogged at it, the duller my mind grew. It must have been days, my mind as numb as my feet, when I fell through the purple weed into a hole. Immediately, everything grew dark, and I felt a pain in my right leg. I felt the blackout coming, and I welcomed its warmth, its rest, its peace.

"Uncle? Uncle? Wake up! Please, wake up!"

I felt slapping against my face, although it felt somehow detached. Agony thundered into my brain, bringing me wide awake. Damned if I didn't break my leg. I looked up and saw the weedy edges of the hole. My rear end was seated in a trickle of water. Zammis squatted next to me.

"What happened?"

Zammis motioned upwards. "This hole was only covered by a thin crust of dirt and plants. The water must have taken the ground away. Are you all right?"

"My leg. I think I broke it." I leaned my back against the muddy wall. "Zammis, you're going to have to go on by yourself."

"I can't leave you, Uncle!"

"Look, if you find anyone, you can send them back for me."

"What if the water in here comes up?" Zammis felt along my leg until I winced. "I must carry you out of here. What must I do for the leg?"

The kid had a point. Drowning wasn't in my schedule. "We need something stiff. Bind the leg so it doesn't move."

Zammis pulled off its pack, and kneeling in the water and mud, went through its pack, then through the tent roll. Using the tent poles, it wrapped my leg with snakeskins torn from the tent. Then, using more snakeskins, Zammis made two loops, slipped one over each of my legs, then propped me up and slipped the loops over its shoulders. It lifted, and I blacked out.

On the ground, covered with the remains of the tent, Zammis shaking my arm. "Uncle? Uncle?"

"Yes?" I whispered.

"Uncle, I'm ready to go." It pointed to my side. "Your food is here, and when it rains, just pull the tent over your face. I'll mark the trail I make so I can find my way back."

I nodded. "Take care of yourself."

Zammis shook its head. "Uncle, I can carry you. We shouldn't separate."

I weakly shook my head. "Give me a break, kid. I couldn't make it. Find somebody and bring 'em back." I felt my stomach flip, and cold sweat drenched my snakeskins. "Go on; get going."

Zammis reached out, grabbed its pack and stood. The pack shouldered, Zammis turned and began running in the direction that the craft had been going. I watched until I couldn't see it. I faced up and looked at the clouds. "You almost got me that time, you *kizlode* sonofabitch, but you didn't figure on the Drac . . . you keep forgetting . . . there's two of us. . . . " I drifted in and out of consciousness, felt rain on my face, then pulled up the tent and covered my head. In seconds, the blackout returned.

"Davidge? Lieutenant Davidge?"

I opened my eyes and saw something I hadn't seen for four Earth years: a human face. "Who are you?"

The face, young, long, and capped by short blond hair, smiled. "I'm Captain Steerman, the medical officer. How do you feel?"

I pondered the question and smiled. "Like I've been shot full of very high grade junk."

"You have. You were in pretty bad shape by the time the survey team brought you in."

"Survey team?"

"I guess you don't know. The United States of Earth and the Dracon Chamber have established a joint commission to supervise the colonization of new planets. The war is over."

"Over?"

"Yes."

Something heavy lifted from my chest. "Where's Zammis?"

"Who?"

"Jeriban Zammis; the Drac that I was with."

The doctor shrugged. "I don't know anything about it, but I suppose the Draggers are taking care of it."

Draggers. I'd once used the term myself. As I listened to it coming out of Steerman's mouth, it seemed foreign: alien, repulsive. "Zammis is a Drac, not a Dragger."

The doctor's brows furrowed, then he shrugged. "Of course. Whatever you say. Just you get some rest, and I'll check back on you in a few hours."

"May I see Zammis?"

The doctor smiled. "Dear, no. You're on your way back to the Delphi USEB. The . . . Drac is probably on its way to Draco." He nodded, then turned and left. God, I felt lost. I looked around and saw that I was in the ward of a ship's sick bay. The beds on either side of me were occupied. The man on my right shook his head and went back to reading a magazine. The one on my left looked angry.

"You damned Dragger suck!" He turned on his left side and presented me his back.

Among humans once again, yet more alone than I had ever been. *Misnuuram va siddeth,* as Mistan observed in the *Talman* from the calm perspective of eight hundred years in the past. Loneliness is a thought—not something done to someone; instead, it is something that someone does to oneself. *Jerry shook its head that one time, then pointed a yellow finger at me as the words it wanted to say came together. "Davidge . . . to me loneliness is a discomfort—a small thing to be avoided if possible, but not feared. I think you would almost prefer death to being alone with yourself."*

Misnuuram yaa va nos misnuuram van dunos. "You who are alone by yourselves will forever be alone with others." Mistan again. On its face, the statement appears to be a contradiction; but the test of reality proves it true. I was a stranger among my own kind because of a hate that I didn't share, and a love that, to them, seemed alien, impossible, perverse. *"Peace of thought with others occurs only in the mind at peace with itself."* Mistan again. Countless times, on the voyage to the Delphi Base, putting in my ward time, then during my processing out of the service, I would reach to my chest to grasp the *Talman* that no longer hung there. What had become of Zammis? The USESF didn't care, and the Drac authorities wouldn't say—none of my affair.

Ex-Force pilots were a drag on the employment market, and there were no commercial positions open—especially not to a pilot who hadn't flown in four years, who had a gimpy leg, and who was a Dragger suck. "Dragger suck" as an invective had the impact of several historical terms—Quisling, heretic, fag, nigger lover—all rolled into one.

I had forty-eight thousand credits in back pay, and so money wasn't a problem. The problem was what to do with myself. After kicking around the Delphi Base, I took transportation to Earth and, for several months, was employed by a small book house translating manuscripts into Drac. It seems that there was a craving among Dracs for Westerns: "Stick 'em up *naagusaat!*"

"Nu Geph, lawman." *Thang, thang!* The guns flashed and the *kizlode shaddsaat* bit the *thessa.*

I quit.

I finally called my parents. *Why didn't you call before, Willy? We've been worried sick . . . Had a few things I had to straighten out, Dad . . . No, not really . . . Well, we understand, son . . . it must have been awful . . . Dad, I'd like to come home for awhile. . . .*

Even before I put down the money on the used Dearman Electric, I knew I was making a mistake going home. I felt the need of a home, but the one I had left at the age of eighteen wasn't it. But I headed there because there was nowhere else to go.

I drove alone in the dark, using only the old roads, the quiet hum of the Dearman's motor the only sound. The December midnight was clear, and I could see the stars through the car's bubble canopy. Fyrine IV drifted into my thoughts, the raging ocean, the endless winds. I pulled off the road onto the shoulder and killed the lights. In a few minutes, my eyes adjusted to the dark and I stepped outside and shut the door. Kansas has a big sky, and the stars seemed close enough to touch. Snow crunched under my feet as I looked up, trying to pick Fyrine out of the thousands of visible stars.

Fyrine is in the constellation Pegasus, but my eyes were not practiced enough to pick the winged horse out from the surrounding stars. I shrugged, felt a chill, and decided to get back in the car. As I put my hand on the doorlatch, I saw a constellation that I did recognize, north, hanging just above the horizon: Draco. The Dragon, its tail twisted around Ursa Minor, hung upside down in the sky. Eltanin, the Dragon's nose, is the homestar of the Dracs. Its second planet, Draco, was Zammis's home.

Headlights from an approaching car blinded me, and I turned toward the car as it pulled to a stop. The window on the driver's side opened and someone spoke from the darkness.

"You need some help?"

I shook my head. "No, thank you." I held up a hand. "I was just looking at the stars."

"Quite a night, isn't it?"

"Sure is."

"Sure you don't need any help?"

I shook my head. "Thanks . . . wait. Where is the nearest commercial spaceport?"

"About an hour ahead in Salina."

"Thanks." I saw a hand wave from the window, then the other car pulled away. I took another look at Eltanin, then got back in my car.

Six months later, I stood in front of an ancient cut-stone gate wondering what in the hell I was doing. The trip to Draco, with nothing but Dracs as companions on the last leg, showed me the truth in Namvaac's words: "Peace is often only war without fighting." The accords, on paper, gave me the right to travel to the planet, but the Drac bureaucrats and their paperwork wizards had perfected the big stall long before the first human step into space. It took threats, bribes, and long days of filling out forms, being checked and rechecked for disease, contraband, reason for visit, filling out more forms, refilling out the forms I had already filled out, more bribes, waiting, waiting, waiting . . .

On the ship, I spent most of my time in my cabin, but since the Drac stewards refused to serve me, I went to the ship's lounge for my meals. I sat alone, listening to the comments about me from other booths. I had figured the path of least resistance was to pretend I didn't understand what they were saying. It is always assumed that humans do not speak Drac.

"Must we eat in the same compartment with the *Irkmaan* slime?"

"Look at it, how its pale skin blotches—and that evil-smelling thatch on top. Feh! The smell!"

I ground my teeth a little and kept my glance riveted to my plate.

"It defies the *Talman* that the universe's laws could be so corrupt as to produce a creature such as that."

I turned and faced the three Dracs sitting in the booth across the aisle from mine. In Drac, I replied: "If your line's elders had seen fit to teach the village *kiz* to use contraceptives, you wouldn't even exist." I returned to my food while the two Dracs struggled to hold the third Drac down.

On Draco, it was no problem finding the Jeriba estate. The problem was getting in. A high stone wall enclosed the property, and from the gate, I could see the huge stone mansion that Jerry had described to me. I told the guard at the gate that I wanted to see Jeriba Zammis. The guard stared at me, then went into an alcove behind the gate. In a few moments, another Drac emerged from the mansion and walked quickly across the wide lawn to the gate. The Drac nodded at the guard, then stopped and faced me. It was a dead ringer for Jerry.

"You are the *Irkmaan* that asked to see Jeriba Zammis?"

I nodded. "Zammis must have told you about me. I'm Willis Davidge."

The Drac studied me. "I am Estone Nev, Jeriba Shigan's sibling. My parent, Jeriba Gothig, wishes to see you." The Drac turned abruptly and walked back to the mansion. I followed, feeling heady at the thought of seeing Zammis again. I paid little attention to my surroundings until I was ushered into a large room with a vaulted stone ceiling. Jerry had told me that the house was four thousand years old. I believed it. As I entered, another Drac stood and walked over to me. It was old, but I knew who it was.

"You are Gothig, Shigan's parent."

The yellow eyes studied me. "Who are you, *Irkmaan?*" It held out a wrinkled, three-fingered hand. "What do you know of Jeriba Zammis, and why do you speak the Drac tongue with the style and accent of my child Shigan? What are you here for?"

"I speak Drac in this manner because that is the way Jeriba Shigan taught me to speak it."

The old Drac cocked its head to one side and narrowed its yellow eyes. "You knew my child? How?"

"Didn't the survey commission tell you?"

"It was reported to me that my child, Shigan, was killed in the battle of Fyrine IV. That was over six of our years ago. What is your game, *Irkmaan?*"

I turned from Gothig to Nev. The younger Drac was examining me with the same look of suspicion. I turned back to Gothig. "Shigan wasn't killed in the battle. We were stranded together on the surface of Fyrine IV and lived there for a year. Shigan died giving birth to Jeriba Zammis. A year later the joint survey commission found us and—"

"Enough! Enough of this, *Irkmaan!* Are you here for money, to use my influence for trade concessions—what?"

I frowned. "Where is Zammis?"

Tears of anger came to the old Drac's eyes. "There is no Zammis, *Irkmaan!* The Jeriba line ended with the death of Shigan!"

My eyes grew wide as I shook my head. "That's not true. I know. I took care of Zammis—you heard nothing from the commission?"

"Get to the point of your scheme, *Irkmaan*. I haven't all day."

I studied Gothig. The old Drac had heard nothing from the

commission. The Drac authorities took Zammis, and the child had evaporated. Gothig had been told nothing. Why? "I was with Shigan, Gothig. That is how I learned your language. When Shigan died giving birth to Zammis, I—"

"*Irkmaan*, if you cannot get to your scheme, I will have to ask Nev to throw you out. Shigan died in the battle of Fyrine IV. The Drac Fleet notified us only days later."

I nodded. "Then, Gothig, tell me how I came to know the line of Jeriba? Do you wish me to recite it for you?"

Gothig snorted. "You say you know the Jeriba line?"

"Yes."

Gothig flipped a hand at me. "Then, recite."

I took a breath, then began. By the time I had reached the hundred and seventy-third generation, Gothig had knelt on the stone floor next to Nev. The Dracs remained that way for the three hours of the recital. When I concluded, Gothig bowed its head and wept. "Yes, *Irkmaan*, yes. You must have known Shigan. Yes." The old Drac looked up into my face, its eyes wide with hope. "And, you say Shigan continued the line—that Zammis was born?"

I nodded. "I don't know why the commission didn't notify you."

Gothig got to its feet and frowned. "We will find out, *Irkmaan* —what is your name?"

"Davidge. Willis Davidge."

"We will find out, Davidge."

Gothig arranged quarters for me in its house, which was fortunate, since I had little more than eleven hundred credits left. After making a host of inquiries, Gothig sent Nev and me to the Chamber Center in Sendievu, Draco's capital city. The Jeriba line, I found, was influential, and the big stall was held down to a minimum. Eventually, we were directed to the Joint Survey Commission representative, a Drac named Jozzdn Vrule. It looked up from the letter Gothig had given me and frowned. "Where did you get this, *Irkmaan*?"

"I believe the signature is on it."

The Drac looked at the paper, then back at me. "The Jeriba line is one of the most respected on Draco. You say that Jeriba Gothig gave you this?"

"I felt certain I said that; I could feel my lips moving—"

Nev stepped in. "You have the dates and the information concerning the Fyrine IV survey mission. We want to know what happened to Jeriba Zammis."

Jozzdn Vrule frowned and looked back at the paper. "Estone Nev, you are the founder of your line, is this not true?"

"It is true."

"Would you found your line in shame? Why do I see you with this *Irkmaan?*"

Nev curled its upper lip and folded its arms. "Jozzdn Vrule, if you contemplate walking this planet in the foreseeable future as a free being, it would be to your profit to stop working your mouth and to start finding Jeriba Zammis."

Jozzdn Vrule looked down and studied its fingers, then returned its glance to Nev. "Very well, Estone Nev. You threaten me if I fail to hand you the truth. I think you will find the truth the greater threat." The Drac scribbled on a piece of paper, then handed it to Nev. "You will find Jeriba Zammis at this address, and you will curse the day that I gave you this."

We entered the imbecile colony feeling sick. All around us, Dracs stared with vacant eyes, or screamed, or foamed at the mouth, or behaved as lower-order creatures. After we had arrived, Gothig joined us. The Drac director of the colony frowned at me and shook its head at Gothig. "Turn back now, while it is still possible, Jeriba Gothig. Beyond this room lies nothing but pain and sorrow."

Gothig grabbed the director by the front of its wraps. "Hear me, insect: If Jeriba Zammis is within these walls, bring my grandchild forth! Else, I shall bring the might of the Jeriba line down upon your pointed head!"

The director lifted its head, twitched its lips, then nodded. "Very well. Very well, you pompous *Kazzmidth!* We tried to protect the Jeriba reputation. We tried! But now you shall see." The director nodded and pursed its lips. "Yes, you overwealthy fashion follower, now you shall see." The director scribbled on a piece of paper, then handed it to Nev. "By giving you that, I will lose my position, but take it! Yes, take it! See this being you call Jeriba Zammis. See it, and weep!"

Among trees and grass, Jeriba Zammis sat upon a stone bench, staring at the ground. Its eyes never blinked, its hands never moved. Gothig frowned at me, but I could spare nothing for Shigan's parent. I walked to Zammis. "Zammis, do you know me?"

The Drac retrieved its thoughts from a million warrens and raised its yellow eyes to me. I saw no sign of recognition. "Who are you?"

I squatted down, placed my hands on its arms and shook them. "Dammit, Zammis, don't you know me? I'm your Uncle. Remember that? Uncle Davidge?"

The Drac weaved on the bench, then shook its head. It lifted an arm and waved to an orderly. "I want to go to my room. Please, let me go to my room."

I stood and grabbed Zammis by the front of its hospital gown. "Zammis, it's me!"

The yellow eyes, dull and lifeless, stared back at me. The orderly placed a yellow hand upon my shoulder. "Let it go, *Irkmaan.*"

"Zammis!" I turned to Nev and Gothig. "Say something!"

The Drac orderly pulled a sap from its pocket, then slapped it suggestively against the palm of its hand. "Let it go, *Irkmaan.*"

Gothig stepped forward. "Explain this!"

The orderly looked at Gothig, Nev, me, and then Zammis. "This one—this creature—came to us professing a love, a *love* mind you, of humans! This is no small perversion, Jeriba Gothig. The government would protect you from this scandal. Would you wish the line of Jeriba dragged into this?"

I looked at Zammis. "What have you done to Zammis, you *kizlode* sonofabitch? A little shock? A little drug? Rot out its mind?"

The orderly sneered at me, then shook its head. "You, *Irkmaan,* do not understand. This one would not be happy as an *Irkmaan vul*—a human lover. We are making it possible for this one to function in Drac society. You think this is wrong?"

I looked at Zammis and shook my head. I remembered too well my treatment at the hands of my fellow humans. "No. I don't think it's wrong . . . I just don't know."

The orderly turned to Gothig. "Please understand, Jeriba Gothig. We could not subject the Jeriba Line to this disgrace. Your grandchild is almost well and will soon enter a reeducation program. In no more than two years, you will have a grandchild worthy of carrying on the Jeriba line. Is this wrong?"

Gothig only shook its head. I squatted down in front of Zammis and looked up into its yellow eyes. I reached up and took its right hand in both of mine. "Zammis?"

Zammis looked down, moved its left hand over and picked up my left hand and spread the fingers. One at a time Zammis pointed at the fingers of my hand, then it looked into my eyes, then examined the hand again. "Yes . . ." Zammis pointed again. "One, two, three, *four, five!*" Zammis looked into my eyes. "Four, five!"

I nodded. "Yes. Yes."

Zammis pulled my hand to its cheek and held it close. "Uncle . . . Uncle. I told you I'd never forget you."

I never counted the years that passed. My beard was back, and I knelt in my snakeskins next to the grave of my friend, Jeriba Shigan. Next to the grave was the four-year-old grave of Gothig. I replaced some rocks, then added a few more. Wrapping my snakeskins tightly against the wind, I sat down next to the grave and looked out to sea. Still the rollers steamed in under the grey-black cover of clouds. Soon, the ice would come. I nodded, looked at my scarred, wrinkled hands, then back at the grave.

"I couldn't stay in the settlement with them, Jerry. Don't get me wrong; it's nice. Damned nice. But I kept looking out my window, seeing the ocean, thinking of the cave. I'm alone, in a way. But it's good. I know what and who I am, Jerry, and that's all there is to it, right?"

I heard a noise. I crouched over, placed my hands upon my withered knees, and pushed myself to my feet. The Drac was coming from the settlement compound, a child in its arms.

I rubbed my beard. "Eh, Ty, so that is your first child?"

The Drac nodded. "I would be pleased, Uncle, if you would teach it what it must be taught: the line, the *Talman,* and about life on Fyrine IV, our planet called 'Friendship'."

I took the bundle into my arms. Chubby three-fingered arms waved at the air, then grasped my snakeskins. "Yes, Ty, this one is a Jeriba." I looked up at Ty. "And how is your parent, Zammis?"

Ty shrugged. "It is as well as can be expected. My parent wishes you well."

I nodded. "And the same to it, Ty. Zammis ought to get out of that air-conditioned capsule and come back to live in the cave. It'll do it good."

Ty grinned and nodded its head. "I will tell my parent, Uncle."

I stabbed my thumb into my chest. "Look at me! You don't see me sick, do you?"

"No, Uncle."

"You tell Zammis to kick that doctor out of there and to come back to the cave, hear?"

"Yes, Uncle." Ty smiled. "Is there anything you need?"

I nodded and scratched the back of my neck. "Toilet paper. Just a couple of packs. Maybe a couple of bottles of whiskey—no, forget the whiskey. I'll wait until Haesni, here, puts in its first year. Just the toilet paper."

Ty bowed. "Yes, Uncle, and may the many mornings find you well."

I waved my hand impatiently. "They will, they will. Just don't forget the toilet paper."

Ty bowed again. "I won't, Uncle."

Ty turned and walked through the scrub forest back to the colony. Gothig had put up the cash and moved the entire line, and all the related lines, to Fyrine IV. I lived with them for a year, but I moved out and went back to the cave. I gathered the wood, smoked the snake, and withstood the winter. Zammis gave me the young Ty to rear in the cave, and now Ty had handed me Haesni. I nodded at the child. "Your child will be called Gothig, and then . . ." I looked at the sky and felt the tears drying on my face. " . . . and then, Gothig's child will be called Shigan." I nodded and headed for the cleft that would bring us down to the level of the cave.

EDWARD BRYANT

✷ *giANTS*

Edward Bryant was born in White Plains, New York, and spent much of his childhood in the small town of Wheatland and on a ranch in Wyoming. He has a B.A. in English (1967), and a M.A. (1968) from the University of Wyoming.

Bryant has been a full-time writer since 1969, appearing in *Omni, Los Angeles Free Press, Penthouse, Writer's Digest, National Lampoon, Analog, New Dimensions, Orbit, Again Dangerous Visions, Universe, Nebula Award Stories, Best from Fantasy and Science Fiction* and *Best Science Fiction Stories of the Year.* His books include *Among the Dead* (1973), *Phoenix Without Ashes* (1975, with Harlan Ellison), *Cinnabar* (1976), *2076: The American Tricentennial* (editor/1977), *Wyoming Sun* (fantasy and science fiction about Wyoming) and *Particle Theory* (scheduled for 1981).

Since 1974, Bryant has participated in the Artists-in-the-Schools Program and similar writer-in-residence projects for state arts councils of Wyoming and Nevada, and for the Western States Arts Foundation. He has taught and spoken at many schools in the West and writes a quarterly column of film criticism for *Eternity* magazine. He has written feature film scripts and his Nebula-nominee story, "The *Hibakusha* Gallery," was produced as a senior film project at UCLA. His short story, "Stone," won the 1979 Nebula. And now you have his 1980 winner, "giANTS."

✷ Winner, Nebula, for Best Short Story of 1979.

Paul Chavez looked from the card on the silver plate to O'Hanlon's face and back to the card. "I couldn't find the tray," she said. "Put the thing away maybe twelve years ago and didn't have time to look. Never expected to need it." Her smile folded like parchment and Chavez thought he heard her lips crackle.

He reached out and took the card. Neat black-on-white printing asserted that one Laynie Bridgewell was a bona fide correspondent for the UBC News Billings bureau. He turned the card over. Sloppy cursive script deciphered as: "Imperitive I talk to you about New Mexico Project." "Children of electronic journalism," Chavez said amusedly. He set the card back on the plate. "I suppose I ought to see her in the drawing room—if I were going to see her, which I'm not."

"She's a rather insistent young woman," said O'Hanlon.

Chavez sat stiffly down on the couch. He plaited his fingers and rested the palms on the crown of his head. "It's surely time for my nap. Do be polite."

"Of course, Dr. Chavez," said O'Hanlon, sweeping silently out of the room, gracefully turning as she exited to close the doors of the library.

Pain simmered in the joints of his long bones. Chavez shook two capsules from his omnipresent pill case and poured a glass of water from the carafe on the walnut desk. Dr. Hansen had said it would

only get worse. Chavez lay on his side on the couch and felt weary
—seventy-two years' weary. He supposed he should have walked
down the hall to his bedroom, but there was no need. He slept
better here in the library. The hardwood panels and the subdued
Mondrian originals soothed him. Endless ranks of books stood
vigil. He loved to watch the wind-blown patterns of the pine
boughs beyond the French windows that opened onto the balcony. He loved to study the colors as sunlight spilled through the
leaded DNA double-helix pane Annie had given him three
decades before.

Chavez felt the capsules working faster than he had expected.
He thought he heard the tap of something hard against glass. But
then he was asleep.

In its basics, the dream never changed.

They were there in the desert somewhere between Al-
buquerque and Alamogordo, all of them: Ben Peterson, the tough
cop; the FBI man Robert Graham; Chavez himself; and Patricia
Chavez, his beautiful, brainy daughter.

The wind, gusting all afternoon, had picked up; it whistled
steadily, atonally, obscuring conversation. Sand sprayed abrasively
against their faces. Even the gaunt stands of spiny cholla bowed
with the wind.

Patricia had struck off on her own tangent. She struggled up the
base of a twenty-foot dune. She began to slip back almost as far as
each step advanced her.

They all heard it above the wind—the shrill, ululating chitter.
"What the hell is that?" Graham yelled.

Chavez shook his head. He began to run toward Patricia. The
sand, the wind, securing the brim of his hat with one hand; all
conspired to make his gait clumsy.

The immense antennae rose first above the crest of the dune.
For a second, Chavez thought they surely must be branches of
windblown cholla. Then the head itself heaved into view, faceted
eyes coruscating with changing hues of red and blue. Mandibles
larger than a farmer's scythes clicked and clashed. The ant paused,
apparently surveying the creatures downslope.

"Look at the size of it," said Chavez, more to himself than to the others.

He heard Peterson's shout. "It's as big as a horse!" He glanced back and saw the policeman running for the car.

Graham's reflexes were almost as prompt. He had pulled his .38 Special from the shoulder holster and swung his arm, motioning Patricia to safety, yelling, "Back, get back!" Patricia began to run from the dune all too slowly, feet slipping on the sand, legs constricted by the ankle-length khaki skirt. Graham fired again and again, the gun popping dully in the wind.

The ant hesitated only a few seconds longer. The wind sleeked the tufted hair on its purplish-green thorax. Then it launched itself down the slope, all six articulated legs churning with awful precision.

Chavez stood momentarily frozen. He heard a coughing stutter from beside his shoulder. Ben Peterson had retrieved a Thompson submachine gun from the auto. Gouts of sand erupted around the advancing ant. The creature never hesitated.

Patricia lost her race in a dozen steps. She screamed once as the crushing mandibles closed around her waist. She looked despairingly at her father. Blood ran from both corners of her mouth.

There was an instant eerie tableau. The Tommy gun fell silent as Peterson let the muzzle fall in disbelief. The hammer of Graham's pistol clicked on a spent cylinder. Chavez cried out.

Uncannily, brutally graceful, the ant wheeled and, still carrying Patricia's body, climbed the slope. It crested the dune and vanished. Its chittering cry remained a moment more before raveling in the wind.

Sand flayed his face as Chavez called out his daughter's name over and over. Someone took his shoulder and shook him, telling him to stop it, to wake up. It wasn't Peterson or Graham.

It was his daughter.

She was his might-have-been daughter.

Concerned expression on her sharp-featured face, she was shaking him by the shoulder. Her eyes were dark brown and enormous. Her hair, straight and cut short, was a lighter brown.

She backed away from him and sat in his worn, leather-covered chair. He saw she was tall and very thin. For a moment he oscillated between dream-orientation and wakefulness. "Patricia?" Chavez said.

She did not answer.

Chavez let his legs slide off the couch and shakily sat up. "Who in the world are you?"

"My name's Laynie Bridgewell," said the young woman.

Chavez's mind focused. "Ah, the reporter."

"Correspondent."

"A semantic distinction. No essential difference." One level of his mind noted with amusement that he was articulating well through the confusion. He still didn't know what the hell was going on. He yawned deeply, stretched until a dart of pain cut the movement short, said, "Did you talk Ms. O'Hanlon into letting you up here?"

"Are you kidding?" Bridgewell smiled. "She must be a great watchdog."

"She's known me a long while. How *did* you get up here?"

Bridgewell looked mildly uncomfortable. "I, uh, climbed up."

"Climbed?"

"Up one of the pines. I shinnied up a tree to the balcony. The French doors were unlocked. I saw you inside sleeping, so I came in and waited."

"A criminal offense," said Chavez.

"They were unlocked," she said defensively.

"I meant sitting and watching me sleep. Terrible invasion of privacy. A person could get awfully upset, not knowing if another human being, a strange one at that, is secretly watching him snore or drool or whatever."

"You slept very quietly," said Bridgewell. "Very still. Until the nightmare."

"Ah," said Chavez. "It was that apparent?"

She nodded. "You seemed really upset. I thought maybe I ought to wake you."

Chavez said, "Did I say anything."

She paused and thought. "Only two words I could make out. A name—Patricia. And you kept saying 'them.'"

"That figures." He smiled. He felt orientation settling around him like familiar wallpaper in a bedroom, or old friends clustering at a departmental cocktail party. "You're from the UBC bureau in Billings?"

"I drove down this morning."

"Work for them long?"

"Almost a year."

"First job?"

She nodded. "First real job."

"You're what—twenty-one?" said Chavez.

"Twenty-two."

"Native?"

"Of Montana?" She shook her head. "Kansas."

"University of Southern California?"

Another shake. "Missouri."

"Ah," he said. "Good school." Chavez paused. "You're here on assignment?"

A third shake. "My own time."

"Ah," said Chavez again. "Ambitious. And you want to talk to me about the New Mexico Project?"

Face professionally sober, voice eager, she said, "Very much. I didn't have any idea you lived so close until I read the alumni bulletin from the University of Wyoming."

"I wondered how you found me out." Chavez sighed. "Betrayed by my alma mater . . ." He looked at her sharply. "I don't grant interviews, even if I occasionally conduct them." He stood and smiled. "Will you be wanting to use the stairs, or would you rather shinny back down the tree?"

"Who is Patricia?" said Bridgewell.

"My daughter," Chavez started to say. "Someone from my past," he said.

"I lost people to the bugs," said Bridgewell quietly. "My parents were in Biloxi at the wrong time. Bees never touched them. The insecticide offensive got them both."

The pain in Chavez's joints became ice needles. He stood—and stared.

Even more quietly, Bridgewell said, "You don't have a daughter. Never had. I did my homework." Her dark eyes seemed even larger. "I don't know everything about the New Mexico Project—that's why I'm here. But I can stitch the rumors together." She paused. "I even had the bureau rent an old print of the movie. I watched it four times yesterday."

Chavez felt the disorientation return, felt exhausted, felt—damn it!—old. He fumbled the container of pain pills out of his trouser pocket, then returned it unopened. "Hungry?" he said.

"You better believe it. I had to leave before breakfast."

"I think we'll get some lunch," said Chavez. "Let's go downtown. Try not to startle Ms. O'Hanlon as we leave."

O'Hanlon had encountered them in the downstairs hall, but reacted only with a poker face. "Would you and the young lady like some lunch, Dr. Chavez?"

"Not today," said Chavez, "but thank you. Ms. Bridgewell and I are going to eat in town."

O'Hanlon regarded him. "Have you got your medicine?"

Chavez patted his trouser leg and nodded.

"And you'll be back before dark?"

"Yes," he said. "Yes. And if I'm not, I'll phone. You're not my mother. I'm older than you."

"Don't be cranky," she said. "Have a pleasant time."

Bridgewell and Chavez paused in front of the old stone house. "Why don't we take my car?" said Bridgewell. "I'll run you back after lunch." She glanced at him. "You're not upset about being driven around by a kid, are you?" He smiled and shook his head. "Okay."

They walked a hundred meters to where her car was pulled off the blacktop and hidden in a stand of spruce. It was a Volkswagen beetle of a vintage Chavez estimated to be a little older than its driver.

As if reading his thoughts, Bridgewell said, "Runs like a watch—the old kind, with hands. Got a hundred and ten thousand on her third engine. I call her Scarlett." The car's color was a dim red like dried clay.

"Do you really miss watches with hands?" said Chavez, opening the passenger-side door.

"I don't know—I guess I hadn't really thought about it. I know I don't miss sliderules."

"*I* miss hands on timepieces." Chavez noticed there were no seatbelts. "A long time ago, I stockpiled all the Timexes I'd need for my lifetime."

"Does it really make any difference?"

"I suppose not." Chavez considered that as Bridgewell drove onto the highway and turned downhill.

"You love the past a lot, don't you?"

"I'm nostalgic," said Chavez.

"I think it goes a lot deeper than that." Bridgewell handled the VW like a racing Porsche. Chavez held onto the bar screwed onto the glove-box door with both hands. Balding radial tires shrieked as she shot the last curve and they began to descend the slope into Casper. To the east, across the city, they could see a ponderous dirigible-freighter settling gracefully toward a complex of blocks and domes.

"Why," she said, "are they putting a pilot fusion plant squarely in the middle of the biggest coal deposits in the country?"

Chavez shrugged. "When man entered the atomic age he opened a door into a new world. What he may eventually find in that new world no one can predict."

"Huh?" Bridgewell said. Then: "Oh, the movie. Doesn't it ever worry you—having that obsession?"

"No," said Chavez. Bridgewell slowed slightly as the road became city street angling past blocks of crumbling budget housing. "Turn left on Rosa. Head downtown."

"Where are we eating? I'm hungry enough to eat coal by-products."

"Close. We're going to the oil can."

"Huh?" Bridgewell said again.

"The Petroleum Tower. Over there." Chavez pointed at a forty-storey cylindrical pile. It was windowed completely with bronze reflective panes. "The rooftop restaurant's rather good."

They left Scarlett in an underground lot and took the high-speed exterior elevator to the top of the Petroleum Tower. Bridgewell closed her eyes as the ground level rushed away from them. At the fortieth floor she opened her eyes to stare at the glassed-in restaurant, the lush hanging plants, the noontime crowd. "Who *are* these people? They all look so, uh, professional."

"They are that," said Chavez, leading the way to the maître d'. "Oil people. Uranium people. Coal people. Slurry people. Shale people. Coal gasification—"

"I've got the point," Bridgewell said. "I feel a little under-dressed."

"They know me."

And so, apparently, they did. The maître d' issued orders and Bridgewell and Chavez were instantly ushered to a table beside a floor-to-ceiling window.

"Is this a perk of being maybe the world's greatest molecular biologist?"

Chavez shook his head. "More a condition of originally being a local boy. Even with the energy companies, this is still a small town at heart." He fell silent and looked out the window. The horizon was much closer than he remembered from his childhood. A skiff of brown haze lay over the city. There was little open land to be seen.

They ordered drinks.

They made small-talk.

They ordered food.

"This is very pleasant," said Bridgewell, "but I'm still a corre-spondent. I think you're sitting on the biggest story of the decade."

"That extraterrestrial ambassadors are shortly to land near Al-buquerque? That they have picked America as a waystation to repair their ship?"

Bridgewell looked bemused. "I'm realizing I don't know when you're kidding."

"Am I now?"

"Yes."

"So why do you persist in questioning me?"

She hesitated. "Because I suspect you want to tell someone. It might as well be me."

He thought about that awhile. The waiter brought the garnish tray and Chavez chewed on a stick of carrot. "Why don't you tell me the pieces you've picked up."

"And then?"

"We'll see," he said. "I can't promise anything."

Bridgewell said, "You're a lot like my father. I never knew when he was kidding either."

"Your turn," said Chavez.

The soup arrived. Bridgewell sipped a spoonful of French onion and set the utensil down. "The New Mexico Project. It doesn't seem to have anything to do with New Mexico. You wouldn't believe the time I've spent on the phone. All my vacation I ran around that state in Scarlett."

Chavez smiled a long time, finally said, "Think metaphorically. The Manhattan Project was conducted under Stagg Field in Chicago."

"I don't think the New Mexico Project has anything to do with nuclear energy," she said. "But I have heard a lot of mumbling about DNA chimeras."

"So far as I know, no genetic engineer is using recombinant DNA to hybridize creatures with all the more loathsome aspects of snakes, goats, and lions. The state of the art improves, but we're not that good yet."

"But I shouldn't rule out DNA engineering?" she said.

"Keep going."

"Portuguese is the official language of Brazil."

Chavez nodded.

"UBC's stringer in Recife has it that, for quite a while now, nothing's been coming out of the Brazilian nuclear power complex at Xique-Xique. I mean there's *news*, but it's all through official release. Nobody's going in or out."

Chavez said, "You would expect a station that new and large to be a concern of national security. Shaking down's a long and complex process."

"Maybe." She picked the ripe olives out of the newly arrived salad and carefully placed them in a line on the plate. "I've got a cousin in movie distribution. Just real scutwork so far, but she knows what's going on in the industry. She told me that the U.S. Department of Agriculture ordered a print from Warner Brothers dubbed in Portuguese and had it shipped to Brazilia. The print was that movie you're apparently so concerned with—*Them!* The one about the ants mutating from radioactivity in the New Mexico desert. The one about giant ants on the rampage."

"Only a paranoid could love this chain of logic," said Chavez.

Her face looked very serious. "If it takes a paranoid to come up with this story and verify it," she said, "then that's what I am. Maybe nobody else is willing to make the jumps. I am. I know nobody else has the facts. I'm going to get them."

To Chavez, it seemed that the table had widened. He looked across the linen wasteland at her. "The formidable Formicidae family . . ." he said. "So have you got a conclusion to state?" He felt the touch of tiny legs on his leg. He felt feathery antennae tickle the hairs on his thigh. He jerked back from the table and his water goblet overturned, the waterstain spreading smoothly toward the woman.

"What's wrong?" said Bridgewell. He heard concern in her voice. He slapped at his leg, stopped the motion, drew a deep breath.

"Nothing." Chavez hitched his chair closer to the table again. A waiter hovered at his shoulder, mopping the water with a towel and refilling the goblet. "Your conclusion." His voice strengthened. "I asked about your theory."

"I know this sounds crazy," said Bridgewell. "I've read about how the Argentine fire ants got to Mobile, Alabama. And I damned well know about the bees—I told you that."

Chavez felt the touch again, this time on his ankle. He tried unobtrusively to scratch and felt nothing. Just the touch. Just the tickling, chitinous touch.

"Okay," Bridgewell continued. "All I can conclude is that somebody in South America's created some giant, mutant ants, and now they're marching north. Like the fire ants. Like the bees."

"Excuse me a moment," said Chavez, standing.

"Your face is white," said Bridgewell. "Can I help you?"

"No." Chavez turned and, forcing himself not to run, walked to the restroom. In a stall, he lowered his trousers. As he had suspected, there was no creature on his leg. He sat on the toilet and scratched his skinny legs until the skin reddened and he felt the pain. "Damn it," he said to himself. "Stop." He took a pill from the case and downed it with water from the row of faucets. Then he stared at himself in the mirror and returned to the table.

"You okay?" Bridgewell had not touched her food.

He nodded. "I'm prey to any number of ailments; goes with the territory. I'm sorry to disturb your lunch."

"I'm apparently disturbing yours more."

"I offered." He picked up knife and fork and began cutting a slice of cold roast beef. "I offered—so follow this through. Please."

Her voice softened. "I have the feeling this all ties together somehow with your wife."

Chavez chewed the beef, swallowed without tasting it. "Did you look at the window?" Bridgewell looked blank. "The stained glass in the library."

Her expression became mobile. "The spiral design? The double helix? I loved it. The colors are incredible."

"It's exquisite; and it's my past." He took a long breath. "Annie gave it to me for my forty-first birthday. As well, it was our first anniversary. Additionally it was on the occasion of the award. It meant more to me than the trip to Stockholm." He looked at her sharply. "You said you did your homework. How much *do* you know?"

"I know that you married late," said Bridgewell, "for your times."

"Forty."

"I know that your wife died of a freak accident two years later. I didn't follow-up."

"You should have," said Chavez. "Annie and I had gone on a picnic in the Florida panhandle. We were driving from Memphis to Tampa. I was cleaning some catfish. Annie wandered off, cataloguing insects and plants. She was an amateur taxonomist. For whatever reason—God only knows—I don't—she disturbed a mound of fire ants. They swarmed over her. I heard her screaming. I ran to her and dragged her away and brushed off the ants. Neither of us had known about her protein allergy—she'd just been lucky enough never to have been bitten or stung." He hesitated and shook his head. "I got her to Pensacola. Annie died in anaphylactic shock. The passages swelled, closed off. She suffocated in the car."

Bridgewell looked stricken. She started to say, "I'm sorry, Dr. Chavez. I had no—"

He held up his hand gently. "Annie was eight months pregnant. In the hospital they tried to save our daughter. It didn't work." He shook his head again, as if clearing it. "You and Annie look a bit alike—coltish, I think is the word. I expect Patricia would have looked the same."

The table narrowed. Bridgewell put her hand across the distance and touched his fingers. "You never remarried."

"I disengaged myself from most sectors of life." His voice was dispassionate.

"Why didn't you re-engage?"

He realized he had turned his hand over, was allowing his fingers to curl gently around hers. The sensation was warmth. "I spent the first half of my life singlemindedly pursuing certain goals. It took an enormous investment of myself to open my life to Annie." As he had earlier in the morning when he'd first met Bridgewell, he felt profoundly weary. "I suppose I decided to take the easier course: to hold onto the past and call it good."

She squeezed his hand. "I won't ask if it's been worth it."

"What about you?" he said. "You seem to be in ferocious pursuit of your goals. Do you have a rest of your life hidden off to the side?"

Bridgewell hesitated. "No. Not yet. I've kept my life directed, very concentrated, since—since everyone died. But someday . . ." Her voice trailed off. "I still have time."

"Time," Chavez said, recognizing the sardonicism. "Don't count on it."

Her voice very serious, she said, "Whatever happens, I won't let the past dictate to me."

He felt her fingers tighten. "Never lecture someone three times your age," he said. "It's tough to be convincing." He laughed and banished the tension.

"This *is* supposed to be an interview," she said, but didn't take her hand away.

"Did you ever have an ant farm as a child?" Chavez said. She shook her head. "Then we're going to go see one this afternoon." He glanced at the food still in front of her. "Done?" She nodded. "Then let's go out to the university field station."

They stood close together in the elevator. Bridgewell kept her back to the panoramic view. Chavez said, "I've given you no unequivocal statements about the New Mexico Project."

"I know."

"And if I should tell you now that there are indeed monstrous ant mutations—creatures large as horses—tramping toward us from the Mato Grosso?"

This time she grinned and shook her head silently.

"You think me mad, don't you?"

"I still don't know when you're kidding," she said.

"There are no giant ants," said Chavez. "Yet." And he refused to elaborate.

The field station of the Wyoming State University at Casper was thirty kilometers south, toward the industrial complex at Douglas-River Bend. Two kilometers off the freeway, Scarlett clattered and protested across the potholed access road, but delivered them safely. They crossed the final rise and descended toward the white dome and the cluster of outbuildings.

"That's huge," said Bridgewell. "Freestanding?"

"Supported by internal pressure," said Chavez. "We needed something that could be erected quickly. It was necessary that we have a thoroughly controllable internal environment. It'll be hell to protect from the snow and wind come winter, but we shouldn't need it by then."

There were two security checkpoints with uniformed guards. Armed men and women dubiously inspected the battered VW and its passengers, but waved them through when Chavez produced his identification.

"This is incredible," said Bridgewell.

"It wasn't my idea," said Chavez. "Rules."

She parked Scarlett beside a slab-sided building that adjoined the dome. Chavez guided her inside, past another checkpoint in the lobby, past obsequious underlings in lab garb who said, "Good afternoon, Dr. Chavez," and into a sterile-appearing room lined with electronic gear.

Chavez gestured at the rows of monitor screens. "We can't go into the dome today, but the entire installation is under surveillance through remotely controlled cameras." He began flipping switches. A dozen screens jumped to life in living color.

"It's all jungle," Bridgewell said.

"Rain forest." The cameras panned past vividly green trees, creepers, seemingly impenetrable undergrowth. "It's a reasonable duplication of the Brazilian interior. Now, listen." He touched other switches.

At first the speakers seemed to be crackling with electronic noise. "What am I hearing?" she finally said.

"What does it sound like?"

She listened longer. "Eating?" She shivered. "It's like a thousand mouths eating."

"Many more," Chavez said. "But you have the idea. Now watch."

The camera eye of the set directly in front of her dollied in toward a wall of greenery wound round a tree. Chavez saw the leaves ripple, undulating smoothly as though they were the surface of an uneasy sea. He glanced at Bridgewell; she saw it too. "Is there wind in the dome?"

"No," he said.

The view moved in for a close-up. "Jesus!" said Bridgewell.

Ants. Ants covered the tree, the undergrowth, the festooned vines.

"You may have trouble with the scale," Chavez said. "They're about as big as your thumb."

The ants swarmed in efficient concert, mandibles snipping like garden shears, stripping everything green, everything alive. Chavez stared at them and felt only a little hate. Most of the emotion had long since been burned from him.

"Behold *Eciton*," said Chavez. "Driver ants, army ants, the *maripunta*, whatever label you'd like to assign."

"I've read about them," said Bridgewell. "I've seen documentaries and movies at one time or another. I never thought they'd be this frightening when they were next door."

"There is fauna in the environment too. Would you like to see a more elaborate meal?"

"I'll pass."

Chavez watched the leaves ripple and vanish, bit by bit. Then he felt the tentative touch, the scurrying of segmented legs along his limbs. He reached out and tripped a single switch; all the pictures flickered and vanished. The two of them sat staring at the opaque gray monitors.

"Those are the giant ants?" she finally said.

"I told you the truth." He shook his head. "Not yet."

"No kidding now," she said.

"The following is a deliberate breach of national security," he said, "so they tell me." He raised his hands. "So what?" Chavez motioned toward the screens. "The *maripunta* apparently are mutating into a radically different form. It's not an obvious physical change, not like in *Them!* It's not by deliberate human agency, as with the bees. It may be through accidental human action—the Brazilian double-X nuclear station is suspected. We just don't know. What we do understand is that certain internal regulators in the *maripunta* have gone crazy."

"And they're getting bigger?" She looked bewildered.

He shook his head violently. "Do you know the square-cube law? No? It's a simple rule of nature. If an insect's dimensions are doubled, its strength and the area of its breathing passages are increased by a factor of four. But the mass is multiplied by eight. After a certain point, and that point isn't very high, the insect can't move or breathe. It collapses under its own mass."

"No giant ants?" she said.

"Not yet. Not exactly. The defective mechanism in the *maripunta* is one which controls the feeding and foraging phases. Ordinarily the ants—all the millions of them in a group—spend about two weeks in a nomadic phase. Then they alternate three weeks in place in a statary phase. That's how it used to be. Now only the nomadic phase remains."

"So they're moving," said Bridgewell. "North?" She sat with hands on knees. Her fingers moved as though with independent life.

"The *maripunta* are ravenous, breeding insanely, and headed our way. The fear is that, like the bees, the ants won't proceed linearly. Maybe they'll leapfrog aboard a charter aircraft. Maybe on a Honduran freighter. It's inevitable."

Bridgewell clasped her hands; forced them to remain still in her lap.

Chavez continued, "Thanks to slipshod internal Brazilian practices over the last few decades, the *maripunta* are resistant to every insecticide we've tried."

"They're unstoppable?" Bridgewell said.

"That's about it," said Chavez.

"And that's why the public's been kept in the dark?"

"Only partially. The other part is that we've found an answer." Chavez toyed with the monitor switches but stopped short of activating them. "The government agencies involved with this project fear that the public will misunderstand our solution to the problem. Next year's an election year." Chavez smiled ruefully. "There's a precedence to politics."

Bridgewell glanced from the controls to his face. "You're part of the solution. How?"

Chavez decisively flipped a switch and they again saw the ant-ravaged tree. The limbs were perceptibly barer. He left the sound down. "You know my background. You were correct in suspecting the New Mexico Project had something to do with recombinant DNA and genetic engineering. You're a good journalist. You were essentially right all down the line." He looked away from her toward the screen. "I and my people here are creating giant ants."

Bridgewell's mouth dropped open slightly. "I—but, you—"

"Let me continue. The purpose of the New Mexico Project has been to tinker with the genetic makeup of the *maripunta*—to create a virus-borne mutagen that will single out the queens. We've got that agent now."

All correspondent again, Bridgewell said, "What will it do?"

"At first we were attempting to readjust the ants' biological clocks and alter the nomadic phase. Didn't work; too sophisticated for what we can accomplish. So we settled for something more basic, more physical. We've altered the ants to make them huge."

"Like in *Them!*"

"Except that *Them!* was a metaphor. It stated a physical impossibility. Remember the square-cube law?" She nodded. "Sometime in the near future, bombers will be dropping payloads all across Brazil, Venezuela, the Guianas . . . anywhere we suspect the ants are. The weapon is dispersal bombs, aerosol cannisters containing the viral mutagen to trigger uncontrolled growth in each new generation of ants."

"The square-cube law . . ." said Bridgewell softly.

"Exactly. We've created monsters—and gravity will kill them."

"It'll work?"

"It should." Then Chavez said very quietly, "I hope I live long enough to see the repercussions."

Bridgewell said equally quietly, "I *will* file this story."

"I know that."

"Will it get you trouble?"

"Probably nothing I can't handle." Chavez shrugged. "Look around you at this multi-million dollar installation. There were many more convenient places to erect it. I demanded it be built here." His smile was only a flicker. "When you're a giant in your field—and needed—the people in power tend to indulge you."

"Thank you, Dr. Chavez," she said.

"Dr. Chavez? After all this, it's still not Paul?"

"Thanks, Paul."

They drove north, back toward Casper, and watched the western photochemical sunset. The sun sank through the clouds in a splendor of reds. They talked very little. Chavez found the silence comfortable.

Why didn't you re-engage?

The question no longer disturbed him. He hadn't truly addressed it. Yet it was no longer swept under the carpet. That made all the difference.

I'll get to it, he thought. Chavez stared into the windshield sun-glare and saw his life bound up in a leaded pane like an ambered insect.

Bridgewell kept glancing at him silently as she drove up the long mountain road to Chavez's house. She passed the stand of spruce where she had hidden Scarlett earlier in the day and braked to a stop in front of the stone house. They each sat still for the moment.

"You'll want to be filing your story," said Chavez.

She nodded.

"Now that you know the way up my tree, perhaps you'll return to visit in a more conventional way?"

Bridgewell smiled. She leaned across the seat and kissed him on the lips. It was, Chavez thought, a more than filial kiss. "Now *I'm* not kidding," she said.

Chavez got out of the Volkswagen and stood on the flagstone walk while Bridgewell backed Scarlett into the drive and turned around. As she started down the mountain, she turned and waved. Chavez waved. He stood there and watched until the car vanished around the first turn.

He walked back to the house and found O'Hanlon waiting, arms folded against the twilight chill, on the stone step. Chavez hesitated beside her and they both looked down the drive and beyond. Casper's lights began to blossom into a growing constellation.

"Does she remind you considerably of what Patricia might have been like?" said O'Hanlon.

Chavez nodded, and then said quickly, "Don't go for easy Freud. There's more to it than that—or there may be."

A slight smile tugged at O'Hanlon's lips. "Did I say anything?"

"Well, no." Chavez stared down at the city. He said, with an attempt at great dignity, "We simply found, in a short time, that we liked each other very much."

"I thought that might be it." O'Hanlon smiled a genuine smile. "Shall we go inside? Much longer out here and we'll be ice. I'll fix some chocolate."

He reached for the door. "With brandy?"

"All right."

"And you'll join me?"

"You know I ordinarily abstain, Dr. Chavez, but—" Her smile impossibly continued. "It is rather a special day, isn't it?" She preceded him through the warm doorway.

Chavez followed with a final look at the city. Below the mountain, Casper's constellation winked and bloomed into the zodiac.

Twelve hours later, the copyrighted story by Laynie Bridgewell made the national news and the wire services.

Eighteen hours later, her story was denied by at least five governmental agencies of two sovereign nations.

Twelve days later, Paul Chavez died quietly in his sleep, napping in the library.

Twenty-two days later, squadrons of jet bombers dropped cargoes of hissing aerosol bombs over a third of the South American continent. The world was saved. For a while, anyway. The grotesquely enlarged bodies of *Eciton burchelli* would shortly litter the laterite tropical soil.

Twenty-seven days later, at night, an intruder climbed up to the balcony of Paul Chavez's house on Casper Mountain and smashed the stained-glass picture in the French doors leading into the library. No item was stolen. Only the window was destroyed.

BEN BOVA

We Have Met the Mainstream...

When you say Ben Bova is a novelist, lecturer and Executive Editor of *Omni,* you have barely begun. A former editor of *Analog,* he received the Hugo as Best Professional Editor six times. Bova has been a newspaperman, aerospace industry executive, motion-picture writer and television consultant. He has worked with leading scientists in advanced research fields and was technical editor on Project *Vanguard.* He has written teaching films for the Physical Sciences Study Committee, working with MIT's physics department and Nobel Laureates from many universities. His lecture audiences range from the U.S. State Department to the Institute on Man and Science, and he has spoken on a wide variety of topics, including "How We Lost the Energy Battle (but May Still Win the War)," "How to Predict the Future," and "The Coming Industrialization of Space." He has directed film courses and taught science fiction at New York's Hayden Planetarium.

With all of this, he has somehow found time to write twenty-three novels and nineteen nonfiction books and to edit eight anthologies. His short stories and articles have appeared in all the major science-fiction magazines as well as in *Harper's, Smithsonian, American Film, Vogue* and *The Writer.* His book *The Fourth State of Matter* was judged one of the best science books of 1971 by the American Library Association.

He is a charter member of the National Space Institute and Science Fiction Writers of America. He was the 1974 recipient of the E. E. Smith Memorial Award for Imaginative Fiction. More? See *Who's Who in the East,* the *International Authors Who's Who, Contemporary Authors,* and *Who's Who In Science Fiction.* Oh, yes, and read his piece here carefully. Bova knows his subject.

... and they are us. Well, almost. Some of us, at least.

In the decade of the Eighties some of the fondest childhood dreams of many a science-fiction writer are coming true. Like most childhood dreams, though, they are not coming true in quite the way we envisaged, 'way back when.

The biggest, most cherished dream of most science-fiction writers has been to break into the mainstream of American literature: to see science fiction respected, admired, and *paid for* just as if it were an integral part of the literary establishment. This is a particularly American dream, because it was mainly in America that science fiction was ghettoized into a narrow corner of the literary marketplace.

Well, the dream is coming true. But in an unexpected way. Science fiction is not breaking into the mainstream, exactly. The mainstream is sort of coming over and engulfing science fiction.

Here's what I mean.

As L. Sprague de Camp has been pointing out for years, the literature of the fantastic *was* the mainstream of world storytelling from the time writing began until the beginning of the Seventeenth Century A.D. From Homer to Cervantes, literature dealt with fantastic landscapes, superhuman heroes, supernatural villains—the domain which today we call science fiction and/or fantasy.

Cervantes's *Don Quixote* was the first major literary work that dealt exclusively with the here-and-now. Its setting was contemporary, its hero and supporting characters were very human.

From that moment on, European literature dealt increasingly with contemporary tales, or with stories out of history. The spread of printing, which helped to foster both the Protestant Reformation and the growth of science, also helped to push fantastic literature into a corner. A middle class rose to power in Europe, and these solid, no-nonsense, practical bourgeoisie demanded solid, no-nonsense, practical fiction. No fantastic landscapes for them! They wanted stories that spoke to them, and of them, and for them.

By the time Hugo Gernsback began publishing *Amazing Stories,* 1926, tales that dealt with fantasy and the future were definitely a minor part of European and American adult literature. Certainly there was an occasional Jules Verne or H. G. Wells, but for every one of those fantasists there were hundreds of Galsworthys, Dickens's, Hardys, Melvilles, and others.

To prove the point, consider the fact that science-fiction enthusiasts often claim that most of the great writers of the past couple of centuries have written science fiction. True enough, you can find tales that could justifiably be called science fiction in the works of Poe, Hale, Swift, even F. Scott Fitzgerald. But their contemporary stories far outnumber their occasional dabbles into futuristic or fantastic tales.

When I was a youngster, growing up during World War II, the popular magazines of the times constantly showed us what marvels the post-war world would bring: privately owned and operated airplanes as commonplace as automobiles; television in every home; super foods at supermarkets; spacious, sunny, electrically-powered individual homes out in the countryside instead of crowded city row houses and tenements.

Most of those marvels are so commonplace today that we complain about them. But there was one private dream of that generation of science-fiction writers which did not materialize in the wonderful post-war world: we wanted to see a magazine as big and colorful and popular as *Life* or *Colliers*—devoted to science and science fiction.

We had to satisfy ourselves with the science-fiction magazines of the era. Which were wonderful, in their way. *Astounding, Galaxy, The Magazine of Fantasy and Science Fiction,* and many others were published in the early 1950's. They kept us busy and happy reading. But these magazines had a very small audience, compared to the readership of *Saturday Evening Post, Reader's Digest,* or even *True.*

Television gobbled up most of those popular magazines, but the hard core audience for science fiction remained loyal, and the top rank of science-fiction magazines remained in publication.

By this time I had left a budding career in newspaper reporting to become a Junior Technical Editor in the thriving aerospace industry. (Of the three words describing my job, only the first one accurately reflected my situation.)

I fought my way through rooms full of personnel executives to win a position on Project *Vanguard,* which in 1956 promised to be "man's first step into space."

There I was, surrounded by engineers who were actually building a satellite-launching rocket! But when I told them that I read science fiction, and was even trying to write some, they shied away. Fast. Even among the elite technologists of the time, science fiction was considered so far removed from established literary values that most people never even looked at it.

(Digression: Even unto this very day, the typical science-fiction enthusiast is described by his or her friends as a science-fiction *nut,* or a science-fiction *freak.* Ever hear of anyone being described as an historical novel freak, or an anthropology nut?)

Well, I left the aerospace industry in 1971, to become the editor of *Analog Science Fiction-Science Fact* magazine. By that time the world had seen Sputnik, a Space Race that culminated with Americans on the Moon, lasers, quasars, superconducting magnets, spy satellites, spacecraft probing Mars and Venus, heart transplants, nuclear submarines, and Howard Cosell brought to you live, from anywhere in the world, via Telstar.

What did all this do for science fiction? Not a hell of a lot, frankly.

Oh, by the time I was ready to leave aerospace, the engineers and scientists were quite willing to talk about science fiction. Many of them even admitted to reading the stuff, back when they were kids. "Think tanks" such as Rand Corporation kept libraries of science-fiction books (paperbacks, to save the taxpayers' money) and invited science-fiction writers in to talk about future breakthroughs in technology.

But they saw us as "futurists." That was a respectable term. No matter that I had written a couple of dozen science-fiction novels, when they invited me out to Rand it was as a "futurist"—i.e., a scientist who specialized in studying the future. Very few science-fiction writers have turned down lucrative speaking engagements because they refused to be described as "futurists."

The science-fiction world seemed as insulated from the rest of the universe as ever, even in 1971. Sure, we dreamed our galaxy-spanning dreams and foresaw more futures than the human race will ever have time to play out. The science-fiction audience grew incrementally—mainly among students.

Back in 1971, when I came to *Analog* following the untimely death of John W. Campbell, Jr., the circulation of the magazine was about 110,000 copies per month. In 1978, when I resigned from *Analog,* the circulation was virtually the same.

And this was the best, most widely-circulated magazine of them all, at that time. The hard core science-fiction audience had not expanded very much.

But although we had not taken over the mainstream of American literature, the mainstream was beginning to take over us.

It happened in an odd way. You would think that with spacecraft whizzing through the solar system and out to the stars, with recombinant DNA scientists tailoring bacteria to produce human insulin, and microcomputers getting down to the size of your thumbnail, that readers would flock to science fiction to see what might be coming next.

None of those events helped science fiction much.

Star Wars is what did it.

George Lucas may not be the Messiah of our history, but he is certainly the prophet (which can also be spelled p-r-o-f-i-t.)

The fast and furious events of the Sixties and Seventies had set the stage for an explosion of popular interest in things science fictional. Yet the publishing industry did not take advantage of this potential market until *Star Wars* began rolling up indecently large profits.

Why did the publishing industry—books and magazines both—fail to capitalize on this huge potential market for science fiction until after the motion picture industry had made its score? Because publishers are—with very rare exceptions—exceedingly cautious.

The publishing industry is based on the marketing strategy of Minimal Success. That is, most publishers base their sales plans around the idea that this or that individual book will make a modest profit for the company, at best. For most publishing houses, only one or two books per season are earmarked for Maximum Success. Those are the top-of-the-line books, the ones that get the ads, the promotion campaigns, the big push with the sales force. If those books flop, heads roll.

But all the other books the publishing house puts out during the year are shipped off to the market like so many loaves of bread. The books are put on the bookstore shelves or paperback racks. Some sell pretty well, others fail miserably. No matter: nobody's going to get fired because a Minimal Success book disappeared without a trace.

In the field of magazine publishing, the strategy of Minimal Success means that some magazines—such as science-fiction magazines—are published and distributed with as small an investment as possible. Shoestring operations, with shoestring results.

The problem with the Minimal Success strategy is that once a book or magazine is earmarked by its publisher for Minimal Success, *it cannot do any better than Minimal Success.*

No matter how the author screams and struggles, the book will sell no more copies than the publisher prints. If the author, through dint of personal valor, wrests a spot on the Johnny Carson Show and seventeen million people run panting to their bookstores the very next morning for a copy of the author's book, what good does that do if the publisher has printed only five thousand copies and most of them are languishing in a warehouse in New Jersey?

Until *Star Wars*, science fiction was a victim of the Minimal Success strategy. Publishers knew that there was a definite hard core audience Out There for science fiction. In fact, the science-fiction audience was so loyal, so persevering, that publishers felt they could sell a certain minimum number of copies of *any* science-fiction book or magazine, without advertising, promotion, sales push, or anything. Just print the books or magazines and ship them out in plain brown boxes. The science-fiction nuts will find them and buy them.

Why risk money on advertising or major print runs? You can make a small but steady profit simply by printing a small but steady number of science-fiction books or magazines. Minimal Success, but steady profits.

John Campbell often said of *Analog* (née *Astounding*) magazine, "It's a gold mine for the publisher. It's only a teeny-weeny gold mine, but it never loses any money for them."

Analog was then published by The Condé Nast Publications, Inc. In 1975, I approached the publisher with an idea: to take advantage of the growing interest in science fiction and the future, we should bring out a new magazine. Now, Condé Nast is no small operation. They publish *Vogue, Glamour, Mademoiselle, House and Garden, Brides,* and many other hugely successful national and international magazines.

As editor of *Analog,* I felt the time was right to bring out a big, slick, new magazine that dealt with science, science fiction, and the future. *Analog* was (and is) a fine magazine, precisely tuned for the hard core science-fiction audience. But there's a market of millions out there ready for this new magazine, I told the executives of Condé Nast. Let's make a Maximum Success out of it.

I even had a name for "my" new magazine: *Tomorrow!* With the exclamation point.

In all fairness, they considered the idea for *Tomorrow!* carefully. But they turned it down and went on to produce another women's magazine, *Self.*

Disheartened, I mentioned my idea to my literary agent, asking him if he knew of any publisher who would seriously consider *Tomorrow!* He shrugged and said (and I quote), "Nobody would go for it, except maybe that madman Guccione."

I thought he was joking.

Then came *Star Wars.* Trivial as that motion picture was in terms of art, it was terrific for business. Not only did film and TV producers hop onto the science-fiction bandwagon (a not unmixed blessing), but publishers began to look at science fiction with new seriousness.

I never tried to contact Bob Guccione about *Tomorrow!* But by June 1978 I resigned from *Analog* to devote myself to writing fulltime. One of the reasons for that decision was that there seemed to be a lot of new markets opening up for writers of science fiction and science fact. Among the new markets was a new magazine published by Bob Guccione: *Omni*.

The birthpangs of *Omni* (née *Nova*) and the story of how I came to be the magazine's Executive Editor are best told elsewhere. Suffice to say that Guccione planned for Maximum Success for his magazine.

And he achieved it.

With its first anniversary issue, *Omni* reached a total sale of more than one million. Independent readership surveys show that the magazine has at least four million readers. Judging from the letters received in the editorial office, those four million read the magazine very thoroughly, indeed. *Omni* is also heavy with advertising; the magazine became profitable before its sixth issue was published—in no small part because Guccione sank millions of dollars of promotion money into it.

And what have the book publishers been doing?

Looking at this week's *New York Times* best-seller lists, I see four works of fantasy or the future on the fiction hardcover list: *The Devil's Alternative*, by Frederick Forsyth; *Jailbird*, by Kurt Vonnegut; *The Dead Zone*, by Stephen King; and *The Third World War*, by a team of NATO generals, no less. Tom Wolfe's *The Right Stuff* has been on the nonfiction hardcover list for months. Among the paperback best sellers are Stephen King's *The Stand* and *The 80's: A Look Back*, edited by Tony Hendra, Christopher Cerf and Peter Elbling.

Within the past year or so, we have seen Len Deighton's *SS-GB*, Carl Sagan's *Broca's Brain* (and his earlier *Dragons of Eden*, which won a Pulitzer Prize), Robert Jastrow's *God and the Astronomers* and many other books of science or science fiction on the bestseller lists around the nation.

The old dream is becoming reality. But not in the way we dreamed it would.

We are not seeing Pulitzer Prizes being pushed on Robert A. Heinlein or Frank Herbert. We are not seeing science-fiction magazines such as *Analog* or *F&SF* blossoming into million-sellers.

We are not taking over the mainstream. It is taking over us.

Many of the novels on the best-seller lists that have nothing to do with the future still use themes and ideas and writing techniques that come straight out of the science-fiction world. The mainstream, the literary establishment, is absorbing the lessons and skills that science-fiction writers have developed over many painful decades. Ten years ago, a novel such as Deighton's *SS-GB* would have been relegated to the science-fiction shelves, to seek its fortune there under the Minimal Success strategy. Today there are enough copies in print, and enough advertising push behind the book, to make it a best seller.

Arthur C. Clarke has never made the best-seller list. Nor has Asimov. Nor Ray Bradbury, Frederik Pohl or any other purely hard core science-fiction writer. Despite the fact that, over the years, their books have sold millions upon millions of copies and been much more profitable to their publishers than most of the books in the *Times'* Top Ten. Frank Herbert's *Dune* novels finally reached best-sellerdom, after a decade of slowly growing sales. Robert A. Heinlein's forty-first book finally became a best seller, forty years after his recognition as the dean of American science-fiction writers.

To capitalize on the general public's newfound interest in science fiction, the publishers are not turning to science-fiction writers. They turn to writers who have proven they can "reach" the general reader and hit the best-seller lists; it is these writers who are bringing science fiction to the general public—in the guise of thrillers, speculative novels, books of horror or the occult.

Once you are labelled as a science-fiction writer, it is very difficult to get a publisher to believe that you can write for anyone other than the hard core science-fiction audience.

Omni magazine is an exception to that rule. At least, we try to be. We have deliberately tried to bring as many science-fiction writers into the magazine's pages as possible, to present both their fiction and their nonfiction to our very wide audience. But it hasn't been easy.

Omni's audience is not accustomed to reading hard core science fiction. So a story that starts with a line such as, "The warpship popped out of hyperspace nine parsecs from Aldebaran IV," would be incomprehensible to most of *Omni*'s readers. To reach that vast audience out there, the writer must get back to basics, stick to a strong human story and eschew the jargon that is perfectly understandable to Us, but opaque to Them.

Many science-fiction writers have tackled this challenge and succeeded beautifully. You can see their work in the magazine. Many others have ignored the challenge, content to work in the same field they have worked in all their lives, unwilling or afraid to lift their eyes toward broader vistas. They are conspicuous by their absence.

Personally, I am committed to reaching as wide an audience as I can. As editor of *Omni*, I want to prove to the literary establishment that science-fiction writers can entertain, excite, even enthrall millions of readers. As a writer, I want to reach the largest number of readers I can—and if this means writing stories in which the characters are more important than the gadgets, then fine, those are the stories I will write.

We have all been happy within the small, snug, comfortable womb of science fiction for many decades. But the bigger, rougher, more rewarding world is calling, and we must respond to that summons. Otherwise, all the work we have done, all the skills and ideas we have developed, all the tales we have to tell, will be appropriated by others while we are ignored.

Science-fiction writers—and readers—have also played the game of Minimal Success. It's time to maximize.

If there is one prediction I would like to see come true in the decade of the Eighties, it is this: that the best writers in science fiction exert themselves to reach the general audience, to prove that what we have to say is worth listening to, and that we can say it well enough to be understood and enjoyed by millions of readers.

The doors of the literary establishment are open to us—a little. This is the decade to push them open all the way.

JOANNA RUSS

The Extraordinary Voyages of Amélie Bertrand

Because Joanna Russ, by her own admission, "does not exist," it falls upon me to—how shall I put this? Explain? Yes, *explain* the situation. You surely will be just as confused afterward as you are now, but I enjoy explaining.

First, remember that when the Cretan said, "All Cretans are liars," he was lying. This in mind, I can report guardedly that someone calling herself Joanna Russ has been seen on the campus of a major university and that "the author of *The Female Man*" is reportedly still writing science fiction as well as work in other categories.

As to "The Extraordinary Voyages of Amélie Bertrand," it began as a dream, then spent two days composing itself in the translatorese by which we (erroneously) know Jules Verne. The story is a homage to Verne and science fiction. You must know that Verne's "extraordinary voyages" (as the books were called at the time) were imaginary—via guidebook, atlas and the author's creative genius. We all travel as Verne did; hence this story. There are science-fiction things all through it. For example, Verne actually did complain (in an interview) that Wells's stories did not "repose on a scientific basis" and he challenged "Cavorite," the anti-gravity material in *The First Men in the Moon,* with "That's all very well, but let him produce it!" You also should be apprised of the French farce ("by Feydeau, I think") called *Occupe-toi d'Amélie* ("Keep Your Eye on Amélie") in which Amélie, left temporarily by her lover, occupies herself much less respectably than Mme. Bertrand, the heroine of the story in this volume, who is a paragon-of-virtue Amélie.

Do you begin to suspect that Joanna Russ exists only in her stories? Ahhh, but you do not find extraordinary women in Joanna Russ stories!

Hommage à Jules Verne

In the summer of 192– there occurred to me the most extraordinary event of my life.

I was traveling on business and was in the French countryside, not far from Lyons, waiting for my train on a small railway platform on the outskirts of a town I shall call Beaulieu-sur-le-Pont. (This is not its name.) The weather was cool, although it was already June, and I shared the platform with only one other passenger: a plump woman of at least forty, by no means pretty but respectably dressed, the true type of our provincial *bonne bourgeoise,* who sat on the bench provided for the comfort of passengers and knitted away at some indeterminate garment.

The station at Beaulieu, like so many of our railway stops in small towns, is provided with a central train station of red brick through which runs an arch of passageway, also of red brick, which thus divides the edifice of the station into a ticket counter and waiting room on one side and a small café on the other. Thus, having attended one's train on the wrong side of the station (for there are railroad tracks on both sides of the edifice), one may occasionally find oneself making the traversal of the station in order to catch one's train, usually at the last minute.

So it occurred with me. I heard the approach of my train, drew out my watch, and found that the mild spring weather had caused me to indulge in a reverie not only lengthy but at a distance from my desired track; the two-fifty-one for Lyons was about to enter

185

Beaulieu, but I was wrongly situated to place myself on board;
were I not quick, no entrainment would take place.

Blessing the good fathers of Beaulieu-sur-le-Pont for their fore-
sight in so dividing their train depot, I walked briskly but with no
excessive haste towards the passage. I had not the slightest doubt
of catching my train. I even had leisure to reflect on the bridge
which figures so largely in the name of the town and to recall that,
according to my knowledge, this bridge had been destroyed in the
time of Caractacus; then I stepped between the buildings. I noticed that my footsteps echoed from the walls of the tunnel, a
phenomenon one may observe upon entering any confined space.
To the right of me and to the left were walls of red brick. The air
was invigoratingly fresh, the weather sunny and clear, and ahead
was the wooden platform, the well-trimmed bushes, and the pot-
ted geraniums of the other side of the Beaulieu train station.

Nothing could have been more ordinary.

Then, out of the corner of my eye, I noticed that the lady I had
seen knitting on the platform was herself entering the passage at
a decorous distance behind me. We were, it seems, to become
fellow passengers. I turned and raised my hat to her, intending to
continue. I could not see the Lyons train, but to judge by the
faculty of hearing, it was rounding the bend outside the station. I
placed my hat back upon my head, reached the center of the
tunnel, or rather, a point midway along its major diameter—

Will you believe me? Probably. You are English; the fogs and
literature of your unfortunate climate predispose you to marvels.
Your winters cause you to read much; your authors reflect to you
from their pages the romantic imagination of a *refugé* from the
damp and cold, to whom anything may happen if only it does so
outside his windows! I am the product of another soil; I am logical,
I am positive, I am French. Like my famous compatriot, I cry,
"Where is this marvel? Let him produce it!" I myself do not believe what happened to me. I believe it no more than I believe that
Phileas Fogg circumnavigated the globe in 187– and still lives
today in London with the lady he rescued from a funeral pyre in
Benares.

Nonetheless I will attempt to describe what happened.

The first sensation was a retardation of time. It seemed to me that I had been in the passage at Beaulieu for a very long time, and the passage itself seemed suddenly to become double its length, or even triple. Then my body became heavy, as in a dream; there was also a disturbance of balance as though the tunnel sloped *down* towards its farther end and some increase in gravity were pulling me in that direction. A phenomenon even more disturbing was the peculiar *haziness* that suddenly obscured the forward end of the Beaulieu tunnel, as if Beaulieu-sur-le-Pont, far from enjoying the temperate warmth of an excellent June day, were actually melting in the heat—yes, heat!—a terrible warmth like that of a furnace, and yet humid, entirely unknown to our moderate climate even in the depths of summer. In a moment my summer clothing was soaked, and I wondered with horror whether I dared offend customary politeness by opening my collar. The noise of the Lyons train, far from disappearing, now surrounded me on all sides as if a dozen trains, and not merely one, were converging upon Beaulieu-sur-le-Pont, or as if a strong wind (which was pushing me forward) were blowing. I attempted to peer into the mistiness ahead of me but could see nothing. A single step farther and the mist swirled aside; there seemed to be a vast spray of greenery beyond—indeed, I could distinctly make out the branches of a large palm tree upon which intense sunlight was beating—and then, directly crossing it, a long, thick, sinuous, gray serpent which appeared to writhe from side to side, and which then fixed itself around the trunk of the palm, bringing into view a gray side as large as the opening of the tunnel itself, four gray columns beneath, and two long ivory tusks.

It was an elephant.

It was the roar of the elephant which brought me to my senses. Before this I had proceeded as in an astonished dream; now I turned and attempted to retrace my steps but found that I could hardly move *up* the steep tunnel against the furious wind which assailed me. I was aware of the cool, fresh, familiar spring of Beaulieu, very small and precious, appearing like a photograph or a scene observed through the diminishing, not the magnifying end, of an opera glass, and of the impossibility of ever attaining it. Then a strong arm seized mine, and I was back on the platform from which I had ventured—it seemed now so long ago!—sitting on the wooden bench while the good bourgeoise in the decent dark dress inquired after my health.

I cried, "But the palm tree—the tropical air—the elephant!"

She said in the calmest way in the world, "Do not distress yourself, monsieur. It was merely Uganda."

I may mention here that Madame Bertrand, although not in her first youth, is a woman whose dark eyes sparkle with extraordinary charm. One must be an imbecile not to notice this. Her concern is sincere, her manner *séduisante,* and we had not been in conversation five minutes before she abandoned the barriers of reserve and explained to me not only the nature of the experience I had undergone, but (in the café of the train station at Beaulieu, over a lemon ice) her own extraordinary history.

"Shortly after the termination of the Great War" (said Madame Bertrand) "I began a habit which I have continued to this day: whenever my husband, Aloysius Bertrand, is away from Beaulieu-sur-le-Pont on business, as often happens, I visit my sister-in-law in Lyons, leaving Beaulieu on one day in the middle of the week and returning on the next. At first my visits were uneventful. Then, one fateful day only two years ago, I happened to depart from the wrong side of the train station after purchasing my ticket, and so found myself seeking to approach my train through that archway or passage where you, Monsieur, so recently ventured. There were the same effects, but I attributed them to an attack of faintness and continued, expecting my hour's ride to Lyons, my sister-in-law's company, the cinema, the restaurant, and the usual journey back the next day.

"Imagine my amazement—no, my stupefaction—when I found myself instead on a rough, wooden platform surrounded on three sides by the massive rocks and lead-colored waters of a place entirely unfamiliar to me! I made inquiries and discovered, to my unbounded astonishment, that I was on the last railway stop or terminus of Tierra del Fuego, the southernmost tip of the South American continent, and that I had engaged myself to sail as supercargo on a whaling vessel contracted to cruise the waters of Antarctica for the next two years. The sun was low, the clouds massing above, and behind me (continuing the curve of the rock-infested bay) was a jungle of squat pine trees, expressing by the irregularity of their trunks the violence of the climate.

"What could I do? My clothing was Victorian, the ship ready to sail, the six months' night almost upon us. The next train was not due until spring.

"To make a long story short, I sailed.

"You might expect that a lady, placed in such a situation, would suffer much that was disagreeable and discommoding. So it was. But there is also a somber charm to the far south which only those who have traveled there can know: the stars glittering on the ice fields, the low sun, the penguins, the icebergs, the whales. And then there were the sailors, children of the wilderness, young, ardent, sincere, especially one, a veritable Apollo with a broad forehead and golden mustachios. To be frank, I did not remain aloof; we became acquainted, one thing led to another, and *enfin* I learned to love the smell of whale oil. Two years later, alighting from the railway train I had taken to Nome, Alaska, where I had gone to purchase my *trousseau* (for having made telegraphic inquiries about Beaulieu-sur-le-Pont, I found that no Monsieur Bertrand existed therein and so considered myself a widow) I found myself, not in my Victorian dress in the bustling and frigid city of Nome, that commercial capital of the North with its outlaws, dogs, and Esquimaux in furs carrying loads of other furs upon their sleds, but in my old, familiar visiting-dress (in which I had started from Beaulieu so long before) on the platform at Lyons, with my sister-in-law waiting for me. Not only that, but in the more than two years I had remained away, no more time had passed in what I am forced to call the real world than the hour required for the train ride from Beaulieu to Lyons! I had expected Garance to fall upon my neck with cries of astonishment at my absence and the strangeness of my dress; instead she inquired after my health, and not waiting for an answer, began to describe in the most ordinary manner and at very great length the roast of veal which she had purchased that afternoon for dinner.

"At first, so confused and grief-stricken was I, that I thought I had somehow missed the train for Nome, and that returning at once from Lyons to Beaulieu would enable me to reach Alaska. I almost cut my visit to Lyons short on the plea of ill-health. But I soon realized the absurdity of imagining that a railway could cross several thousand miles of ocean, and since my sister-in-law was already suspicious (I could not help myself during the visit and often burst out with a *'Mon cher Jack!'*) I controlled myself and gave vent to my feelings only on the return trip to Beaulieu— which, far from ending in Nome, Alaska, ended at the Beaulieu train station and at exactly the time predicted by the railway timetable.

"I decided that my two-years' holiday had been only what the men of psychological science would entitle an unusually complete and detailed dream. The ancient Chinese were, I believe, famous for such vivid dreams; one of their poets is said to have experienced an entire lifetime of love, fear, and adventure while washing his feet. This was my case exactly. Here was I not a day —nay, not an hour—older, and no one knew what had passed in the Antarctic save I myself.

"It was a reasonable explanation, but it had one grave defect, which rendered it totally useless.

"It was false.

"Since that time, Monsieur, I have gone on my peculiar voyages, my holidays, *mes vacances*, as I call them, not once but dozens of times. My magic carpet is the railway station at Beaulieu, or to be more precise, the passageway between the ticket office and the café at precisely ten minutes before three in the afternoon. A traversal of the passage at any other time brings me merely to the other side of the station, but a traversal of the passage at this particular time brings me to some far, exotic corner of the globe. Perhaps it is Ceylon with its crowds of variegated hue, its scent of incense, its pagodas and rickshaws. Or the deserts of Al-Iqah, with the crowds of Bedawi, dressed in flowing white and armed with rifles, many of whom whirl round about one another on horseback. Or I will find myself on the languid islands of Tahiti, with the graceful and dusky inhabitants bringing me bowls of *poi* and garlands of flowers whose beauty is unmatched anywhere else in the tropical portion of the globe. Nor have my holidays been entirely confined to the terrestrial regions. Last February I stepped through the passage to find myself on the sands of a primitive beach under a stormy, gray sky; in the distance one could perceive the roarings of saurians and above me were the giant saw-toothed, purple leaves of some palmaceous plant, one (as it turned out) entirely unknown to botanical science.

"No, Monsieur, it was not Ceylon; it was Venus. It is true that I prefer a less overcast climate, but still one can hardly complain. To lie in the darkness of the Venerian night, on the silky volcanic sands, under the starry leaves of the *laradh,* while imbibing the million perfumes of the night-blooming flowers and listening to the music of the *karakh*—really, one does not miss the blue sky. Although only a few weeks ago I was in a place that also pleased me: imagine a huge, whitish-blue sky, a desert with giant mountains on the horizon, and the lean, hard-bitten water-prospectors with their dowsing rods, their high-heeled boots, and their large hats, worn to protect faces already tanned and wrinkled from the intense sunlight.

"No, not Mars, Texas. They are marvelous people, those American pioneers, the men handsome and laconic, the women sturdy and efficient. And then one day I entrained to Lyons only to find myself on a railway platform that resembled a fishbowl made of tinted glass, while around me rose mountains fantastically slender into a black sky where the stars shone like hard marbles, scarcely twinkling at all. I was wearing a glass helmet and clothes that resembled a diver's. I had no idea where I was until I rose, and then to my edified surprise, instead of rising in the usual manner, I positively bounded into the air!

"I was on the Moon.

"Yes, Monsieur, the Moon, although some distance in the future, the year two thousand eighty and nine, to be precise. At that date human beings will have established a colony on the Moon. My carriage swiftly shot down beneath one of the Selenic craters to land in their principal city, a fairy palace of slender towers and domes of glass, for they use as building material a glass made from the native silicate gravel. It was on the Moon that I gathered whatever theory I now have concerning my peculiar experiences with the railway passage at Beaulieu-sur-le-Pont, for I made the acquaintance there of the principal mathematician of the twenty-first century, a most elegant lady, and put the problem to her. You must understand that on the Moon *les nègres, les juifs,* even *les femmes* may obtain high positions and much influence; it is a true republic. This lady introduced me to her colleague, a black physicist of more-than-normal happenings, or *le paraphysique* as they call it, and the two debated the matter during an entire day (not a Selenic day, of course, since that would have amounted to a time equal to twenty-eight days of our own). They could not agree, but in brief, as they told me, either the railway tunnel at Beaulieu-sur-le-Pont has achieved infinite connectivity or it is haunted. To be perfectly sincere, I regretted leaving the Moon. But one has one's obligations. Just as my magic carpet here at Beaulieu is of the nature of a railway tunnel, and just as I always find myself in *mes vacances* at first situated on a railway platform, thus my return must also be effected by that so poetically termed road of iron; I placed myself into the railway that connects two of the principal Selenic craters, and behold!—I alight at the platform at Lyons, not a day older.

"Indeed, Monsieur" (and here Madame Bertrand coughed delicately) "as we are both people of the world, I may mention that certain other of the biological processes also suspend themselves, a fact not altogether to my liking, since my dear Aloysius and myself are entirely without family. Yet this suspension has its advantages; if I had aged as I have lived, it would be a woman of seventy who speaks to you now. In truth, how can one age in worlds that are, to speak frankly, not quite real? Though perhaps if I had remained permanently in one of these worlds, I too would have begun to age along with the other inhabitants. That would be a pleasure on the Moon, for my mathematical friend was aged two hundred when I met her, and her acquaintance, the professor of *le paraphysique,* two hundred and five."

Here Madame Bertrand, to whose recital I had been listening with breathless attention, suddenly ceased speaking. Her lemon ice stood untouched upon the table. So full was I of projects to make the world acquainted with this amazing history that I did not at first notice the change in Madame Bertrand's expression, and so I burst forth:

"The National Institute—the Académie—no, the universities, and the newspapers also—"

But the charming lady, with a look of horror, had risen from the table, crying, "*Mon dieu!* My train! What will Garance think? What will she say? Monsieur, not a word to anyone!"

Imagine my consternation when Madame Bertrand here

precipitously departed from the café and began to cross the station towards that ominous passageway. I could only expostulate, "But, madame, consider! Ceylon! Texas! Mars!"

"No, it is too late," said she. "Only at the former time in the train schedule. Monsieur, remember, please, not a word to anyone!"

Following her, I cried, "But if you do not return—" and she again favored me with her delightful smile, saying rapidly, "Do not distress yourself, Monsieur. By now I have developed certain sensations—a *frisson* of the neck and shoulder blades—which warns me of the condition of the passageway. The later hour is always safe. But my train—!"

And so Madame Bertrand left me. Amazing woman! A traveler not only to the far regions of the earth but to those of imagination, and yet perfectly respectable, gladly fulfilling the duties of family life, and punctually (except for this one time) meeting her sister-in-law, Mademoiselle Garance Bertrand, on the train platform at Lyons.

Is that the end of my story? No, for I was fated to meet Amélie Bertrand once again.

My business, which I have mentioned to you, took me back to Beaulieu-sur-le-Pont at the end of that same summer. I must confess that I hoped to encounter Madame Bertrand, for I had made it my intention to notify at least several of our great national institutions of the extraordinary powers possessed by the railway passage at Beaulieu, and yet I certainly could not do so without Madame Bertrand's consent. Again it was shortly before three in the afternoon; again the station platform was deserted. I saw a figure which I took to be that of Madame Bertrand seated upon the bench reserved for passengers and hastened to it with a glad cry—

But it was not Amélie Bertrand. Rather it was a thin and elderly female, entirely dressed in the dullest of black and completely without the charm I had expected to find in my fellow passenger. The next moment I heard my name pronounced and was delighted to perceive, issuing from the ticket office, Madame Bertrand herself, wearing a light-colored summer dress.

But where was the gaiety, the charm, the pleasant atmosphere of June? Madame Bertrand's face was closed, her eyes watchful,

her expression determined. I would immediately have opened to
her my immense projects, but with a shake of her head the lady
silenced me, indicating the figure I have already mentioned.

"My sister-in-law, Mademoiselle Garance," she said. I confess
that I nervously expected that Aloysius Bertrand himself would
now appear. But we were alone on the platform. Madame Bertrand continued: "Garance, this is the gentleman who was the
unfortunate cause of my missing my train last June."

Mademoiselle Garance, as if to belie the reputation for loquacity
I had heard applied to her earlier in the summer, said nothing, but
merely clutched to her meager bosom a small train case.

Madame Bertrand said to me, "I have explained to Garance the
occasion of your illness last June and the manner in which the
officials of the station detained me. I am glad to see you looking
so well."

This was a clear hint that Mademoiselle Garance was to know
nothing of her sister-in-law's history; thus I merely bowed and
nodded. I wished to have the opportunity of conversing with Madame Bertrand more freely, but I could say nothing in the presence of her sister-in-law. Desperately I began: "You are taking the
train today—"

"For the sake of nostalgia," said Madame Bertrand. "After today
I shall never set foot in a railway carriage. Garance may if she likes,
but I will not. Aeroplanes, motor cars, and ships will be good
enough for me. Perhaps like the famous American, Madame Ear-
hart, I shall learn to fly. This morning Aloysius told me the good
news: a change in his business arrangements has enabled us to
move to Lyons, which we are to do at the end of the month."

"And in the intervening weeks—?" said I.

Madame Bertrand replied composedly, "There will be none.
They are tearing down the station."

What a blow! And there sat the old maid, Mademoiselle Garance, entirely unconscious of the impending loss to science! I
stammered something—I know not what—but my good angel
came to my rescue; with an infinitesimal movement of the fingers,
she said:

"Oh, Monsieur, my conscience pains me too much! Garance,
would you believe that I told this gentleman the most preposter-

ous stories? I actually told him—seriously, now—that the passage-way of this train station was the gateway to another world! No, many worlds, and that I had been to all of them. Can you believe it of me?" She turned to me. "Oh, Monsieur," she said, "you were a good listener. You only pretended to believe. Surely you cannot imagine that a respectable woman like myself would leave her husband by means of a railway passage which has achieved infinite connectivity?"

Here Madame Bertrand looked at me in a searching manner, but I was at a loss to understand her intention in so doing and said nothing.

She went on, with a little shake of the head. "I must confess it; I am addicted to storytelling. Whenever my dear Aloysius left home on his business trips, he would say to me, *'Occupe-toi, occupe-toi, Amélie!'* and, alas, I have occupied myself only too well. I thought my romance might divert your mind from your ill-health and so presumed to tell you an unlikely tale of extraordinary voyages. Can you forgive me?"

I said something polite, something I do not now recall. I was, you understand, still reeling from the blow. All that merely a fable! Yet with what detail, what plausible circumstance Madame Bertrand had told her story. I could only feel relieved I had not actually written to the National Institute. I was about to press both ladies to take some refreshment with me, when Madame Bertrand (suddenly putting her hand to her heart in a gesture that seemed to me excessive) cried, "Our train!" and turning to me, remarked, "Will you accompany us down the passage?"

Something made me hesitate; I know not what.

"Think, Monsieur," said Madame Bertrand, with her hand still pressed to her heart, "where will it be this time? A London of the future, perhaps, enclosed against the weather and built entirely of glass? Or perhaps the majestic, high plains of Colorado? Or will we find ourselves in one of the underground cities of the moons of Jupiter, into whose awesome skies the mighty planet rises and sets with a visual diameter greater than that of the terrestrial Alps?"

She smiled with humor at Mademoiselle Garance, remarking, "Such are the stories I told this gentleman, dear Garance; they were a veritable novel," and I saw that she was gently teasing her

sister-in-law, who naturally did not know what any of this was
about.

Mademoiselle Garance ventured to say timidly that she "liked
to read novels."

I bowed.

Suddenly I heard the sound of the train outside Beaulieu-sur-le-
Pont. Madame Bertrand cried in an utterly prosaic voice, "Our
train! Garance, we shall miss our train!" and again she asked,
"Monsieur, will you accompany us?"

I bowed, but remained where I was. Accompanied by the thin,
stooped figure of her sister-in-law, Madame Bertrand walked
quickly down the passageway which divides the ticket room of the
Beaulieu-sur-le-Pont station from the tiny café. I confess that
when the two ladies reached the midpoint of the longitudinal axis
of the passageway, I involuntarily closed my eyes, and when I
looked again, the passage was empty.

What moved me then I do not know, but I found myself quickly
traversing the passageway, seeing in my mind's eye Madame Bertrand boarding the Lyons train with her sister-in-law, Mademoiselle Garance. One could certainly hear the train; the sound of its
engine filled the whole station. I believe I told myself that I wished
to exchange one last polite word. I reached the other side of the
station—

And there was no Lyons train there.

There were no ladies on the platform.

There is, indeed, no two-fifty-one train to Lyons whatsoever, not
on the schedule of any line!

Imagine my sensations, my dear friend, upon learning that Madame Bertrand's story was true, all of it! It is true, all too true, all
of it is true, and my Amélie is gone forever!

"My" Amélie I call her; yet she still belongs (in law) to Aloysius
Bertrand, who will, no doubt, after the necessary statutory period
of waiting is over, marry again, and thus become a respectable and
unwitting bigamist.

That animal could never have understood her!

Even now (if I may be permitted that phrase) Amélie Bertrand
may be drifting down one of the great Venerian rivers on a gon-
dola, listening to the music of the *karakh;* even now she may

perform acts of heroism on Airstrip One or chat with her mathematical friend on a balcony that overlooks the airy towers and flower-filled plazas of the Selenic capitol. I have no doubt that if you were to attempt to find the places Madame Bertrand mentioned by looking in the Encyclopedia or a similar work of reference, you would not succeed. As she herself mentioned, they are "not quite real." There are strange discrepancies.

Alas, my friend, condole with me; by now all such concern is academic, for the train station at Beaulieu-sur-le-Pont is gone, replaced by a vast erection swarming with workmen, a giant *hangar* (I learned the name from one of them), or edifice for the housing of aeroplanes. I am told that large numbers of these machines will soon fly from *hangar* to *hangar* across the country.

But think: these aeroplanes, will they not in time be used for ordinary business travel, for scheduled visits to resorts and other places? In short, are they not even now the railways of the new age? Is it not possible that the same condition, whether of infinite connectivity or of hauntedness, may again obtain, perhaps in the same place where the journeys of my vanished angel have established a precedent or predisposition?

My friend, collude with me. The *hangar* at Beaulieu will soon be finished, or so I read in the newspapers. I shall go down into the country and establish myself near this *hangar;* I shall purchase a ticket for a ride in one of the new machines, and then we shall see. Perhaps I will enjoy only a pleasant ascension into the air and a similar descent. Perhaps I will instead feel that *frisson* of the neck and shoulder blades of which Madame Bertrand spoke; well, no matter: my children are grown, my wife has a generous income, the *frisson* will not dismay me. I shall walk down the corridor or passageway in or around the *hangar* at precisely nine minutes before three and into the space between the worlds; I shall again feel the strange retardation of time, I shall feel the heaviness of the body, I shall see the haziness at the other end of the tunnel, and then through the lashing wind, through the mistiness which envelops me, with the rushing and roaring of an invisible aeroplane in my ears, I shall proceed. Madame Bertrand was kind enough to delay her own holiday to conduct me back from Uganda; she was generous enough to offer to share the traversal of the passage with me a second time. Surely such kindness and generosity must have its effect! This third time I will proceed. Away from my profession, my daily newspaper, my chess games, my *digestif*—in short, away from all those habits which, it is understood, are given us to take the place of happiness. Away from the petty annoyances of life I shall proceed, away from a dull old age, away from the confusions and terrors of a Europe grown increasingly turbulent, to—

—*What?*

The above copy of a letter was found in a volume of the Encyclopedia (U–Z) in the Bibliothèque Nationale. *It is believed from the evidence that the writer disappeared at a certain provincial town (called "Beaulieu-sur-le-Pont" in the manuscript) shortly after purchasing a ticket for a flight in an aeroplane at the flying field there, a pastime popular among holiday-makers.*

He has never been seen again.

"There's a new sound north of here, east of here: Christian
aroldsen, and he'll tear out your heart with his songs."
The Listeners came, a few to whom variety was everything first,
en those to whom novelty and vogue mattered most, and at last
ose who valued beauty and passion above everything else. They
me and stayed out in Christian's woods and listened as his music
s played through perfect speakers on the roof of his house.
en the music stopped and Christian came out of his house, he
ld see the Listeners moving away. He asked and was told why
y came; he marveled that the things he did for love on his
trument could be of interest to other people.
He felt, strangely, even more lonely to know that he could sing
he Listeners and yet never be able to hear their songs.
But they have no songs," said the woman who came to bring
food every day. "They are Listeners. You are a Maker. You
e songs, and they listen."
Why?" asked Christian, innocently.
e woman looked puzzled. "Because that's what they want
to do. They've been tested, and they are happiest as Listen-
You are happiest as a Maker. Aren't you happy?"
es," Christian answered, and he was telling the truth. His life
erfect, and he wouldn't change anything, not even the sweet
ss of the backs of the Listeners as they walked away at the
f his songs.
ristian was seven years old.

FIRST MOVEMENT

the third time the short man with glasses and a strangely
opriate mustache dared to wait in the underbrush for Chris-
come out. For the third time he was overcome by the
of the song that had just ended, a mournful symphony that
the short man with glasses feel the pressure of the leaves
him, even though it was summer and they had months left
they would fall. The fall was still inevitable, said Christian's
rough all their life the leaves hold within them the power
nd that must color their life. The short man with glasses
but when the song ended and the other Listeners moved
e hid in the brush and waited.

ORSON SCOTT CARD

Unaccompanied Sonata

Orson Scott Card began publishing science fiction with stories in
Analog and "branched out" from there. He has three novels, the most
recent, *Songmaster* (1980), which includes Nebula nominee "Mikal's
Songbird" as an episode. His newest work, however, is historical, not
science fiction, and he is currently working on "a huge novel, *Saints*,
due in 1981." That could mean you may never again see his work in
pages such as these, but certainly not because of the caliber of his
writing. He insists, though, that his work is moving away from science
fiction, "becoming more and more either fantasy or mainstream. I'm
more comfortable with the limitations of history than with the limitations of the conventions in science fiction."

For the time being, Card teaches a science fiction-fantasy writing
course at the University of Utah, where he is working on a graduate
degree in English. He has worked as a copyeditor and book editor and
was staff writer-assistant editor on a magazine before turning freelance.
Card also has written "several dozen" plays, most produced in Utah.
He says he lost $20,000 on theater in Utah and "still manages to lose
a few thousand a year on plays."

Card and his wife, Kristine Allen, live near Salt Lake City. They have
a son, Geoffrey, and are expecting a second child. Of "Unaccompanied
Sonata," he says, it began as hard science fiction "but quickly degenerated to the sort of story I'd rather tell . . . a sort of *Paradise Lost* with
a nice Satan." *Degenerated,* that was his own word. This could mean
he is not completely lost to us; perhaps he senses that being *more
comfortable* is not all that inspiring.

❧

❧

When Christian Haroldsen was six months old, preliminary tests showed a predisposition toward rhythm and a keen awareness of pitch. There were other tests, of course, and many possible routes still open to him. But rhythm and pitch were the governing signs of his own private zodiac, and already the reinforcement began. Mr. and Mrs. Haroldsen were provided with tapes of many kinds of sound and instructed to play them constantly, whether Christian was awake or asleep.

When Christian Haroldsen was two years old, his seventh battery of tests pinpointed the path he would inevitably follow. His creativity was exceptional; his curiosity, insatiable; his understanding of music, so intense that on top of all the tests was written "Prodigy."

Prodigy was the word that took him from his parents' home to a house in deep deciduous forest where winter was savage and violent and summer, a brief, desperate eruption of green. He grew up, cared for by unsinging servants, and the only music he was allowed to hear was bird song and wind song and the crackling of winter wood; thunder and the faint cry of golden leaves as they broke free and tumbled to the earth; rain on the roof and the drip of water from icicles; the chatter of squirrels and the deep silence of snow falling on a moonless night.

These sounds were Christian's only conscious music. He grew

up with the symphonies of his early years only distant an[d] ble-to-retrieve memories. And so he learned to hea[r] unmusical things—for he had to find music, even when none to find.

He found that colors made sounds in his mind: Sunli[ght in sum]mer was a blaring chord; moonlight in winter, a thin[ ] wail; new green in spring, a low murmur in almost (bu[t not quite]) random rhythms; the flash of a red fox in the leave[s a] sudden startlement.

And he learned to play all those sounds on his Instru[ment. The] world were violins, trumpets, and clarinets, as there [had been for] centuries. Christian knew nothing of that. Only hi[s Instrument] was available. It was enough.

Christian lived in one room in his house, which he [ ] most of the time. He had a bed (not too soft), a chai[r and a table, a] silent machine that cleaned him and his clothing, a[nd a] light.

The other room contained only his Instrument. I[t was large, filled] with many keys and strips and levers and bars, [and when he] touched any part of it, a sound came out. Ever[y key made a] different sound; every point on the strips made a [ ] every lever modified the tone; every bar altered [the structure of] the sound.

When he first came to the house, Christian pla[yed (as children] will) with the Instrument, making strange and fu[nny noises. It was] his only playmate; he learned it well, could prod[uce any sound he] wanted to. At first he delighted in loud, blarin[g] began to learn the pleasure of silences and rhyt[hms.] began to play with soft and loud and to play tw[o sounds at once] and to change those two sounds together to mak[e] to play again a sequence of sounds he had pla[yed]

Gradually, the sounds of the forest outside hi[s house found their] way into the music he played. He learned t[o] through his Instrument; he learned to make [ ] songs he could play at will. Green with its in[ ] his most subtle harmony; the birds cried out [ ] with all the passion of Christian's loneliness.

And the word spread to the licensed Liste[ners]

200

This time his wait was rewarded. Christian came out of his house, walked among the trees, and came toward where the short man with glasses waited. The man admired the easy, unpostured way that Christian walked. The composer looked to be about thirty, yet there was something childish in the way he looked around him, the way his walk was aimless and prone to stop so he would just touch (and not break) a fallen twig with his bare toes.

"Christian," said the short man with glasses.

Christian turned, startled. In all these years, no Listener had ever spoken to him. It was forbidden. Christian knew the law.

"It's forbidden," Christian said.

"Here," the short man with glasses said, holding out a small black object.

"What is it?"

The short man grimaced. "Just take it. Push the button and it plays."

"Plays?"

"Music."

Christian's eyes opened wide. "But that's forbidden. I can't have my creativity polluted by hearing other musicians' work. That would make me imitative and derivative, instead of original."

"Reciting," the man said. "You're just reciting that. This is Bach's music." There was reverence in his voice.

"I can't," Christian said.

And then the short man shook his head. "You don't know. You don't know what you're missing. But I heard it in your song when I came here years ago, Christian. You want this."

"It's forbidden," Christian answered, for to him the very fact that a man who knew an act was forbidden still wanted to perform it was astounding, and he couldn't get past the novelty of it to realize that some action was expected of him.

There were footsteps, and words being spoken in the distance, and the short man's face became frightened. He ran at Christian, forced the recorder into his hands, then took off toward the gate of the preserve.

Christian took the recorder and held it in a spot of sunlight coming through the leaves. It gleamed dully. "Bach," Christian said. Then, "Who the hell is Bach?"

But he didn't throw the recorder down. Nor did he give the recorder to the woman who came to ask him what the short man with glasses had stayed for. "He stayed for at least ten minutes."

"I only saw him for thirty seconds," Christian answered.

"And?"

"He wanted me to hear some other music. He had a recorder."

"Did he give it to you?"

"No," Christian said. "Doesn't he still have it?"

"He must have dropped it in the woods."

"He said it was Bach."

"It's forbidden. That's all you need to know. If you should find the recorder, Christian, you know the law."

"I'll give it to you."

She looked at him carefully. "You know what would happen if you listened to such a thing."

Christian nodded.

"Very well. We'll be looking for it, too. I'll see you tomorrow, Christian. And next time somebody stays after, don't talk to him. Just come back in and lock the doors."

"I'll do that," Christian said.

There was a summer rainstorm that night, wind and rain and thunder, and Christian found that he could not sleep. Not because of the music of the weather—he'd slept through a thousand such storms. It was the recorder that lay against the wall behind the Instrument. Christian had lived for nearly thirty years surrounded only by this wild, beautiful place and the music he himself made. But now . . .

Now he could not stop wondering. Who was Bach? Who *is* Bach? What is his music? How is it different from mine? Has he discovered things that I don't know?

What is his music? What is his music? What is his music?

Wondering. Until dawn, when the storm was abating and the wind had died. Christian got out of his bed, where he had not slept but only tossed back and forth all night, and took the recorder from its hiding place and played it.

At first it sounded strange, like noise; odd sounds that had nothing to do with the sounds of Christian's life. But the patterns were clear, and by the end of the recording, which was not even a half-hour long, Christian had mastered the idea of fugue, and the sound of the harpsichord preyed on his mind.

Yet he knew that if he let these things show up in his music, he would be discovered. So he did not try a fugue. He did not attempt to imitate the harpsichord's sound.

And every night he listened to the recording, learning more and more until finally the Watcher came.

The Watcher was blind, and a dog led him. He came to the door, and because he was a Watcher, the door opened for him without his even knocking.

"Christian Haroldsen, where is the recorder?" the Watcher asked.

"Recorder?" Christian asked, then knew it was hopeless. So he took the machine and gave it to the Watcher.

"Oh, Christian," said the Watcher, and his voice was mild and sorrowful. "Why didn't you turn it in without listening to it?"

"I meant to," Christian said. "But how did you know?"

"Because suddenly there are no fugues in your work. Suddenly your songs have lost the only Bach-like thing about them. And you've stopped experimenting with new sounds. What were you trying to avoid?"

"This," Christian said, and he sat down and on his first try duplicated the sound of the harpsichord.

"Yet you've never tried to do that until now, have you?"

"I thought you'd notice."

"Fugues and harpsichord, the two things you noticed first—and the only things you didn't absorb into your music. All your other songs for these last weeks have been tinted and colored and influenced by Bach. Except that there was no fugue, and there was no harpsichord. You have broken the law. You were put here because you were a genius, creating new things with only nature for your inspiration. Now, of course, you're derivative, and truly new creation is impossible for you. You'll have to leave."

"I know," Christian said, afraid, yet not really understanding what life outside his house would be like.

"We'll train you for the kinds of jobs you can pursue now. You won't starve. You won't die of boredom. But because you broke the law, one thing is forbidden to you now."

"Music."

"Not all music. There is music of a sort, Christian, that the common people, the ones who aren't Listeners, can have. Radio and television and record music. But live music and new music— those are forbidden to you. You may not sing. You may not play an instrument. You may not tap out a rhythm."

"Why not?"

The Watcher shook his head. "The world is too perfect, too at peace, too happy, for us to permit a misfit who broke the law to go about spreading discontent. And if you make more music, Christian, you will be punished drastically. Drastically."

Christian nodded, and when the Watcher told him to come, he came, leaving behind the house and the woods and his Instrument. At first he took it calmly, as the inevitable punishment for his infraction; but he had little concept of punishment, or of what exile from his Instrument would mean.

Within five hours he was shouting and striking out at anyone who came near him, because his fingers craved the touch of the Instrument's keys and levers and strips and bars, and he could not have them, and now he knew that he had never been lonely before.

It took six months before he was ready for normal life. And when he left the Retraining Center (a small building, because it was so rarely used), he looked tired and years older, and he didn't smile at anyone. He became a delivery-truck driver, because the tests said that this was a job that would least grieve him and least remind him of his loss and most engage his few remaining aptitudes and interests.

He delivered doughnuts to grocery stores.

And at night he discovered the mysteries of alcohol; and the alcohol and the doughnuts and the truck and his dreams were enough that he was, in his way, content. He had no anger in him. He could live the rest of his life, without bitterness.

He delivered fresh doughnuts and took the stale ones away with him.

SECOND MOVEMENT

"With a name like Joe," Joe always said, "I had to open a bar and grill, just so I could put up a sign saying 'Joe's Bar and Grill.' " And he laughed and laughed, because, after all, Joe's Bar and Grill was a funny name these days.

But Joe was a good bartender, and the Watchers had put him in the right kind of place. Not in a big city but in a small town: a town just off the freeway, where truck drivers often came; a town not far from a large city, so that interesting things were nearby to be talked about and worried about and bitched about and loved.

Joe's Bar and Grill was, therefore, a nice place to come, and many people came there. Not fashionable people, and not drunks, but lonely people and friendly people in just the right mixture. "My clients are like a good drink. Just enough of this and that to make a new flavor that tastes better than any of the ingredients." Oh, Joe was a poet; he was a poet of alcohol, and like many another person these days, he often said, "My father was a lawyer, and in the old days I would have probably ended up a lawyer, too. And I never would have known what I was missing."

Joe was right. And he was a damn good bartender, and he didn't wish he were anything else, so he was happy.

One night, however, a new man came in, a man with a doughnut delivery truck and a doughnut brand name on his uniform. Joe noticed him because silence clung to the man like a smell—wherever he walked, people sensed it, and though they scarcely looked at him, they lowered their voices or stopped talking at all, and they got reflective and looked at the walls and the mirror behind the bar. The doughnut deliveryman sat in a corner and had a watered-down drink that meant he intended to stay a long time and didn't want his alcohol intake to be so rapid that he was forced to leave early.

Joe noticed things about people, and he noticed that this man kept looking off in the dark corner where the piano stood. It was an old, out-of-tune monstrosity from the old days (for this had been a bar for a long time), and Joe wondered why the man was fascinated by it. True, a lot of Joe's customers had been interested, but they had always walked over and plunked on the keys, trying to find a melody, failing with the out-of-tune keys, and finally giving up. This man, however, seemed almost afraid of the piano, and didn't go near it.

At closing time, the man was still there, and, on a whim, instead of making the man leave, Joe turned off the piped-in music, turned off most of the lights, and went over and lifted the lid and exposed the gray keys.

The deliveryman came over to the piano. *Chris*, his name tag said. He sat and touched a single key. The sound was not pretty. But the man touched all the keys one by one and then touched them in different orders, and all the time Joe watched, wondering why the man was so intense about it.

"Chris," Joe said.

Chris looked up at him.

"Do you know any songs?"

Chris's face went funny.

"I mean, some of those old-time songs, not those fancy ass-twitchers on the radio, but *songs*. 'In a Little Spanish Town.' My mother sang that one to me." And Joe began to sing, "In a little Spanish town, 'twas on a night like this. Stars were peek-a-booing down, 'twas on a night like this."

Chris began to play as Joe's weak and toneless baritone went on with the song. But his playing wasn't an accompaniment, not anything Joe could call an accompaniment. It was, instead, an opponent to his melody, an enemy to it, and the sounds coming out of the piano were strange and unharmonious and, by God, beautiful. Joe stopped singing and listened. For two hours he listened, and when it was over he soberly poured the man a drink and poured one for himself and clinked glasses with Chris the doughnut deliveryman who could take that rotten old piano and make the damn thing sing.

Three nights later, Chris came back, looking harried and afraid. But this time Joe knew what would happen (had to happen), and instead of waiting until closing time, Joe turned off the piped-in music ten minutes early. Chris looked up at him pleadingly. Joe misunderstood—he went over and lifted the lid to the keyboard and smiled. Chris walked stiffly, perhaps reluctantly, to the stool and sat.

"Hey, Joe," one of the last five customers shouted, "closing early?"

Joe didn't answer. Just watched as Chris began to play. No preliminaries this time; no scales and wanderings over the keys. Just power, and the piano was played as pianos aren't meant to be played; the bad notes, the out-of-tune notes, were fit into the music so that they sounded right, and Chris's fingers, ignoring the strictures of the twelve-tone scale, played, it seemed to Joe, in the cracks.

None of the customers left until Chris finished an hour and a half later. They all shared that final drink and went home, shaken by the experience.

The next night Chris came again, and the next, and the next. Whatever private battle had kept him away for the first few days after his first night of playing, he had apparently won it or lost it. None of Joe's business. What Joe cared about was the fact that when Chris played the piano, it did things to him that music had never done, and he wanted it.

The customers apparently wanted it, too. Near closing time people began showing up, apparently just to hear Chris play. Joe began starting the piano music earlier and earlier, and he had to discontinue the free drinks after the playing, because there were so many people it would have put him out of business.

It went on for two long, strange months. The delivery van pulled up outside, and people stood aside for Chris to enter. No one said anything to him. No one said anything at all, but everyone waited until he began to play the piano. He drank nothing at all. Just played. And between songs the hundreds of people in Joe's Bar and Grill ate and drank.

But the merriment was gone. The laughter and the chatter and the camaraderie were missing, and after a while Joe grew tired of the music and wanted to have his bar back the way it was. He toyed with the idea of getting rid of the piano, but the customers would have been angry at him. He thought of asking Chris not to come any more, but he could not bring himself to speak to the strange, silent man.

And so finally he did what he knew he should have done in the first place. He called the Watchers.

They came in the middle of a performance, a blind Watcher with a dog on a leash, and an earless Watcher who walked unsteadily, holding onto things for balance. They came in the middle of a song and did not wait for it to end. They walked to the piano and closed the lid gently, and Chris withdrew his fingers and looked at the closed lid.

"Oh, Christian," said the man with the seeing-eye dog.

"I'm sorry," Christian answered. "I tried not to."

"Oh, Christian, how can I bear doing to you what must be done?"

"Do it," Christian said.

And so the man with no ears took a laser knife from his coat pocket and cut off Christian's fingers and thumbs, right where they rooted into his hands. The laser cauterized and sterilized the wound even as it cut, but still some blood spattered on Christian's uniform. And, his hands now meaningless palms and useless knuckles, Christian stood and walked out of Joe's Bar and Grill. The people made way for him again, and they listened intently as the blind Watcher said, "That was a man who broke the law and was forbidden to be a Maker. He broke the law a second time, and the law insists that he be stopped from breaking down the system that makes all of you so happy."

The people understood. It grieved them; it made them uncomfortable for a few hours, but once they had returned home to their exactly right homes and got back to their exactly right jobs, the sheer contentment of their lives overwhelmed their momentary sorrow for Chris. After all, Chris had broken the law. And it was the law that kept them all safe and happy.

Even Joe. Even Joe soon forgot Chris and his music. He knew he had done the right thing. He couldn't figure out, though, why a man like Chris would have broken the law in the first place, or what law he would have broken. There wasn't a law in the world that wasn't designed to make people happy—and there wasn't a law Joe could think of that he was even mildly interested in breaking.

Yet. Once, Joe went to the piano and lifted the lid and played every key on the piano. And when he had done that he put his head down on the piano and cried, because he knew that when

Chris lost that piano, lost even his fingers so he could never play again—it was like Joe's losing his bar. And if Joe ever lost his bar, his life wouldn't be worth living.

As for Chris, someone else began coming to the bar driving the same doughnut delivery van, and no one ever saw Chris again in that part of the world.

THIRD MOVEMENT

"Oh, what a beautiful mornin'!" sang the road-crew man who had seen *Oklahoma!* four times in his home town.

"Rock my soul in the bosom of Abraham!" sang the road-crew man who had learned to sing when his family got together with guitars.

"Lead, kindly light, amid the encircling gloom!" sang the road-crew man who believed.

But the road-crew man without hands, who held the signs telling the traffic to Stop or Go Slow, listened but never sang.

"Whyn't you never sing?" asked the man who liked Rogers and Hammerstein; asked all of them, at one time or another.

And the man they called Sugar just shrugged. "Don't feel like singin'," he'd say, when he said anything at all.

"Why they call him Sugar?" a new guy once asked. "He don't look sweet to me."

And the man who believed said, "His initials are *CH*. Like the sugar. C & H, you know." And the new guy laughed. A stupid joke, but the kind of gag that makes life easier on the road building crew.

Not that life was that hard. For these men, too, had been tested, and they were in the job that made them happiest. They took pride in the pain of sunburn and pulled muscles, and the road growing long and thin behind them was the most beautiful thing in the world. And so they sang all day at their work, knowing that they could not possibly be happier than they were this day.

Except Sugar.

Then Guillermo came. A short Mexican who spoke with an accent, Guillermo told everyone who asked, "I may come from Sonora, but my heart belongs in Milano!" And when anyone asked why (and often when no one asked anything), he'd explain: "I'm an Italian tenor in a Mexican body,'" and he proved it by singing every note that Puccini and Verdi ever wrote. "Caruso was nothing," Guillermo boasted. "Listen to this!"

Guillermo had records, and he sang along with them, and at work on the road crew he'd join in with any man's song and harmonize with it or sing an obbligato high above the melody, a soaring tenor that took the roof off his head and filled the clouds. "I can sing," Guillermo would say, and soon the other road-crew men answered, "Damn right, Guillermo! Sing it again!"

But one night Guillermo was honest and told the truth. "Ah, my friends, I'm no singer."

"What do you mean? Of course you are!" came the unanimous answer.

"Nonsense!" Guillermo cried, his voice theatrical. "If I am this great singer, why do you never see me going off to record songs? Hey? This is a great singer? Nonsense! Great singers they raise to be great singers. I'm just a man who loves to sing but has no talent! I'm a man who loves to work on the road crew with men like you and sing his guts out, but in the opera I could never be! Never!"

He did not say it sadly. He said it fervently, confidently. "Here is where I belong! I can sing to you who like to hear me sing! I can harmonize with you when I feel a harmony in my heart. But don't be thinking that Guillermo is a great singer, because he's not!"

It was an evening of honesty, and every man there explained why it was he was happy on the road crew and didn't wish to be anywhere else. Everyone, that is, except Sugar.

"Come on, Sugar. Aren't you happy here?"

Sugar smiled. "I'm happy. I like it here. This is good work for me. And I love to hear you sing."

"Then why don't you sing with us?"

Sugar shook his head. "I'm not a singer."

But Guillermo looked at him knowingly. "Not a singer, ha! Not a singer. A man without hands who refuses to sing is not a man who is not a singer. Hey?"

"What the hell did that mean?" asked the man who sang folk songs.

"It means that this man you call Sugar, he's a fraud. Not a singer! Look at his hands. All his fingers gone! Who is it who cuts off men's fingers?"

The road crew didn't try to guess. There were many ways a man could lose fingers, and none of them were anyone's business.

"He loses his fingers because he breaks the law and the Watchers cut them off! That's how a man loses fingers. What was he doing with his fingers that the Watchers wanted him to stop? He was breaking the law, wasn't he?"

"Stop," Sugar said.

"If you want," Guillermo said, but the others would not respect Sugar's privacy.

"Tell us," they said.

Sugar left the room.

"Tell us," and Guillermo told them. That Sugar must have been a Maker who broke the law and was forbidden to make music any more. The very thought that a Maker—even a lawbreaker—was working on the road crew with them filled the men with awe. Makers were rare, and they were the most esteemed of men and women.

"But why his fingers?"

"Because," Guillermo said, "he must have tried to make music again afterward. And when you break the law a second time, the power to break it a third time is taken away from you." Guillermo spoke seriously, and so to the road-crew men Sugar's story sounded as majestic and terrible as an opera. They crowded into Sugar's room and found the man staring at the wall.

"Sugar, is it true?" asked the man who loved Rogers and Hammerstein.

"Were you a Maker?" asked the man who believed.

"Yes," Sugar said.

"But Sugar," the man who believed said, "God can't mean for a man to stop making music, even if he broke the law."

Sugar smiled. "No one asked God."

"Sugar," Guillermo finally said. "There are nine of us on the crew, nine of us, and we're miles from any other human beings. You know us, Sugar. We swear on our mother's graves, every one of us, that we'll never tell a soul. Why should we? You're one of us. But sing, dammit man, sing!"

"I can't," Sugar said.

"It isn't what God intended," said the man who believed. "We're all doing what we love best, and here you are, loving music and not able to sing a note. Sing for us! Sing with us! And only you and us and God will know!"

They all promised. They all pleaded.

And the next day as the man who loved Rogers and Hammerstein sang "Love, Look Away," Sugar began to hum. As the man who believed sang "God of Our Fathers," Sugar sang softly along. And as the man who loved folk songs sang, "Swing Low, Sweet Chariot," Sugar joined in with a strange, piping voice, and all the men laughed and cheered and welcomed Sugar's voice to the songs.

Inevitably Sugar began inventing. First harmonies, of course, strange harmonies that made Guillermo frown and then, after a while, grin as he joined in, sensing as best he could what Sugar was doing to the music.

And after harmonies, Sugar began singing his own melodies, with his own words. He made them repetitive, the words simple and the melodies simpler still. And yet he shaped them into odd shapes and built them into songs that had never been heard of before, that sounded wrong and yet were absolutely right. It was not long before the man who loved Rogers and Hammerstein and the man who sang folk songs and the man who believed were learning Sugar's songs and singing them joyously or mournfully or angrily or gaily as they worked along the road.

Even Guillermo learned the songs, and his strong tenor was changed by them until his voice, which had, after all, been ordinary, became something unusual and fine. Guillermo finally said to Sugar one day, "Hey, Sugar, your music is all wrong, man. But I like the way it feels in my nose! Hey, you know? I like the way it feels in my mouth!"

Some of the songs were hymns: "Keep me hungry, Lord," Sugar sang, and the road crew sang it, too.

Some of the songs were love songs: "Put your hands in someone else's pockets," Sugar sang angrily; "I hear your voice in the morning," Sugar sang tenderly; "Is it summer yet?" Sugar sang sadly; and the road crew sang them, too.

Over the months, the road crew changed, one man leaving on Wednesday and a new man taking his place on Thursday, as different skills were needed in different places. Sugar was silent when each newcomer arrived, until the man had given his word and the secret was sure to be kept.

What finally destroyed Sugar was the fact that his songs were so unforgettable. The men who left would sing the songs with their new crews, and those crews would learn them and teach them to others. Crew men taught the songs in bars and on the road; people learned them quickly and loved them; and one day a blind Watcher heard the songs and knew, instantly, who had first sung them. They were Christian Haroldsen's music, because in those melodies, simple as they were, the wind of the north woods still whistled and the fall of leaves still hung oppressively over every note and—and the Watcher sighed. He took a specialized tool from his file of tools and boarded an airplane and flew to the city closest to where a certain road crew worked. And the blind Watcher took a company car with a company driver up the road, and at the end of it, where the road was just beginning to swallow a strip of wilderness, he got out of the car and heard singing. Heard a piping voice singing a song that made even an eyeless man weep.

"Christian," the Watcher said, and the song stopped.

"You," said Christian.

"Christian, even after you lost your fingers?"

The other men didn't understand—all the other men, that is, except Guillermo.

"Watcher," said Guillermo. "Watcher, he done no harm."

The Watcher smiled wryly. "No one said he did. But he broke the law. You, Guillermo, how would you like to work as a servant in a rich man's house? How would you like to be a bank teller?"

"Don't take me from the road crew, man," Guillermo said.

"It's the law that finds where people will be happy. But Christian Haroldsen broke the law. And he's gone around ever since, making people hear music they were never meant to hear."

Guillermo knew he had lost the battle before it began, but he couldn't stop himself. "Don't hurt him, man. I was meant to hear his music. Swear to God, it's made me happier."

The Watcher shook his head sadly. "Be honest, Guillermo. You're an honest man. His music's made you miserable, hasn't it? You've got everything you could want in life, and yet his music makes you sad. All the time, sad."

Guillermo tried to argue, but he was honest, and he looked into his own heart. And he knew that the music was full of grief. Even the happy songs mourned for something; even the angry songs wept; even the love songs seemed to say that everything dies and contentment is the most fleeting of things. Guillermo looked in his own heart, and all Sugar's music stared back up at him; and Guillermo wept.

"Just don't hurt him, please," Guillermo murmured as he cried.

"I won't," the blind Watcher said. Then he walked to Christian, who stood passively waiting, and he held the special tool up to Christian's throat. Christian gasped.

"No," Christian said, but the word only formed with his lips and tongue. No sound came out. Just a hiss of air. "No."

"Yes," the Watcher said.

The road crew watched silently as the Watcher led Christian away. They did not sing for days. But then Guillermo forgot his grief one day and sang an aria from *La Bohème,* and the songs went on from there. Now and then they sang one of Sugar's songs, because the songs could not be forgotten.

In the city, the blind Watcher furnished Christian with a pad of paper and a pen. Christian immediately gripped the pencil in the crease of his palm and wrote: "What do I do now?"

The blind Watcher laughed. "Have we got a job for you! Oh, Christian, have we got a job for you!"

APPLAUSE

In all the world there were only two dozen Watchers. They were secretive men who supervised a system that needed little supervision because it actually made nearly everybody happy. It was a good system, but like even the most perfect of machines, here and there it broke down. Here and there someone acted madly and damaged himself, and to protect everyone and the person himself, a Watcher had to notice the madness and go to fix it.

For many years the best of the Watchers was a man with no fingers, a man with no voice. He would come silently, wearing the uniform that named him with the only name he needed—Authority. And he would find the kindest, easiest, yet most thorough way of solving the problem and curing the madness and preserving the system that made the world, for the first time in history, a very good place to live. For practically everyone.

For there were still a few people—one or two each year—who were caught in a circle of their own devising, who could neither adjust to the system nor bear to harm it, people who kept breaking the law despite their knowledge that it would destroy them.

Eventually, when the gentle maimings and deprivations did not cure their madness and set them back into the system, they were given uniforms, and they, too, went out. Watching.

The keys of power were placed in the hands of those who had most cause to hate the system they had to preserve. Were they sorrowful?

"I am," Christian answered in the moments when he dared to ask himself that question.

In sorrow he did his duty. In sorrow he grew old. And finally the other Watchers, who reverenced the silent man (for they knew he had once sung magnificent songs), told him he was free. "You've served your time," said the Watcher with no legs, and he smiled.

Christian raised an eyebrow, as if to say, "And?"

"So wander."

Christian wandered. He took off his uniform, but lacking neither money nor time he found few doors closed to him. He wandered where in his former lives he had once lived. A road in the mountains. A city where he had once known the loading entrance of every restaurant and coffee shop and grocery store. And, at last, a place in the woods where a house was falling apart in the weather because it had not been used in forty years.

Christian was old. The thunder roared, and it only made him realize that it was about to rain. All the old songs. All the old songs, he mourned inside himself, more because he couldn't remember them than because he thought his life had been particularly sad.

As he sat in a coffee shop in a nearby town to stay out of the rain, he heard four teenagers who played the guitar very badly singing a song that he knew. It was a song he had invented while the asphalt poured on a hot summer day. The teenagers were not musicians and certainly were not Makers. But they sang the song from their hearts, and even though the words were happy, the song made everyone who heard it cry.

Christian wrote on the pad he always carried, and showed his question to the boys. "Where did that song come from?"

"It's a Sugar song," the leader of the group answered. "It's a song by Sugar."

Christian raised an eyebrow, making a shrugging motion.

"Sugar was a guy who worked on a road crew and made up songs. He's dead now, though," the boy answered.

Christian smiled. Then he wrote (and the boys waited impatiently for this speechless old man to go away): "Aren't you happy? Why sing sad songs?"

The boys were at a loss for an answer. The leader spoke up, though, and said, "Sure, I'm happy. I've got a good job, a girl I like, and man, I couldn't ask for more. I got my guitar. I got my songs. And my friends."

And another boy said, "These songs aren't sad, mister. Sure, they make people cry, but they aren't sad."

"Yeah," said another. "It's just that they were written by a man who knows."

Christian scribbled on his paper. "Knows what?"

"He just knows. Just knows, that's all."

And then the teenagers turned back to their clumsy guitars and their young, untrained voices, and Christian walked to the door to leave because the rain had stopped and because he knew when to leave the stage. He turned and bowed just a little toward the singers. They didn't notice him, but their voices were all the applause he needed. He left the ovation and went outside where the leaves were just turning color and would soon, with a slight inaudible sound, break free and fall to the earth.

For a moment he thought he heard himself singing. But it was just the last of the wind, coasting madly through the wires over the street. It was a frenzied song, and Christian thought he had recognized his voice.

APPENDIX A

Nebula Awards 1979

The results of the Nebula Awards voting for 1979 were as follows:

NOVEL

WINNER: THE FOUNTAINS OF PARADISE by Arthur C. Clarke (Harcourt Brace Jovanovich, Inc.)

Runners-up: JEM by Frederik Pohl (St. Martin's Press)

JUNIPER TIME by Kate Wilhelm (Harper & Row)

ON WINGS OF SONG by Thomas M. Disch (St. Martin's Press)

THE ROAD TO CORLAY by Richard Cowper (Pocket Books)

TITAN by John Varley (Berkley/Putnam)

NOVELLA

WINNER: "Enemy Mine" by Barry B. Longyear *(Isaac Asimov's Science Fiction Magazine)*

Runners-up: "The Battle of the Abaco Reef" by Hilbert Schenck *(The Magazine of Fantasy and Science Fiction)*

"Fireship" by Joan Vinge *(Analog)*

"Mars Masked" by Frederik Pohl *(Isaac Asimov's Science Fiction Magazine)*

"The Story Writer" by Richard Wilson *(Destinies)*

"The Tale of Gorgik" by Samuel R. Delany *(Isaac Asimov's Science Fiction Magazine)*

NOVELETTE

WINNER: "Sandkings" by George R. R. Martin *(Omni)*
Runners-up: "The Angel of Death" by Michael Shea *(The Magazine of
             Fantasy and Science Fiction)*
          "Camps" by Jack Dann *(The Magazine of Fantasy and
             Science Fiction)*
          "Options" by John Varley *(Universe 9)*
          "The Pathways of Desire" by Ursula K. Le Guin *(New
             Dimensions 9)*
          "The Ways of Love" by Poul Anderson *(Destinies 2)*

SHORT STORY

WINNER: "giANTS" by Edward Bryant *(Analog)*
Runners-up: "The Extraordinary Voyages of Amélie Bertrand" by
             Joanna Russ *(The Magazine of Fantasy and Science
             Fiction)*
          "Red as Blood" by Tanith Lee *(The Magazine of Fantasy
             and Science Fiction)*
          "Unaccompanied Sonata" by Orson Scott Card *(Omni)*
          "Vernalfest Morning" by Michael Bishop *(Chrysalis 3)*
          "The Way of the Cross and Dragon" by George R. R.
             Martin *(Omni)*

Fifteen Years of Nebula Winners

The first Nebula Awards were presented on March 11, 1966 for the best science fiction of 1965. Since that time they have been *the* mark of excellence in the field. A complete list of winners follows:

NOVELS

DUNE *by Frank Herbert*
FLOWERS FOR ALGERNON *by Daniel Keyes* (tie)
BABEL-17 *by Samuel R. Delany* (tie)
THE EINSTEIN INTERSECTION *by Samuel R. Delany*
RITE OF PASSAGE *by Alexei Panshin*
THE LEFT HAND OF DARKNESS *by Ursula K. Le Guin*
RINGWORLD *by Larry Niven*
A TIME OF CHANGES *by Robert Silverberg*
THE GODS THEMSELVES *by Isaac Asimov*
RENDEZVOUS WITH RAMA *by Arthur C. Clarke*
THE DISPOSSESSED *by Ursula K. Le Guin*
THE FOREVER WAR *by Joe Haldeman*
MAN PLUS *by Frederik Pohl*
GATEWAY *by Frederik Pohl*
DREAMSNAKE *by Vonda N. McIntyre*
THE FOUNTAINS OF PARADISE *by Arthur C. Clarke*

NOVELLAS

"He Who Shapes" *by Roger Zelazny* (tie)

"The Saliva Tree" *by Brian W. Aldiss* (tie)
"The Last Castle" *by Jack Vance*
"Behold the Man" *by Michael Moorcock*
"Dragonrider" *by Anne McCaffrey*
"A Boy and His Dog" *by Harlan Ellison*
"Ill Met in Lankhmar" *by Fritz Leiber*
"The Missing Man" *by Katherine MacLean*
"A Meeting with Medusa" *by Arthur C. Clarke*
"The Death of Dr. Island" *by Gene Wolfe*
"Born With the Dead" *by Robert Silverberg*
"Home Is the Hangman" *by Roger Zelazny*
"Houston, Houston, Do You Read?" *by James Tiptree, Jr.*
"Stardance" *by Spider and Jeanne Robinson*
"The Persistence of Vision" *by John Varley*
"Enemy Mine" *by Barry B. Longyear*

NOVELETTES

"The Doors of His Face, The Lamps of His Mouth" *by Roger Zelazny*
"Call Him Lord" *by Gordon R. Dickson*
"Gonna Roll the Bones" *by Fritz Leiber*
"Mother to the World" *by Richard Wilson*
"Time Considered as a Helix of Semi-Precious Stones" *by Samuel R. Delany*
"Slow Sculpture" *by Theodore Sturgeon*
"The Queen of Air and Darkness" *by Poul Anderson*
"Goat Song" *by Poul Anderson*
"Of Mist, and Grass, and Sand" *by Vonda N. McIntyre*
"If the Stars Are Gods" *by Gordon Eklund and Gregory Benford*
"San Diego Lightfoot Sue" *by Tom Reamy*
"The Bicentennial Man" *by Isaac Asimov*
"The Screwfly Solution" *by Raccoona Sheldon*
"A Glow of Candles, A Unicorn's Eye" *by Charles L. Grant*
"Sandkings" *by George R. R. Martin*

SHORT STORIES

" 'Repent, Harlequin!' Said the Ticktockman" *by Harlan Ellison*

"The Secret Place" *by Richard McKenna*
"Aye, and Gomorrah" *by Samuel R. Delany*
"The Planners" *by Kate Wilhelm*
"Passengers" *by Robert Silverberg*
No Award (for 1970)
"Good News From the Vatican" *by Robert Silverberg*
"When It Changed" *by Joanna Russ*
"Love is the Plan, The Plan is Death" *by James Tiptree, Jr.*
"The Day Before the Revolution" *by Ursula K. Le Guin*
"Catch That Zeppelin!" *by Fritz Leiber*
"A Crowd of Shadows" *by Charles L. Grant*
"Jeffty Is Five" *by Harlan Ellison*
"Stone" *by Edward Bryant*
"giANTS" *by Edward Bryant*

DRAMATIC PRESENTATIONS

SOYLENT GREEN *by Stanley R. Greenberg* (1973)
SLEEPER *by Woody Allen* (1974)
YOUNG FRANKENSTEIN *by Mel Brooks, Gene Wilder, and Mary Wollstonecraft Shelley* (1975)

GRAND MASTERS

Robert A. Heinlein (awarded in 1975)
Jack Williamson (awarded in 1976)
Clifford D. Simak (awarded in 1977)
L. Sprague de Camp (awarded in 1979)